THE

LAST

SUMMER

I

REMEMBER

KATHY WINSLOWER

DEDICATION

*For the summers that stayed with us long after
they were gone.*

CONTENTS

CHAPTER 1: THE PERFECT DAY

They say your life flashes before your eyes in a moment of crisis. If that's true, mine would look like a perfectly curated Instagram feed—bright, happy, filtered to perfection. And if you zoomed in on the details, you'd find exactly what I thought was a perfect life. Spoiler alert: I was wrong.

On the surface, everything looked perfect that morning. There's something about mornings in Grey Lake. The sun filters through my window in pale golden beams, the kind that makes everything feel clean and new, even the chipped paint on the windowsill. Outside, the air smells faintly of rain from the night before, the sky soft and watercolor blue.

Downstairs, my mom's humming drifts up, a familiar melody from the 80s she's been singing for years. The faint sound of my brother Trevor blasting some obnoxious YouTuber fills the background. Same as always. A soundtrack of normalcy. Stability.

I stretch out on my bed, letting my fingers trace the soft patches of the quilt Mom sewed for me when

I was seven. It's faded in some places, the stitching uneven, but it's mine.

This is my world—safe, predictable, wrapped in the warm cocoon of family. Perfect, on the surface.

The smell of coffee and cinnamon drifts up the stairs, coaxing me out of my morning daze. I take a moment to savor it, pulling myself into the present. I liked my routines. I liked that I could count on Trevor's terrible taste in YouTube videos, the sticky sweetness of Mom's cinnamon rolls, and the way Dad always poked his head in my room with the same greeting.

"Natalie-bean!" Dad's voice booms from the hallway a second before he appears in my doorway, brandishing the local newspaper like it's a prized trophy. "Guess who made the Honor Roll again?"

I groan, but it's the good kind of groan. "Dad, seriously? You still read that thing?"

"Absolutely. And don't pretend you're not secretly proud of this, Ms. High Achiever." He tosses the paper onto my desk, ruffles my hair like I'm six instead of seventeen, and grins. "Breakfast's ready. Don't make me drag you down."

"Okay, okay, I'm coming." I sit up and swing my legs over the edge of the bed. Dad's energy is inescapable. Some dads are stoic and reserved. Mine is the opposite—big, loud, and unapologetically alive. He's the kind of guy who'll bust out bad dance moves at weddings and laugh louder than anyone at his own jokes.

"Nat, let's go!" Trevor's voice barrels down the hall, cracking mid-shout, and I cringe. Thirteen-year-old boys have an uncanny knack for destroying any illusion of peace.

"I'm coming!" I shout back, grabbing my phone off the nightstand and padding across the hall to the bathroom.

Inside, I catch a glimpse of myself in the mirror. My hair's a mess—half of it sticking out like a bird's nest. I sigh, pulling it into a quick ponytail, and splash water on my face. It's one of those mornings where everything feels just...right. The kind of right you don't notice until later, when you're looking back, trying to piece together how everything fell apart.

By the time I'm dressed in my favorite hoodie and jeans, Trevor's pounding on the door. "You take forever!" he complains as I yank it open.

"You're welcome," I say sweetly, dodging his glare. "The bathroom's all yours."

The day started slipping into place, every moment clicking together like pieces of a puzzle I'd put together a hundred times before. Everything about it was ordinary—so blissfully, deceptively ordinary.

Downstairs, Dad was at his usual spot by the kitchen island, still in his plaid pajama pants and the faded World's Okayest Golfer T-shirt that Mom always threatened to throw away. A steaming mug of coffee rested in his hand as he flipped through the paper like it contained the secrets of the universe. "Ah there she is," he said as I wandered in, my hair still damp from the shower. "Honor Roll Donovan strikes again."

"Dad," I groaned, but I couldn't help smiling.

Across the room, Mom was a whirlwind of domestic efficiency. She flipped cinnamon rolls onto a plate with the practiced ease of a magician pulling off a sleight of hand, her apron dusted with flour. The radio was on low, playing an old Fleetwood Mac song she swayed to as she moved. The scent of cinnamon and sugar hung in the air like a warm hug, and for a moment, I just stood there, soaking it all in.

"Good morning, superstar," she said, sliding a roll onto a plate and passing it to me. "Big day ahead?"

"Just the usual," I replied, snagging the plate before Trevor could grab it. I perched on a stool at the island, letting the sticky sweetness melt on my tongue.

Trevor stormed in a second later, already mid-complaint. "Mom, Natalie's gotta drive me to the mall after school!" His voice cracked, halfway between a demand and a whine, and I had to bite my lip to keep from laughing.

"Don't talk with your mouth full," I said automatically, watching him shove half a cinnamon roll in his mouth and scatter crumbs like confetti.

"Why does he need to go to the mall?" I asked, washing my roll down with a sip of coffee.

"Shoes," Mom answered, not looking up from her task of cleaning the counter. "His cleats are practically disintegrating."

"Because someone didn't take care of them," I teased, ruffling his hair as I walked by.

"Stop!" Trevor squawked, ducking away.

Dad snorted, sipping his coffee. "You know, Trev, you might shock us all one day by chewing your food."

"Doubt it," I muttered, stealing the last cinnamon roll from Trevor's plate.

"Natalie!" Trevor howled. "That was mine!"

"Mom says sharing is caring," I said sweetly, though I licked a streak of frosting off the roll before tossing it back onto his plate.

"You're disgusting," Trevor shot back, though he was grinning. It was our thing—bantering until someone got the last word. Usually him, because I let him win.

Mom wiped her hands on her apron and turned to me, raising an eyebrow. "You are driving him, Natalie."

I sighed dramatically. "Fine. But he's picking the music."

"Deal," Trevor said, stuffing the rest of his roll into his mouth with the triumphant air of someone who'd just won a court case.

He launched into a detailed retelling of something dumb his best friend, Logan, had done during PE yesterday. I wasn't really listening—Trevor's stories always veered wildly off course—but his voice filled the room, blending with the clinking of dishes and the low hum of the coffeemaker.

It was the kind of morning that felt untouched by time, like it could stretch on forever. Everything was so normal, so perfectly normal, that I didn't think to memorize it.

If I'd known what was coming, maybe I would've paid more attention to the way the sunlight hit the kitchen tiles or the way Dad hummed under his breath as he read. Maybe I would've committed every laugh, every cinnamon-scented second, to memory.

But hindsight only comes when it's too late,

doesn't it?

The day started like a puzzle I'd solved a hundred times before. It wasn't until later that I realized some of the pieces didn't quite fit.

At school, everything fell into its usual rhythm. The hallway buzzed with overlapping conversations, sneakers squeaking against the polished floors, and lockers slamming shut in a disharmony of routine chaos.

Ryan Maxwell was waiting for me at my locker, leaning against it like he didn't have a care in the world. But I knew better. His glasses had slid halfway down his nose, and his phone was out, probably showing an article on AI, space travel, or one of the million things he "nerded" out over. He looked up when he saw me, a lopsided grin breaking across his face.

"Morning, Natalie," he said, tucking his phone into his pocket. "So, are we taking bets on how fast Mr. Allen falls asleep during first period?"

I laughed, spinning the combination on my lock. "Ryan, it's an 8:00 a.m. lecture on macroeconomics. He doesn't stand a chance."

Ryan pushed his glasses up. "I give him ten minutes."

"Fifteen, tops," I replied, yanking my math

textbook free from the cramped locker space.

He leaned closer, feigning seriousness. "You're too generous. Twelve minutes and he'll be out like a light."

"Deal," I said, shoving my bag closed. "Loser has to buy the winner coffee from the cafeteria."

"That's hardly a punishment," he deadpanned. "Their coffee tastes like burned regret."

I grinned, falling into step beside him. The warning bell shrieked, sending a wave of students scurrying to their classrooms. Ryan kept a steady stream of chatter as we walked to class, his hands gesturing animatedly while he explained the latest coding app he was working on.

Ryan was like that—always brimming with ideas, his brain running at a speed I could never quite keep up with. He'd been my best friend since middle school, the day he showed me how to hack my school-issued laptop to bypass the web filter. We'd been inseparable ever since, with him as the brains and me...well, I wasn't sure what I brought to the table, but Ryan didn't seem to mind.

"You're not even listening," he accused, his tone mock-hurt.

"I am!" I protested. "Something about...a feature

that prevents people from accidentally deleting their files?"

He rolled his eyes. "Close enough."

By the time we reached the classroom, the conversation had shifted. Ryan slid into the seat next to me, nudging my arm with his elbow. "Okay, real talk—are we doing this senior prank or not?"

I groaned, pulling my notebook from my bag. "Ryan, we've been over this. I can't afford to get caught doing something dumb. My grades—"

"Are perfect," he interrupted. "Which is exactly why you need to loosen up. You've spent high school being responsible. Don't you want to do at least one thing that people will remember?"

"You mean the way they remember that time Jake Muller got caught releasing frogs in the cafeteria?" I shot back.

Ryan snorted. "That's different. Our prank would be legendary."

"Legendary for getting us suspended," I countered. "And besides, you're a genius. You can get into any tech school you want without worrying about a single prank on your record."

He leaned back in his chair, his expression suddenly serious. "It's not that simple, Nat."

"What do you mean?"

Ryan hesitated, his fingers drumming lightly against the desk. "Everyone keeps telling me where I should go. MIT. Stanford. Caltech. It's like...I don't even know if it's what I want anymore."

I frowned. "Ryan, you're literally the smartest person I know. You could go anywhere. Don't let anyone else decide that for you."

He shrugged, his gaze shifting to the window. "Yeah, but...it'd be nice to have some certainty, you know? Like knowing where my friends will be."

"Friends?" I teased. "You mean me? Because I'm pretty sure I'm your only friend."

Ryan smirked but didn't deny it. "Hey, one's all I need."

The bell rang, cutting off any further conversation. As Mr. Allen shuffled to the front of the room, droning on about supply and demand curves, I glanced at Ryan. He was doodling absentmindedly in the margins of his notebook, his focus somewhere else entirely.

It hit me then—how much I took Ryan for granted. How much I assumed he'd always be there, waiting by my locker with his sarcastic comments and easy smile.

But the thing about certainty is that it's rarely as solid as it seems. If I'd known how much I'd be questioning everything in just a few weeks, maybe I'd have paid more attention to the cracks starting to form.

By lunch, the sun had burned off the morning fog, leaving the sky a sharp, cloudless blue. It was the kind of weather that made Grey Lake look like it belonged on the cover of a lifestyle magazine. Perfect little houses with their perfect little yards. Main Street with its rows of mom-and-pop shops, each one more charming than the last. But there was a hollowness to it, too, like everything had been designed to be admired from a distance—not lived in.

I picked at the corner of my peanut butter sandwich, watching as a glob of jelly oozed out onto my napkin. Across the table, Ryan was mid-sentence, rattling off specs for some AI model he was programming.

"And if I can figure out how to streamline the neural pathways," he said, oblivious to my zoning out, "then it could cut processing time by at least 30 percent."

I nodded vaguely, letting his words wash over me. Across the cafeteria, Sadie Caldwell sat with her usual crew, all glossy blonde hair and polished nails, tossing her head back as she laughed at something one of her friends said. It was one of those loud, over-the-top laughs that made me want to roll my eyes.

Then, just for a second, her gaze flicked toward me. It wasn't hostile, exactly, but it wasn't warm, either. A reminder that in the unspoken hierarchy of Grey Lake High, people like Sadie were on one level, and people like me were...not.

"Hey," Ryan said, snapping his fingers in front of my face. "Earth to Natalie. You still with me, or did I lose you at 'algorithm'?"

"Sorry." I forced a smile, crunching the napkin in my fist. "Lost in thought. Keep going."

Ryan gave me a look but didn't press. That was the thing about him—he never pushed when he knew I didn't want to talk.

Sometimes, I wondered how my life would've been different if we'd lived somewhere else. If my parents had a little more money, maybe I wouldn't be sitting in this cafeteria at all. Private school, maybe, or one of those fancy prep academies you see in movies where the students wear uniforms and have trust funds.

But we weren't that kind of family. My parents had gotten married right out of high school—high school sweethearts who'd had their whole lives figured out at eighteen. Mom liked to tell me how Dad proposed on prom night, down on one knee in the middle of the gymnasium with the disco ball spinning above them.

"And everyone clapped," she'd say, her face lighting up like it always did when she talked about Dad. "It was like something out of a movie."

I used to love that story when I was younger. But now, at seventeen, it just felt...claustrophobic. Like their love story had set this invisible expectation that I was supposed to find my happily-ever-after in Grey Lake, too. Except I didn't want that.

I wanted something bigger.

Not just college or a career, but a life that didn't feel so small, so suffocating. Sometimes, I'd sit in my room at night, scrolling through travel blogs or Instagram accounts of people living in big cities, and wonder what it'd be like to be one of them. Someone with a view of the skyline instead of the same old streets I'd known my whole life.

"Nat," Ryan said, nudging my arm. "You've got that faraway look again. You good?"

"Yeah," I said quickly, taking a bite of my sandwich to buy myself a second. "Just...thinking."

"About?"

I hesitated, then shrugged. "Nothing important."

Ryan frowned like he didn't believe me but let it drop. Instead, he launched into another tangent about the potential applications for his app, his voice filling the empty space in my head.

I should've been grateful for him, for the way he grounded me. But even then, I couldn't shake the feeling that no matter how good my life looked on the outside, something was missing.

What that something was, though—I had no idea.

After school, I rode my bike home.

I know what you're thinking—aren't high schoolers supposed to be driving a car by now? Well, I wasn't ready yet to unleash my inner driving goddess. Okay, fine, I was terrified of driving. There, I said it. But no way was I letting Ryan drive me home, either. If he ever found out about my fear, I'd never hear the end of it. So instead, I leaned into the eco-girl narrative. Save the planet, one bike ride at a time.

The streets were quiet, lined with the same maple trees that had been here since forever. Their leaves were just starting to turn gold at the edges, a hint of fall creeping in. My backpack weighed me down like an anchor, full of textbooks I probably wouldn't open tonight, and my thoughts were already on dinner. Dad had promised to make his famous burgers—his pre-trip tradition.

Fishing was Dad's thing. His escape. He called it his "soul reset," and even though he joked about it, I knew it meant something deeper to him.

"Hey, Dad!" I called as I walked into the house, the smell of sawdust and engine oil greeting me before I even made it to the garage.

He was there, as expected, fiddling with his fishing rod. The radio played some old country song in the background, the kind of twangy ballad that made me cringe, but he loved it. Humming off-key, he didn't notice me at first.

"You all set for tomorrow?" I asked, leaning against the doorframe.

"Just about," he said, looking up with his signature warm smile. "Gotta make sure I've got everything. Can't come home empty-handed, or your mom will never let me hear the end of it."

"She just wants an excuse to make fish tacos," I teased, stepping closer.

He laughed, a deep, belly-shaking sound that made me smile despite myself. "And you love 'em."

He wasn't wrong. Mom's fish tacos were legendary—a blend of crispy, spicy, and tangy that tasted like summer in every bite.

"Where's Mom?" I asked, glancing around.

"She took Trevor to the mall. Something about sneakers and bribing him with pretzels. You've got the house to yourself for a bit. Lucky you."

"Phew," I said dramatically, sinking onto the old bench by the worktable. "Peace and quiet at last."

Dad chuckled, setting the fishing rod aside and wiping his hands on a rag. "Enjoy it while it lasts, kiddo. So, what's on your mind? You've got that look."

"What look?"

"That 'I've got a question but I don't know how to ask it' look."

I hesitated, biting my lip. "It's nothing. Just...how did you know Mom was the one?"

Dad's expression softened, and he leaned back against the counter, crossing his arms. "Ah, the big question. You want the honest answer?"

I nodded.

"Well," he said, rubbing the back of his neck, "we didn't exactly have it all figured out back in high school. Life kind of...happened."

"Life?"

He sighed, but it wasn't the heavy kind. More like the weight of a secret finally being set down. "You.

Your mom and I, we found out we were having you, and, well, that sped up the timeline a bit. But I'll tell you this, Nat. Even when it felt like we were flying blind, there wasn't a single moment I regretted it."

"Not even a little?"

He walked over and crouched in front of me, his hands on my shoulders. His eyes, the same green as mine, held nothing but certainty. "Not even a second. Especially not having you. You were the best surprise we ever got."

Something in my chest tightened, like a knot I hadn't realized was there. "Thanks, Dad."

He kissed the top of my head and stood up, his smile back in full force. "Anytime, peanut. Now, go set the table before your mom gets home and decides I'm slacking."

As I walked toward the kitchen, I couldn't shake the warmth spreading through me. Dad always had a way of making everything feel okay, even when nothing about life felt certain. Maybe I didn't have all the answers yet, but in that moment, it didn't matter.

For now, this was enough.

That night, over burgers and laughter, everything felt normal. Safe. I didn't know it was the last night I'd see Dad as the man I thought I knew.

The next morning, Dad was already up, sitting at the kitchen table in his fishing gear. His tan cargo vest bulged with lures and tackle, pockets stuffed to the brim. A crossword puzzle sat in front of him, half-filled, the corners of the newspaper smudged with coffee rings. He was humming an old song under his breath, the same one he always did before a fishing trip.

I slid into my usual chair and reached across the table to snag a crispy slice of bacon from Trevor's plate.

"Hey!" Trevor protested, his mouth still full of cereal. "That was mine!"

"Finders keepers," I said, crunching it in half, savoring the salty bite.

"Dad, you do know you're supposed to actually catch fish on these trips, right?" Trevor teased, waving his spoon in the air like a judge delivering a verdict.

Dad looked up, feigning an exaggerated look of offense. "Oh, I plan to. You're the one who should be worried. Who do you think's teaching you how to fish this summer?"

Trevor groaned dramatically, dragging his hand down his face. "Can't wait for that."

Mom breezed into the kitchen, already dressed for work, her apron tied neatly over her blouse. She moved with her usual efficiency, somehow managing to pour herself a coffee, kiss Dad's cheek, and straighten Trevor's bedhead all in one motion.

"Don't be late getting home," she reminded Dad, brushing a stray blonde hair behind her ear. "You know how Natalie worries."

"Mom," I said, my voice dripping with mock annoyance.

"What? It's true," she said, a small smile tugging at her lips.

"Nat's got nothing to worry about," Dad said, standing and stretching. He grabbed his thermos and tucked it under his arm. "Same lake, same boat, same me. I'll be back by sundown with enough fish to make a feast. You better have those tortillas ready."

Mom shook her head, laughing. "Tortillas are the easy part. You just make sure the fish show up."

Out on the porch, I followed him as he loaded his gear into the back of his old Jeep. The early morning air was crisp, and the scent of dewy grass mingled with the familiar smell of his peppermint gum.

"Think I'll catch the big one today?" he asked, holding up a shiny new lure he'd bought on our last hardware store run.

"Definitely," I said, leaning my head briefly

against his shoulder. Dad was solid, warm, like a living piece of home.

He smiled down at me, his green eyes crinkling at the corners. "You know, one of these days, you're coming with me. Maybe for your graduation? You, me, and the open water. Sound good?"

"Only if I get to steer the boat," I said, grinning.

"Deal," he said, ruffling my hair.

As he climbed into the driver's seat, he leaned out the window, lowering his voice. "Don't tell your mom, but I might stay out a little longer this time. The fish bite better at dusk."

"Mom's gonna kill you," I said, laughing.

"She'll forgive me when she tastes those fish tacos," he said with a wink.

"Be back by sundown!" I called as the Jeep rolled down the driveway. "Catch something big!"

"Always do!" he shouted back, the words carrying over the sound of the engine.

I stood there on the porch for a moment, watching until his Jeep disappeared around the bend. It was one of those small moments you don't think twice about at the time.

Because why would I?

That was just Dad. Reliable. Unshakable. Perfect

on the surface.

I idolized him more than I probably should've admitted—to him or to anyone else. He was the kind of man who could fix anything: a broken chair, a busted bike chain, or even a bad day. And when he'd promised to take me fishing for my graduation, it felt like more than just a trip. It was his way of saying, I'm proud of you.

I carried that with me all day, not knowing how much I'd need it when everything started to unravel.

CHAPTER 2: THE VANISHING ACT

Grandpa closed up his shop early that day to join us at the house. He claimed it was because he wanted to spend time with the family, but I suspected it had more to do with the promise of Mom's fresh tortillas. Grandpa was Mom's dad, the original fisherman in our family. He was the one who'd taught Dad everything he knew.

While Mom rolled out the tortillas in the kitchen, Grandpa took up his station by the stove, expertly flipping each one over the open flame. I was in charge of the side dishes—cutting tomatoes for salsa and slicing avocados just thin enough for Grandpa's approval.

"Perfect slices, mija," he said, nodding as I lined them up on a plate. "You're finally learning."

"Finally?" I teased, tossing a handful of chopped cilantro into a bowl. "I've been doing this since I could hold a knife."

He chuckled, a low, rumbling sound. "Just like your mom. Except she used to sneak bites when she thought I wasn't looking."

Mom threw a playful glare over her shoulder. "And you never said anything."

"Of course not," Grandpa said, his eyes twinkling. "I figured I owed her that much, raising six siblings and all."

Mom came from a big family—four sisters and two brothers—all scattered across the country now. They only made it back for Christmas or Thanksgiving every other year. Our small house always felt bursting at the seams when they visited, filled with laughter, card games, and the smell of roasting turkey or tamales. Compared to Dad, an only child, Mom's world had always been noisier, more chaotic.

Dad used to joke that marrying into Mom's family was like stepping into a tornado, but it was clear he loved it. He'd started working for Grandpa at the fishing store not long after they got married, learning the ins and outs of bait supplies, boat rentals, and how to talk shop with old-timers who treated fishing like a religion. It became his routine, his second home.

By sundown, though, Dad still wasn't back.

Trevor, restless as ever, decided to fire up the grill for practice. "I'll get it started so we're ready when Dad comes home with his haul," he said confidently, waving a pair of tongs in the air like a baton.

"You sure you know what you're doing?" Mom asked, raising an eyebrow.

"Please. How hard can it be?"

Five minutes later, the grill flared up too high, sending a lick of flames across Trevor's arm. He yelped, dropping the tongs. Mom rushed him inside to treat the burn, the calm precision in her voice betraying the panic in her eyes.

"Grandpa," I said, as the two of us sat alone in the quiet kitchen. "Something feels off. Dad's never this late."

Grandpa, seated at the table with a fresh tortilla in hand, didn't look worried. "Fishing takes patience, Natalie. Sometimes the best catches come when the rest of the world is asleep."

"But Dad said he'd be back by sundown."

He patted my hand, his calloused fingers warm and steady. "Your dad's a good fisherman. He knows what he's doing."

We sat there a while, talking about fishing and how Grandpa used to take Mom and her siblings out to the lake when they were kids. He painted a picture of simpler times—skipping stones, packing sandwiches, and the excitement of catching even the smallest fish.

It should've been comforting, but I couldn't shake the nagging feeling growing in my chest.

When Mom and Trevor came back from the hospital, the tension was palpable. Trevor had a bandage wrapped around his arm, and he looked more embarrassed than hurt.

"Still no word from him?" Mom asked, her voice tight as she set her purse down.

I shook my head.

"Let's call him again," she said, pulling her phone from her pocket.

It rang once. Twice. Then, faintly, we heard it—his ringtone, coming from the living room.

Trevor picked up Dad's phone from where it sat on the coffee table, right next to his empty coffee mug from the morning. "He forgot it," he said, holding it up.

Mom's face paled. "He never forgets his phone."

The clock on the stove glowed 10:42 p.m. The house felt too quiet. Dad was never late—not like this.

His trips were short, predictable, like everything about him. By now, his gear should've been cleaned, his tackle box neatly stacked on its shelf in the garage.

Mom paced in the kitchen, her arms crossed tightly over her chest. "He probably lost track of time," she said, but her voice wavered. "You know how he gets when he's fishing."

I nodded, but a cold knot twisted in my stomach. Dad didn't lose track of time.

By midnight, Mom was on the phone with the police.

"He's not answering his phone," she said, her voice rising with every word. "He was supposed to be back hours ago."

The calm voice on the other end did little to reassure us. "Ma'am, we understand your concern, but we typically require 24 hours before filing a missing person's report. Is it possible he decided to stay longer or—"

"No!" Mom snapped, her face flushing with frustration. "It's not possible. Something's wrong."

I stared at the table, tracing the woodgrain with my finger. My thoughts were a chaotic tangle, each one more unsettling than the last.

Dad wasn't late.

Dad was missing.

The house felt like a tomb that night. We all stayed awake, hearts heavy and eyes trained on the clock, waiting for something—anything—that might explain Dad's absence. The low hum of the ceiling fan did little to break the unbearable silence. Trevor fidgeted in his seat, flipping channels on the TV without actually watching, while Mom sat at the kitchen table, her phone clutched tightly in her hand, willing it to ring.

Grandpa, calm and steady as ever, finally stood and cleared his throat. "It's late," he said, his deep voice resonating in the stillness. "John's been fishing his whole life. These things happen sometimes. He probably stayed out too long and got embarrassed about coming back empty-handed."

"Embarrassed?" Mom snapped, her voice cracking. "He wouldn't do this. Not to us."

Grandpa didn't flinch. Instead, he placed a reassuring hand on her shoulder. "He'll be back by morning, Marisol. You'll see. But we need our rest if we're going to handle whatever comes next."

His words were calm, but his eyes betrayed a flicker of doubt. He ushered Trevor and me toward our rooms like we were kids again. I didn't argue. There was no point.

But sleep wouldn't come. I lay in bed, staring at the ceiling, my mind spinning with worst-case scenarios. The house was too quiet, the kind of quiet that presses down on you, making it hard to breathe.

When the first streaks of dawn peeked through my window, I couldn't take it anymore. I threw on a hoodie, grabbed my bike, and pedaled toward Grey Lake.

The cool morning air stung my face, sharp and biting, but it didn't slow me down. My legs pumped furiously, my thoughts a chaotic blur. I kept replaying Dad's last laugh over burgers, the way his eyes crinkled at the corners when he teased me about graduation. It felt impossible that he could just...vanish.

The lake emerged through the trees, its surface eerily calm, like glass reflecting the soft pinks and oranges of sunrise. Normally, I found Grey Lake beautiful, peaceful even. But today, it felt wrong. Too still.

And then I saw it.

Dad's kayak.

It floated near the shore, tilted slightly, one paddle drifting a few feet away. His tackle box bobbed nearby, half-submerged, its lid open. Hooks and lures spilled out like scattered confetti.

"Dad!" I yelled, my voice breaking the quiet.

I dropped my bike in the grass and stumbled toward the water's edge, my heart pounding so loud it drowned out everything else.

"Dad!" I screamed again, my voice echoing across the lake.

Nothing. Just the soft lapping of water against the shore.

My hands shook as I pulled out my phone and dialed Mom. She answered on the first ring.

"Mom," I choked out, barely able to form the words. "It's his kayak. It's here. But he's not."

There was a beat of silence, then the sound of her sharp inhale. "Where are you?" she demanded.

"At the lake," I admitted, bracing myself.

"You left the house? Natalie, you should've—"

"I had to," I said, cutting her off. My voice cracked as tears blurred my vision. "I had to, Mom. Dad's gone."

She was there within twenty minutes, Trevor and Grandpa in tow. The moment Mom stepped out of the car, her eyes locked on the kayak. For a second, she didn't say anything, just clutched the door like it was the only thing keeping her upright.

"What were you thinking?" she finally said,

spinning toward me. "You don't just take off like that without telling anyone!"

I opened my mouth to respond, but the words wouldn't come. Instead, I burst into tears. Hot, angry, helpless tears. "I just wanted to find him," I whispered.

Mom's face softened, and she pulled me into a hug, but it didn't help. Nothing could. Dad wasn't here. His kayak was, his jeep parked in its usual spot nearby, but he was nowhere to be found.

By mid-morning, the police arrived. Yellow tape went up around the area where Dad's kayak had been found, creating a boundary between us and the growing search effort. Officers combed the shore, their voices calm and measured, but their faces told another story. This wasn't a rescue anymore—it was a recovery.

A search-and-rescue team launched boats into the water, their motors breaking the lake's silence. They moved with grim efficiency, scanning every inch of the surface and sending divers below.

Detective Maxwell, Ryan's dad, approached us. He was a tall man with kind eyes and a voice meant to reassure, though it did little to ease the weight pressing on my chest.

"We'll do everything we can to find him," he said, his tone steady but somber.

Mom nodded, her grip tightening on my arm. Trevor stood silent, his face pale and drawn. Grandpa, usually so composed, rubbed the back of his neck, his gaze fixed on the water.

I didn't look at any of them. My eyes stayed on the lake, scanning every ripple, every shadow, every possible sign of Dad. But the water gave nothing away, its surface as calm and unyielding as a secret too big to share.

Dad was missing. And for the first time, it felt real.

By the time the search intensified at Grey Lake, the police insisted we stay home. "Just in case your dad calls," Detective Maxwell had said, though his tone suggested he wasn't holding his breath. It was the kind of careful optimism they used to soften the blow of reality.

I hated being stuck in the house, waiting for a phone call that I knew deep down wasn't coming. The walls seemed to close in on us as the hours stretched into an unbearable silence. Grandpa sat in his armchair, his brow furrowed in thought, while Trevor hadn't said much of anything since the morning. He just stared at his phone, opening and closing apps like it might distract him from the weight in the room.

Mom was the worst. She paced the living room

like a caged animal, her phone glued to her hand, cheeks tear-streaked. By nightfall, she had dissolved into sobs that wracked her entire body, shaking like she might crumble at any moment. I didn't know how to comfort her—I didn't know how to comfort myself.

The first day ended with no news, no sign of Dad. Something inside me shifted as the sun dipped below the horizon. It felt like the moment when a balloon slips out of your grasp and drifts upward, too far to catch but impossible to look away from.

It felt like he wasn't coming back.

The Garners, our neighbors and Dad's closest friends, were devastated. They were practically family, their house just across the street a second home when I was younger. They'd known Dad longer than I'd been alive, and the weight of his disappearance hit them almost as hard as it hit us.

Mr. Garner had joined the search efforts every day since it began, his wiry frame and sun-weathered face a constant presence at the lake. Meanwhile, Mrs. Garner became our self-appointed caretaker, filling our fridge with casseroles, soups, and pies we barely touched. Her way of hovering reminded me of a protective hen, bustling around with worried eyes.

While the adults talked inside, Jamie Garner sat

with me on our front porch. Jamie had always been a little different—sharper in some ways, quieter in others. His autism made him unpredictable at times, though not in the ways people usually assumed. It just meant his brain worked in a different rhythm, one that took a little extra patience to understand.

He sat cross-legged on the steps, picking at the seam of his jeans. "Mom's freaking out," he said suddenly. "She thinks your dad...well, you know."

I stared at the yard, the grass dry and patchy in the midsummer heat. "Yeah. I know."

Jamie fidgeted, his sneaker scraping against the wood. "But your dad's smart. He wouldn't just—" He stopped himself, as if trying to wrestle his words into something that wouldn't upset me. "It's weird, though, right? Like, if he drowned, someone would've found him by now."

I turned to look at him, startled. Jamie rarely said things so bluntly. He wasn't trying to be cruel—he just didn't believe in tiptoeing around the truth.

"What are you saying?" I asked, my voice low.

"I don't know. It just doesn't add up." He started picking at the seam again, his fingers moving in quick, repetitive motions. "Your dad knew that lake better than anyone. Like...better than my dad even. He wouldn't just fall in. And if it was an accident, wouldn't they have found...something?"

His words lodged in my chest like a splinter. He was saying out loud what I hadn't let myself consider: what if this wasn't an accident? What if someone had taken him—or worse?

"What if someone hurt him?" I whispered, the thought taking shape for the first time.

Jamie paused, his hands stilling. "Maybe." He glanced at me, his eyes unusually serious. "But who'd wanna hurt your dad? He's, like, the nicest guy."

I didn't answer. My mind raced with possibilities I didn't want to think about—people Dad had argued with, the stranger who'd stopped by the shop last month looking for fishing gear but seemed too interested in our schedules. It was like pulling the thread on a sweater; the more I thought about it, the more it unraveled.

Jamie tilted his head, studying me the way he did when he was trying to solve a puzzle. "You think it was on purpose, don't you?"

"I don't know," I admitted, my voice barely audible. "I just...I feel like we're missing something."

We sat in silence after that, the cicadas buzzing loud in the sticky evening air. For all his awkwardness,

Jamie had a way of seeing straight to the heart of things. His questions left me with an unease that refused to fade, a nagging voice in the back of my mind whispering: What if this wasn't an accident?

By the time I went inside, my stomach was churning with doubt. The possibility of my dad being gone forever was unbearable, but the idea that someone might've done something to him? That was worse.

I realized Jamie had cracked open a door in my mind, one I wasn't sure I was ready to walk through. But now that it was open, I couldn't ignore it. Something about Dad's disappearance didn't feel right.

And the more I thought about it, the more certain I became that this was just the beginning.

Days blurred together, a tangle of casseroles we didn't eat, whispered prayers that filled the silence, and faces shadowed by pity. The church vigil was supposed to be a comfort, but all it did was underline the hollow ache that had taken up residence in my chest.

The entire town seemed to crowd into the community center that night. Candles flickered in trembling hands, casting soft glows over worried faces. Grandpa stood apart from the throng, his cowboy hat clutched tightly in his hands, his lips pressed in a thin, grim line. Trevor stuck close to the edges, his shoulders hunched like he wanted to fold in on himself. Mom stayed at the center, leaning into Mrs. Garner as though she might collapse without her.

Even my aunts and uncles had flown in, their presence making everything feel more official. If it had just been us, maybe it could still feel temporary, like Dad might walk through the door at any moment. But their somber faces, their long embraces—they spoke of permanence, of inevitability.

The pastor's voice echoed softly over the gathering. I barely registered his words, my gaze locked on the makeshift memorial near the stage. A photo of Dad sat perched on an easel, his grin bright and sunburned from his last fishing trip. Surrounding it were clusters of flowers, handwritten notes from neighbors, and a few of Dad's old lures that someone thought to include.

As the first chords of Amazing Grace filled the room, I squeezed my candle tight, the wax beginning to soften under my grip. With closed eyes, I whispered the same silent prayer I had every night since he disappeared: Come back, Dad. Please. Just come back.

The search stretched on for weeks. Divers plunged into the depths of Green Lake, their heads surfacing occasionally with shakes that sent cold dread down my spine. Search dogs sniffed tirelessly along the wooded edges, their handlers urging them on with sharp commands. Even helicopters joined the effort, their rotors slicing through the air, shadows flitting over the water like restless ghosts.

Every day ended the same. Nothing. No signs, no answers. Just an aching emptiness that seemed to expand with every passing hour.

Eventually, my aunts and uncles had to return to their lives. "We'll be back if you need us," Aunt Celia said as she hugged me tightly, her familiar perfume bringing a fleeting sense of comfort. "Call anytime, sweetheart."

But their absence left the house even quieter than before, their laughter and clinking coffee cups replaced by silence.

Neighbors continued to stop by, their faces drawn with concern. They dropped off casseroles, pies, and pots of soup, as if food could fill the gaps where answers should have been.

"You're in our prayers," Mrs. Thompson said, her weathered hands gripping Mom's.

"God has a plan," Mr. Jeffries offered solemnly, setting a tray of lasagna on the counter.

I nodded and thanked them because that's what I was supposed to do. But their pity wrapped around me like a heavy coat, thick and suffocating. I hated how it felt. How it made me feel like a character in a tragedy, a girl to be pitied instead of someone who could do something about it.

School wasn't much better. Teachers offered extensions on assignments I hadn't even thought about, their voices dripping with sympathy. My classmates avoided eye contact, their whispers trailing behind me like smoke. It wasn't cruelty—it was worse. It was pity.

The only constant was Ryan Maxwell. He didn't tiptoe around me or offer empty words. He just…showed up. At lunch, in the hallway, during study periods.

His easy confidence had dulled into something quieter, softer, but he stayed close. He walked me to class, filled the silence when I didn't have the energy to talk, and occasionally cracked jokes that pulled a reluctant smile from me.

It was one of those afternoons, where I found him leaning against my locker, twirling a pen between his fingers.

"Hey," he said.

"Hey."

There was a pause before I blurted out the question that had been nagging me. "Has your dad said anything? About the investigation?"

Ryan hesitated, his usual smirk replaced by something softer. "He doesn't really talk about work at home," he admitted.

I nodded. Detective Maxwell was nothing if not methodical.

"But don't give up hope," Ryan added, his tone careful. "They're still looking. There's always a chance—"

I cut him off, my voice sharper than I intended. "Be realistic, Ryan. No one survives underwater for weeks. My dad is dead. Everyone knows it—they're just too scared to say it out loud."

The words hung in the air between us, heavy and undeniable. Ryan didn't argue. Instead, he shifted closer, his shoulder brushing mine, and said softly, "You don't have to believe that yet. Not if you're not ready."

But I did believe it. And the weight of that belief was slowly crushing me.

The words hung between us, heavy and unspoken until now. Ryan didn't flinch, but his shoulders sagged slightly, like he didn't know how to argue with the truth.

"Maybe," he said quietly. "But I'm here. For whatever happens next."

For a moment, his presence was the only thing holding me together.

And maybe that was enough.

CHAPTER 3: CRACKS IN THE STORY

By the end of the second week, the search had shifted from rescue to recovery. The change in language was subtle but devastating. It was no longer about finding Dad alive. It was about bringing back…whatever was left.

But deep down, I couldn't accept it. Not fully. How could the world keep turning without him? How could life just go on when everything in me had stopped?

At home, the silence was thicker than ever. Grandpa stopped coming by as often. When he did, he sat quietly at the kitchen table, his hands folded over the brim of his hat, his eyes fixed on a point only he could see.

"He blames himself," Mom said one night when we were doing dishes together—a rare moment of normalcy in the haze.

"For what?" I asked, scrubbing at a plate harder

than I needed to.

"For letting your dad go out that night. He thinks he should've stopped him."

I shook my head, anger flaring unexpectedly. "That's stupid. How could anyone have known?"

Mom sighed, wiping her hands on a dish towel. "Grief doesn't always make sense, Nat."

Neither did anything else, I wanted to say, but I swallowed the words.

Somehow, life stumbled forward, dragging us along with it. There was school—hallways filled with stares that lingered too long and teachers who gave me extensions I didn't want. There was home—too quiet, too empty. Mom had stopped cooking, and the laundry piled up until I couldn't take it anymore and started doing it myself.

It wasn't like I wanted to be the one keeping things running, but someone had to. And it wasn't going to be Trevor.

Trevor had retreated into his own world, headphones permanently glued to his ears. When he wasn't at school, he was in his room, playing video games or scrolling on his phone. He barely spoke to me or Mom, but I couldn't blame him. We were all just trying to survive in our own ways.

One Saturday, I found him in the garage, sitting cross-legged on the cold concrete floor, surrounded by Dad's things.

"What are you doing?" I asked, stepping over a box labeled Fishing Gear.

Trevor shrugged, his eyes fixed on a stack of old Polaroids. "Looking."

"For what?"

He held up a picture of Dad grinning proudly next to a huge fish, the lake glittering in the background. "I don't know. Something."

I sat down beside him, the concrete chilling me through my jeans. Together, we sifted through the boxes, uncovering pieces of Dad's life. An old baseball glove, its leather cracked and worn. A stack of maps, the edges dog-eared and smudged with dirt. A tin of coins from all the places he'd traveled.

"This was his favorite," Trevor said, holding up a fish bait shaped like a tiny rainbow trout.

I took it, running my fingers over the smooth, painted surface. "He used this on our last trip to the lake. He said it was lucky."

Trevor snorted, but his voice wavered. "Guess it wasn't lucky enough."

I didn't say anything. Instead, I slipped it into my

pocket. It felt like a piece of Dad I could keep with me, even if the rest of him was gone.

That night, as I lay in bed, I thought about the garage, about dad's lucky fish bait, still in my pocket. I thought about Dad's smile in the Polaroids, about his laugh echoing through the house.

And I thought about what Trevor had said: "I don't know. Something."

Because that's what I felt too. That there was something missing. Something we weren't seeing. Something about Dad's disappearance that didn't add up.

And I couldn't let it go.

But weeks turned into a month. The rescue efforts had stopped, and the word from the authorities was official: Dad was presumed drowned.

Presumed dead.

The words echoed in my head like a drumbeat, hollow and relentless. They didn't feel like closure. They felt like a question mark—something unfinished, unresolved, left hanging in the air like an unanswered call.

I couldn't stand it.

One morning, after another night of tossing and turning, I grabbed my bike and pedaled to the police station. The ride was cold, the November air biting against my cheeks, but I barely noticed. My thoughts were a tangled knot of anger and desperation.

Detective Maxwell was at his desk when I walked in, looking tired and older than I remembered. When he saw me, he frowned.

"Natalie," he said, his tone cautious, "does your mom know you're here?"

"No," I said, standing as straight as I could. "But I need answers."

He sighed, rubbing a hand over his face. "Natalie, we've done everything we can. The divers, the dogs, the helicopters... We've scoured that lake. There's nothing more—"

"You don't know that!" I cut him off, my voice rising. "What if he didn't drown? What if he's out there, and you're just giving up?"

His expression softened, but it only made me angrier.

"I know this is hard," he said quietly. "I know you want to believe there's more we can do. But sometimes...sometimes, people don't come back."

I stared at him, my throat tight. "You're wrong," I said, my voice barely above a whisper. "He's not gone. He can't be."

But even as I said it, the weight of his words settled over me like a suffocating blanket.

At school, I wasn't just Natalie Donovan anymore. I was Natalie Donovan, the girl with the dead dad. That was my identity now, whether I wanted it or not.

People treated me differently. Teachers offered me extensions on assignments with pitying smiles. Classmates whispered when they thought I couldn't hear. Their words were overly careful, their sympathy suffocating.

"I'm so sorry for your loss," said Kelly Crawford, a girl from my history class, her voice syrupy sweet.

"Thanks," I mumbled, turning away before she could say more.

I hated it all—the stares, the whispers, the way people avoided eye contact. But most of all, I hated that I couldn't stop waiting.

Waiting for the phone to ring. Waiting for Dad to walk through the door with some ridiculous story about how this had all been a misunderstanding. Waiting for him to come back and make everything right again.

Because I couldn't accept that he wouldn't.

The day Mom decided we had to bury an empty

casket, it felt like the ground beneath me had been ripped away.

"It has to be done," she said, her voice brittle, as though the words themselves might shatter her. "For the insurance."

I stared at her. "What insurance?"

Her hands shook as she set down her coffee cup. "Your dad took out a policy. Three weeks before he…" She trailed off, unable to say the word.

The room spun. I gripped the edge of the counter, trying to make sense of it. "Why would he do that?"

"I don't know," Mom whispered, tears filling her eyes. "But we need it, Natalie. We can't survive without it."

Her words hung heavy in the air, the weight of them pressing down on me. Three weeks before he went missing. My mind raced, trying to piece together what it meant.

"Do you think he…planned this?" I asked, the question tasting bitter on my tongue.

"Don't," Mom said sharply, her voice breaking. "Don't say that. Your father loved us. He wouldn't— he couldn't—"

But she didn't finish, and the silence between us said everything.

The day of the funeral was gray and cold. The empty casket sat at the front of the church, draped in flowers. People spoke in hushed tones, their eyes flickering to us with a mix of pity and curiosity.

Mom held Trevor's hand tightly, her face pale and drawn. Grandpa sat stiffly in the front pew, his hat clutched in his lap. I felt like I was watching it all from a distance, like it was happening to someone else.

When the pastor spoke, his words felt hollow, bouncing off the walls of my mind without sinking in.

"He was a loving husband, a devoted father, and a cherished member of this community," the pastor said.

But all I could think was: He's not here. None of this is real.

When it was over, I stood by the casket, staring at the polished wood as the church emptied. My hands trembled, and I clenched them into fists to keep from crying.

"I don't believe it," I whispered. "I don't believe you're gone."

Because deep down, I didn't.

But life has this cruel way of moving on, even when you're standing still. The world keeps spinning, the sun rises and sets, and people fall back into their routines as if nothing has changed. Except everything had changed.

And I had changed most of all.

The Natalie Donovan I used to be—the one who stayed up late perfecting essays and double-checking math homework, who took pride in her spot on the honor roll—felt like a stranger now. I'd stare at my old certificates taped to my bedroom wall, their crisp gold lettering mocking me. That girl was organized, determined, and confident. She had her whole life mapped out like a series of bullet points in a planner.

Now, I was someone else. Someone who barely had the energy to open her textbooks, let alone ace a test. The math problems that used to click effortlessly in my mind looked like an alien language. Words jumbled together on the page whenever I tried to write an essay. And every time I picked up a pencil, the weight of everything I wasn't anymore pressed down harder.

It wasn't even a wakeup call, when Mrs. McAllister, the school guidance counselor, had pulled me into her office.

"Natalie, we need to talk about your future," she'd said in her careful, counselor voice, the kind that's supposed to make you feel safe but really just makes you want to shut down.

I slouched in the chair, crossing my arms. "What future?"

Her eyebrows lifted slightly, like she was deciding whether or not to push back. "You've always been a high achiever," she began, shuffling through a stack of papers on her desk. "But your recent grades... They're concerning."

I shrugged, my eyes on the fraying hem of my hoodie sleeve. "So? Plenty of people have bad grades."

Mrs. McAllister sighed. "Natalie, you're a bright student with so much potential. But if you keep going like this, you're going to have a hard time getting into a decent college."

"So I'll go to community college," I shot back, my tone sharp enough to cut. "Who cares?"

Her lips pressed into a thin line. "That's not what you wanted a few months ago. You were aiming for Ivy League schools."

I looked away, letting my eyes wander to the motivational posters on her wall. One read, Believe in Yourself! in bold, cheerful letters. It felt like a bad joke.

"Ivy League doesn't matter anymore," I said flatly.

But that was a lie. It did matter. It mattered more than I wanted to admit, but the weight of everything—

Dad's disappearance, the whispers at school, the pitying looks—had buried me so deep I didn't know how to dig myself out.

I was late for last period when Ryan found me at my locker.

"Hey," he said softly, leaning against the row of metal doors. His usual mischievous grin was gone, replaced by a tentative look that made my chest ache.

"Hey," I muttered, keeping my head down as I fumbled with the lock.

"Let's skip," he said, nudging my shoulder lightly.

I froze, glancing up at him. "Are you serious?"

He shrugged, his lips twitching in the ghost of a smile. "Dead serious. Let's get out of here."

"I can't," I said, though the thought of sitting through algebra made my stomach churn.

"Sure you can," he said, his voice light. "I mean, it's not like one more missed class is gonna ruin your perfect attendance record or anything."

The joke was so unexpected, so absurdly Ryan, that a laugh escaped me before I could stop it. It wasn't much, but it felt like breathing again after holding my breath for too long.

"Come on," he said, his smile growing. "We'll take a ride. You can tell me about that time your dad almost sank his boat."

The mention of Dad made my throat tighten, but Ryan's tone wasn't pitying—just familiar, like he was pulling me back to the version of myself that didn't feel so broken.

I nodded, and together we slipped out through the gym doors.

Ryan's car was an old silver hatchback with a peeling bumper sticker that read, I Brake for Tacos. My bike barely fit in the back, wedged awkwardly between a gym bag and a stack of empty energy drink bottles.

"You're gonna drive," he announced as we pulled into an empty parking lot by the track.

I stared at him. "What?"

"You heard me," he said, tossing me the keys.

"Absolutely not."

"Absolutely yes," he countered, grinning. "You can't bike everywhere forever, Natalie."

"I'm not driving your car," I said firmly. "Cars are…not economically efficient."

Ryan raised an eyebrow. "Oh, come on. At least make up a better excuse. What about electric cars?"

I opened my mouth, then closed it again. Busted.

Reluctantly, I slid into the driver's seat, the key trembling in my hand.

"It's easy," Ryan said, climbing into the passenger side. "Gas, brake, steer. That's it."

"That's it," I muttered, gripping the wheel like it might attack me.

It was not "it."

Within five minutes, I had accidentally hit the windshield wipers, honked the horn twice, and nearly reversed into a trash can. Ryan was laughing so hard he was doubled over, tears streaming down his face.

"Stop laughing!" I yelled, my face hot with embarrassment.

"You're—" he gasped, trying to catch his breath. "You're terrible at this."

I glared at him, but a reluctant smile tugged at the corners of my mouth.

Then I hit the gas too hard, and the car lurched forward. Ryan grabbed the dashboard, howling with laughter.

"Okay, we're done!" I said, slamming on the brake and throwing the car into park.

But the laughter faded as I stared out at the empty parking lot, my chest tightening. "This was supposed to be Dad's job," I whispered, the words spilling out before I could stop them.

Ryan's grin disappeared. "Natalie…"

Tears blurred my vision, and I pressed my forehead against the steering wheel. "He was supposed to teach me how to drive. How to change a tire. How to—" My voice cracked, and I couldn't finish.

Ryan didn't say anything. He just reached over and put a hand on my shoulder, solid and steady, like he was anchoring me to the moment.

"It's okay," he said quietly. "You're allowed to miss him."

And for the first time in weeks, I let myself cry.

When I got back home, the air inside the house felt heavy, like the walls themselves were weighed down by the absence of Dad. It was as if the place knew he wasn't coming back and had decided to mourn him in its own way—creaking floorboards, dim lighting, the faint scent of wood polish and dust.

Trevor had buried himself in his room, drowning his pain in the glow of his gaming setup. I could hear the muted sound of gunfire and shouted commands coming through his door. Mom, on the other hand, had stopped pretending entirely.

I found her in the living room, curled up on the couch, clutching one of Dad's old flannel shirts. It was the blue one he wore to every barbecue, now wrinkled and soft from too many washes. Her hair was pulled into a messy bun, and her eyes were rimmed red.

"Mom?" I said softly, stepping closer.

She looked up at me, her expression raw and tired. "I don't know how to do this," she whispered. Her voice cracked like glass, and something inside me cracked too.

I hesitated for a moment before sitting down beside her. "I don't think we're supposed to know how," I said, my voice barely above a whisper.

For a moment, we just sat there, the silence filled with the faint hum of the dishwasher in the kitchen. Then, without warning, she leaned into me, her body trembling with sobs.

I held her, my arms awkward and uncertain, even as tears welled in my own eyes. It was the first time I'd seen her let go like this, and it scared me. She was supposed to be the strong one—the glue that held us together. But now she was unraveling, and I didn't know how to stop it.

Dinner was a quiet, fragmented affair. I reheated leftovers and arranged plates like a robot, moving through the motions without thinking too much. The dining table sat empty; none of us ate there anymore. Mom had retreated back to the couch with a mug of tea she barely touched, and Trevor was, predictably, holed up in his room.

I carried his plate down the hall, knocking gently on his door.

"Trevor?" I called, my voice muffled by the sound of his game.

There was a pause, then the sound of his voice, low and hurried. "Hang on. One sec."

I stood there for a moment, waiting for him to open the door. But he didn't.

I could hear him talking to someone on the other end of his headset, his words quick and clipped. Probably one of his online gaming friends.

Sighing, I placed the plate on the floor by the door. "Dinner's here," I said quietly.

No response.

I turned and walked back to my room, feeling the ache of loneliness settle in my chest. It wasn't just the physical absence of Dad that hurt—it was the way we were all pulling away from each other, retreating into our own separate worlds.

Later, I lay in bed staring at the ceiling, the darkness pressing in around me. At night, when the house was quiet, I let myself feel everything I couldn't during the day. The ache. The confusion. The anger.

I replayed every moment of that day—the day

Dad vanished—over and over like a bad movie. Had I missed something? A sign? A clue?

I couldn't stop thinking about the way people said it: presumed drowned. As if they didn't really know. As if they were guessing.

The doubt gnawed at me constantly. It wasn't just grief holding me back—it was the questions. The ones no one wanted to answer.

And maybe that was the worst part. Everyone else seemed ready to accept what had happened and move on. Even Mom, in her own detached way. But not me.

I wasn't ready to move on. I wasn't ready to let go of the possibility that Dad was still out there somewhere.

And I wasn't ready to admit that I didn't know how to move forward if he wasn't.

I didn't know when I fell asleep, but the low murmur of voices downstairs woke me. At first, I thought I was dreaming. My room was bathed in moonlight, and the house was silent except for the faint hum of the air conditioner. But the voices persisted, low and urgent.

Curiosity tugged at me, and I tiptoed down the hall, careful to avoid the creaky third step on the staircase. The voices grew clearer as I approached the kitchen. I stopped just short of the doorway, pressing myself against the wall.

"It's not typical," a man said. I recognized the sheriff's gravelly tone. "The laptop being wiped suggests premeditation. It's possible he planned this."

Planned what?

I clamped a hand over my mouth to keep from gasping.

"You think he…?" Mom's voice cracked, breaking mid-sentence. "No. That doesn't make sense. He wouldn't just—"

"Mrs. Donovan," the sheriff interrupted gently, "we're keeping all possibilities open."

I didn't hear the rest. My legs felt like lead as I turned and crept back upstairs. My heart was pounding so hard I could feel it in my ears. What were they saying? That Dad hadn't drowned? That he'd planned something?

I sat at my desk, trying to focus on anything else, but my thoughts were a jumbled mess of questions. I grabbed an old notebook, flipping through it aimlessly, hoping the familiar scrawl of old math problems and doodles would calm me.

That's when I noticed it.

The snow globe.

It hadn't been there before.

I froze, staring at it. It was small, with a miniature Eiffel Tower encased in glass. When I picked it up, it glinted faintly in the moonlight streaming through my window.

This snow globe had been Dad's favorite. He'd kept it on his desk for as long as I could remember.

The memory hit me before I could stop it.

"Paris," Dad had said, holding the snow globe up to the light. I was ten, and we were sitting on the porch, the summer air thick and buzzing with fireflies. "My favorite city in the world."

"You've been there?" I'd asked, wide-eyed.

"Once," he replied, his voice tinged with nostalgia. "Back in my gap year. My friends and I spent two weeks there, eating crepes, sketching by the Seine. I promised myself I'd go back someday."

"What happened?" I'd asked.

He smiled, but it didn't quite reach his eyes. "Life happened, kiddo. It always does."

Now, holding the snow globe in my hand, my breath caught.

How had it ended up here?

I'd been through this room a thousand times since Dad disappeared. I knew what was on every shelf, every surface. This wasn't supposed to be here.

My fingers tightened around the globe as a strange feeling settled over me—a mix of dread and hope that made my chest ache.

Was this a coincidence? Or was it something else?

And why did it feel like Dad's way of leaving me a clue?

I sat back in my chair, staring at the tiny Eiffel Tower encased in its glass dome. The weight of it in my hand felt heavier than it should have, as if it carried secrets I wasn't ready to uncover.

But I had to try.

Because now, more than ever, I was certain of one thing.

Dad wasn't just gone. He'd left something behind for me to find.

CHAPTER 4: SECRETS UNVEILED

By the time I found Ryan at his locker, the knot of unease in my chest had tightened into something sharp and restless. I needed to tell someone what I'd overheard, and Ryan was the only person who might actually understand.

"Hey," I said, catching his arm as he pulled a book from the top shelf.

"Hey." His smile flickered, but it vanished the second he saw my face. "What's wrong?"

I glanced around, lowering my voice. "I heard something last night. About my dad."

Ryan's brow furrowed as he shut his locker with a soft click. "Okay…what kind of something?"

I told him everything in a rush, the words tumbling out like they'd been trapped behind a dam.

About the sheriff's theory, about the wiped laptop. I didn't stop until my chest felt hollow and my throat burned.

When I finished, Ryan leaned against the lockers, rubbing the back of his neck. "The laptop…" he muttered, staring at the floor like it held the answer.

"What?" I pressed, gripping the strap of my bag so tightly my fingers ached.

He looked up, guilt written all over his face. "I should've thought to check it before the cops took it. I mean, I was there. I was right there. I could've…"

"This isn't your fault," I said quickly, cutting him off.

"But what if—"

"It's not your fault," I repeated firmly. "None of this is. If anyone should've seen it coming, it's me. He's my dad."

The words hung between us, heavy and bitter.

Ryan reached out and touched my shoulder lightly. "Nat, this isn't on you either. Whatever's going on, your dad didn't want anyone to see it."

His words settled over me like a cold fog. He was right, but that didn't make it any easier to accept.

After school, Ryan insisted on driving me to the precinct.

"I don't know what you're expecting," he said as we pulled into the parking lot. His old Subaru creaked as he shifted into park. "But my dad's not exactly the sharing type."

"I have to try," I said, gripping the snow globe I'd stuffed into my jacket pocket. The weight of it was both comforting and unnerving.

Inside, the precinct smelled like stale coffee and copier ink. Ryan led the way to the front desk, where his dad, Detective Maxwell, was sorting through a stack of files.

"Dad," Ryan said, stepping up. "Can you talk to Natalie? Just for a minute?"

Detective Maxwell glanced up, his eyes narrowing slightly when he saw me. "What's this about?"

"It's about my dad," I said, stepping forward. My voice wavered, but I pushed through. "Please, Detective Maxwell. I just need to know if there's anything—anything at all that can help me understand."

His expression softened, but he shook his head. "Natalie, you know I can't share details of an active investigation. It's not personal—it's protocol."

"But it is personal," I shot back, my voice rising. "It's my dad. Everyone thinks he's dead or worse, and

I don't even know what to believe anymore. How is that not personal?"

For a moment, he looked like he might say something—like he wanted to. But instead, he sighed and adjusted his hat. "Stay out of it, kid. Trust me. You don't want to know everything."

His words hit me like a slap. Before I could stop myself, I spun on my heel and stormed out of the station.

"Nat, wait!" Ryan called, hurrying after me.

I was already halfway down the steps when he caught up, grabbing my arm gently. "I'm sorry," he said, his voice low. "He's just—he thinks he's protecting you."

"Yeah, well, I don't feel very protected," I snapped, yanking my arm away. Tears blurred my vision, but I blinked them back, refusing to let them fall.

Ryan sighed, shoving his hands into his jacket pockets. "You're right. It's not fair. But you're not alone in this, okay? We'll figure it out."

I didn't respond. Instead, I stared out at the parking lot, the snow globe pressing into my palm like a silent reminder.

How was I supposed to figure this out when it felt

like every answer just led to more questions?

But the next day, everything changed.

I'd been standing by the hallway mirror, pretending to adjust my hair, when Mom's voice drifted down the hall. I wasn't trying to eavesdrop, not at first, but her tone stopped me cold.

"…What do you mean, chats? With who?"

Chats?

My fingers froze on my ponytail. I leaned closer, the words becoming sharper as they cut through the silence.

"I don't care if it was innocent! A French woman? No, I didn't know… Wait, what's this about a passport?"

A passport.

The words landed like a brick in my stomach, heavy and wrong. Passport? French woman?

Mom's voice rose, her anger cracking at the edges. "Why wouldn't he tell me? Why would he—" She stopped abruptly, as if the answer had hit her midsentence. The silence that followed was deafening.

I stood there, caught in a strange limbo between needing to know more and being too terrified to ask. When I heard the click of her ending the call, I bolted out the door before she could catch me.

Outside, the crisp winter air slapped my cheeks, but it did nothing to clear the storm brewing in my mind.

A French woman? Passport? It felt impossible, like I'd stepped into someone else's life. Dad wasn't the type of person to…what? Have secrets? Keep things from us? But then again, I wasn't sure what type of person Dad was anymore.

I walked without thinking, my boots crunching against patches of leftover snow. My hands were stuffed deep in my jacket pockets, but the cold had still found its way in, numbing my fingers.

Questions swirled around me like a whirlwind I couldn't escape. Had the snow globe been some sort of clue? Was this connected? How much did Mom know, and how much had she been hiding?

And most terrifying of all—what if the dad I thought I knew had never really existed?

When I finally stopped, I was at the park. The place where Dad used to take Trevor and me when we were kids, back when life felt simpler, brighter.

I sank onto a bench, pulling the snow globe from my pocket. The tiny Eiffel Tower inside glittered as I turned it over in my hands.

I wanted to feel angry, or sad, or even betrayed.

But mostly, I felt lost—adrift in a sea of questions with no land in sight.

A sudden gust of wind sent a flurry of leaves skittering across the pavement, and for a moment, I imagined Dad sitting beside me, telling me one of his stories. He'd always had a way of making things seem less scary, more manageable.

But now, it felt like he'd left me alone in the middle of a puzzle I wasn't sure I wanted to solve.

Ryan's call came just as I was getting ready to leave the park. My fingers were frozen, but I fumbled the phone out of my pocket, swiping to answer.

"Hey," I said, my voice shaky from the cold—or maybe everything else.

"Natalie," Ryan said, urgency threading his tone. "Can I see you? It's important."

I glanced around the park, the empty swings swaying gently in the breeze. "I'm at the park," I replied. "Dad's spot."

"I'll be there in ten," he said before hanging up.

I sat back on the bench, clutching the snow globe in my lap. My thoughts churned like the gray clouds overhead. The idea of someone having answers—any answers—was enough to make me stay put, despite the cold seeping into my bones.

When Ryan arrived, the first thing he did was frown.

"You haven't eaten today, have you?" he said, not even bothering with hello.

I opened my mouth to argue but realized I couldn't. My stomach growled softly, betraying me.

Ryan sighed, pulling his car keys from his pocket. "Come on," he said, tilting his head toward his car. "Let's get food first. You can't think on an empty stomach."

I wanted to argue, to tell him I didn't have time for food. But the look in his eyes—equal parts concern and stubbornness—made me give in.

The diner was warm and smelled like pancakes and syrup, even though it was past noon. We slid into a booth by the window, the vinyl seats cracked in places but still comfortable. A waitress in a worn apron handed us menus, but Ryan didn't even look at his.

"Two cheeseburgers, fries, and coffee," he said, glancing at me. "Unless you want something else?"

I shook my head. My appetite had started creeping back, though it felt like a distant echo of hunger rather than the real thing.

Once the waitress left, I leaned forward. "Okay, what's so important?"

Ryan hesitated, fiddling with the salt shaker. "Let's wait until the food gets here."

"Ryan," I said, exasperated. "Just tell me."

He pulled out his phone, setting it on the table between us. "A friend of mine at the sheriff's office sent me something," he said, his voice low. "Natalie…you need to see this."

The diner felt both too loud and too quiet at the same time as I scrolled through the screenshots on Ryan's phone. My hands shook, but I wasn't sure if it was from the cold earlier or the words staring back at me.

"They found his online chats," I whispered, my voice barely audible over the clatter of dishes around us. "He was talking to someone. A woman in France."

Ryan leaned closer, his brows knitting together. "That doesn't make sense. Why would your dad—"

"And he got a new passport," I interrupted, my voice rising despite myself. "They think he crossed the Canadian border two days after."

The information hung heavy between us, a weight I didn't know how to carry.

"So…" Ryan started, his words careful. "Are they saying your dad ran away?"

I shook my head, though the motion felt hollow.

"I don't know what they're saying. But if he's alive…"

The sentence trailed off, unfinished, but the thought filled the space between us.

If Dad was alive, why hadn't he reached out?

The waitress returned with our food, but I barely noticed. The burger sat untouched in front of me as my mind spiraled into questions I couldn't answer.

Ryan reached over, nudging the plate closer. "Eat," he said gently. "You'll think clearer with food."

I picked at the fries, my appetite caught somewhere between the need for answers and the knot in my stomach.

"How am I supposed to eat when—" I started, but Ryan cut me off.

"Because you're going to need your strength for this, Nat," he said, his voice firm but kind. "Whatever's happening, it's big. And I'll help you figure it out. But you can't run on empty."

For a moment, I hated him for being right. But then I took a bite, because what else could I do?

And as the warmth of the food settled in my stomach, so did the realization: this was only the beginning.

But when I got home, the air was thick with the acrid smell of smoke and something else—loss, maybe.

It was the kind of smell that seeped into your skin, clinging to you like a memory you couldn't shake.

I followed the trail of smoke to the backyard, my stomach dropping as I stepped onto the patio. Mom stood by the barbecue grill, her hands shaking as she threw another bundle onto the flames.

"Mom!" I screamed, running toward her. "What the hell are you doing?"

She didn't answer right away. Her eyes were wild, her cheeks streaked with tears. "I'm done," she said finally, her voice trembling with something between anger and despair. "I'm done with the lies, the secrets. He's not coming back, Natalie. He's not!"

I watched in horror as she picked up another box—a box I recognized as Dad's—and dumped it onto the fire. His flannel shirts curled and blackened in the heat, the smell of burning fabric rising in the air.

"No!" I shouted, lunging forward. My hand shot out to grab the corner of a photo album sticking out of the flames. My fingers brushed the burning paper, and a sharp, searing pain shot up my arm.

"Natalie!" Mom screamed, her voice cutting through the crackling of the fire. She rushed toward me as I dropped the album onto the ground, clutching my burned hand.

In the kitchen, the cold towel she wrapped around my hand should have soothed the sting, but it didn't. Not really. Her touch was gentle, but her face was closed off, her lips pressed into a thin, unyielding line.

"You didn't have to do that," she said, her voice quiet but sharp.

I looked at her, my eyes burning with unshed tears. "You didn't have to burn his stuff."

She didn't respond right away. The hum of the fridge filled the silence, a stark contrast to the chaos of the backyard.

"I just want to move on," she said finally, breaking the stillness. Her voice cracked, but she didn't cry. Her eyes, shiny but dry, seemed to stare right through me. "I can't keep holding onto someone who's not here."

Her words hit me like a punch to the stomach. "But what if he is?" I whispered, my voice barely audible.

She shook her head, her gaze hardening. "He's not, Natalie. And even if he is, he made his choice."

I didn't respond. I couldn't. The weight of her words settled in my chest, a dull ache that I knew would linger long after the sting in my hand faded.

She finished wrapping my hand in silence, her movements precise and practiced, like she'd done this a hundred times before. But there was no warmth in her touch, no comfort in her presence.

I stared at the bandage as she stepped away, my mind a tangled mess of anger, confusion, and hurt. How could she give up so easily? How could she decide to let go when I wasn't ready?

The house felt too big, too quiet, too heavy. I wanted to scream, to cry, to demand answers from a world that refused to give them.

Instead, I sat there, staring at my hand, the faint smell of smoke still clinging to me.

And for the first time since Dad disappeared, I wasn't sure who I was angrier with—him, for leaving us, or her, for giving up on him.

That night, I lay in bed, the weight of the day pressing down on me like a suffocating blanket. My room was dark except for the faint glow of the streetlamp outside, its light casting fractured shadows through the blinds.

The snow globe sat on my nightstand, catching the faintest bit of light, the glitter inside suspended like a thousand frozen moments. When I shook it earlier, the glitter swirled in a chaotic storm, tiny pieces spinning endlessly in the small glass world. Now it had settled, but I hadn't.

Paris. A passport. A woman in France.

The words were fragments in my mind, like puzzle pieces from two completely different boxes. They didn't fit together, but somehow, they still belonged to the same story. His story.

If Dad had made his choice…I couldn't finish the thought. My throat tightened, and my eyes burned with unshed tears. It wasn't fair. None of it was.

Mom's words echoed in my head. Even if he is alive, he made his choice.

What choice? To disappear? To leave us? To start over without us?

I hated the uncertainty. It gnawed at me, more painful than the truth I was too scared to uncover. If he was alive, why hadn't he reached out? If he wasn't…

I couldn't bring myself to think about that either.

Anger and sadness twisted together inside me, an ugly knot I couldn't untangle. It felt like I was stuck in limbo, suspended between holding on and letting go. I wanted to scream, to cry, to break something. Instead, I reached for the snow globe and shook it again.

The glitter swirled violently, catching the dim light and creating the illusion of tiny stars trapped in a spinning galaxy.

I stared at it, my chest aching. "What are you

trying to tell me, Dad?" I whispered into the stillness of my room. But the snow globe offered no answers. It just sat there, silent and unyielding, like the rest of the world.

I rolled onto my side, clutching my pillow tightly as a tear slid down my cheek. The ache in my chest didn't fade. If anything, it deepened, stretching into the corners of my being until it felt like I might shatter.

And yet, somewhere beneath the ache, a flicker of something stirred. Hope, maybe. Or defiance.

I wasn't ready to accept Mom's version of the truth. Not yet. Not without answers. If Dad had made a choice, I needed to know what it was.

CHAPTER 5: FRACTURED FAMILY

The house was quieter than usual that evening. Trevor had barely spoken a word to anyone for days, retreating into the dim, shadowed corners of his room, where I could barely hear his footsteps. Mom hadn't said much either—she was always in the kitchen now, her movements slow and methodical, too focused on her wine glass to care about much else.

It was like the house had become a hollow shell. The silence was more suffocating than the shouting, more oppressive than the confusion that hung in the air. But, surprisingly, Trevor came out of his room that evening. He didn't say anything at first, just walked through the hallway and into the kitchen, looking down at the floor. For the first time in what felt like forever, we sat at the dinner table together, even though the food was cold and untouched.

We didn't talk about Dad, but we didn't need to. It felt like a small, hesitant step—like maybe, just maybe, we were moving toward some sort of normal, even if we were both too broken to find the right words. Trevor started talking about his day, about how he'd almost finished a history project he hated, and how the math teacher had assigned extra homework. It wasn't much, but it was something. It was a start.

"Did you hear about Brad Carter?" he asked, pushing the edge of his plate around with his fork. "He's a total jerk."

I didn't respond right away. Brad Carter was a name I hadn't even thought about in ages. He was the kind of guy who lived for gossip and drama, always looking for someone to tear down. Trevor's eyes were dark, and I knew exactly what he was getting at.

"Yeah, I heard," I said softly.

Trevor scoffed, his voice bitter. "That guy's a walking cliché. It's like he's auditioning for some high school drama where he's the villain."

I nodded, trying to mask the anger that bubbled beneath my skin. Brad's words—Maybe he's got a new family in Paris. Wonder if they're better looking than you—sliced through me like a blade, but I didn't let it show. Not to Trevor. He was dealing with enough of his own demons.

I tried to joke, though. "I think he just wants your attention. He probably misses being the center of every joke in the cafeteria."

Trevor snorted, but it didn't feel like laughter. He shoved his chair back and stood abruptly. "I can't just sit here and pretend like everything's fine. You don't know what it's like."

I opened my mouth to say something, but he was already gone, the front door slamming behind him. The sound was sharp and final, like a bullet shot through a glass window.

The silence that followed was deafening.

Later, when I tried to knock on his door, he didn't answer. His silence was like a wall between us, a wall I couldn't scale, no matter how hard I tried. I slid down to the floor outside his room, feeling the weight of everything crashing down on me. We were falling apart, piece by piece, and I didn't know how to fix it.

The smell of wine lingered from the kitchen, and I could hear Mom's soft, distant hums as she stood in front of the open fridge, reaching for another bottle. Her movements were slower now, almost deliberate, like she was trying to avoid facing the truth. But I could see it—the cracks were starting to show, the ones I'd ignored for so long.

She wasn't just grieving Dad. She was drowning in something deeper, something darker.

And it was only a matter of time before it swallowed her whole.

I pushed myself off the floor, feeling the weight of the house press in on me again. Trevor was shut in his room, my mom was lost somewhere in her own sorrow, and me? I didn't know what I was doing anymore. There was no plan, no escape, just this endless waiting for something to break wide open.

But everything I had once known felt like it was slipping through my fingers, and I didn't have the strength to hold on anymore.

How much longer could we keep pretending?

The answer, I realized with a sickening clarity, was not much longer at all.

Trevor didn't leave his room for days. The house felt empty, even though we were all still here, stuck in our own separate worlds, each of us trying to survive in our own way. I missed the noise—the laughter, the teasing, the constant hum of him raiding the fridge or blasting some obnoxious pop-punk song at full volume. That was Trevor, the guy who used to FaceTime his friends at ungodly hours and make dumb jokes about everything, never seeming to care what anyone thought. Now, his room was a fortress. The door never opened.

I tried. I really did. "Trevor, let's go get milkshakes," I'd call through his door, my voice sickly sweet, almost like I could convince him with some sugary treat.

Nothing.

"Trevor, it's movie night. Your pick," I said the next night. I threw in my best smile through the cracks in his door, but he didn't bite.

When Mom tried, it was worse. She wasn't as good at pretending. She knocked a few times, her voice getting tight. "You don't get to shut us out, Trevor! Not when—"

She stopped, the words hanging in the air like smoke. She didn't finish. Not when your dad abandoned us. It was on the tip of her tongue, but she couldn't say it, or maybe she didn't want to, even though it was true. But Trevor didn't come out.

And then there was the world outside. The house felt like it was folding in on itself, collapsing into this tight, uncomfortable space. It wasn't just that Trevor was shut in, or that Mom was quieter than ever, but it was the looks, the whispers, the pity that followed us everywhere we went.

I would walk down the street and feel their eyes on my back. Mrs. Garner, who had been my best friend's mom when I was younger, didn't even make eye contact anymore. Not that I blamed her. It was like we were a disease, a contagion that could be caught if you got too close. We were the family with the man who pretended to drown, who ran off for another woman. The kind of family that made you uncomfortable when you were around, like a bad omen hanging in the air.

At school, I overheard whispers in the hallways, a couple of girls giggling behind me. "You hear? Her dad ran away with some woman in Paris. Can you imagine?" One of them laughed, but there was no humor in it. Only judgment.

It was like we were the family that everyone felt sorry for, but not in the way that made you want to help. No, it was the kind of pity that made people avoid you, like somehow they thought we'd catch whatever made Dad leave.

The pity was everywhere. It seeped into every conversation, every glance, even when people didn't say anything at all. We were the abandoned family. The ones who didn't deserve a father anymore.

It felt like being invisible, but at the same time, it felt like everyone was looking at me. Like there was some glaring neon sign above my head saying, Her dad left. Her dad chose someone else over her.

And then there was Mom. She'd retreated, like I knew she would. The woman who used to talk to me about everything, who would drag me to every garage sale in a ten-mile radius just to spend time together, was now a shell. She walked around the house like a ghost, her eyes empty, her movements slow and mechanical. She didn't speak much, only when she had to, and her words were always clipped, icy.

"Dinner's in the fridge," she'd say, or, "Don't forget to take the trash out." Simple things, short things. Nothing that felt like us.

And Trevor? Trevor, the boy who used to tear through the house like a tornado, had become a shadow of himself. It wasn't just that he shut himself away, it was that he was gone, even when he was here. He never looked at me anymore, never responded when I said his name. And I couldn't get through to him. Not when I was drowning, too.

It was unbearable.

I had no idea how to make it stop. How to put the pieces back together when everything was falling apart. The house felt too small, too cramped with all the things we weren't saying, all the emotions we were pretending didn't exist. The silence was too loud.

Sometimes, late at night, I'd lie awake in my room, staring at the ceiling, feeling like I was losing everyone I loved. Trevor had pulled away, Mom was slipping further into herself, and I couldn't even think about Dad without feeling this knot twist in my stomach. If he was really gone, why did it still feel like he was here? If he really chose someone else, why did I keep wondering if he would come back?

And what if he didn't?

What if we never saw him again?

What did that make us, then?

What do I even have left?

I lay on my bed, staring at the books that had once meant something to me. They sat there, long forgotten now, piles of homework, notes from teachers, assignments I couldn't find the energy to care about anymore. My grades, once a source of pride, felt so insignificant. Everything around me was falling apart, and I couldn't stop it. And worse, I could feel myself falling, too. Falling deep into something I didn't know how to climb out of.

They called it "functioning depression" online. I could go through the motions—get up, shower, eat, talk when I had to—but none of it felt real. I didn't feel like I was really living. I was just… existing.

I sat at my desk, Dad's snow globe resting in my palm, its tiny storm of glitter swirling with every shake. The soft sound of its bell tinkled in my ears, almost mocking me. Staring at my laptop, I felt a strange pull. The police had found his chats, right? That meant there was a digital trail somewhere. There had to be something they missed, some clue they hadn't connected yet. Maybe something that would give me answers. Maybe something that would make sense of all of this.

The weight of the snow globe in my hand grounded me. It felt oddly comforting, as if it could shield me from the uncertainty of the world outside. But I knew I had to dig deeper.

I opened his email account first. The password, "Fishing4Days," was the one I'd guessed years ago after catching him scrolling through online fishing stores late at night. He'd always said it was for his weekend trips, but I'd gotten curious once and snooped to see what he was getting me for Christmas. Of course, I hadn't found out anything useful then, but I hadn't forgotten the password either. And it still worked.

The inbox was a mess of mundane receipts, subscription confirmations, and the usual spam—junk about lawn care and endless requests to buy new gear. Nothing stood out. Nothing was out of the ordinary. I was about to give up when my eyes stopped on something. An email address I didn't recognize: MargauxL27@gmail.com

I clicked it, my heart pounding in my throat. I don't know why I felt this sense of urgency—maybe because it was something new. Something that could make sense of everything.

The message itself was short. Too short.

"Looking forward to chat you soon, my love. It's been too long. – Margaux"

My stomach churned. The words hit me like a slap. My love.

A cold, sick feeling crawled through my body. I clicked the sender's name, desperate to know more. But there was nothing else. Just this one message, sitting there in Dad's inbox, hidden among the rest of the meaningless noise.

I let out a shaky breath, my fingers trembling as I gripped the edge of the desk.

I didn't know what to think. A million questions flooded my mind—Who was Margaux? Was she the woman from Paris? Was this the reason Dad left us? And if he really was still alive—why hadn't he reached out? Why hadn't he ever mentioned her? Why was this secret buried in his emails, hidden behind a smile that I thought I knew?

I clicked through a few more of his emails, but the words blurred in front of my eyes. The screen seemed to spin, and my hands started to feel numb. This was real. This was proof. Dad wasn't just gone. He had chosen to leave us for someone else.

The feeling of betrayal was suffocating. I wanted to slam the laptop shut, throw it across the room, but I couldn't. I couldn't stop staring at that email. At the words. My love.

The sound of footsteps outside my door broke my concentration. I quickly closed the laptop and shoved it away. My heart was hammering in my chest, and I tried to push the wave of nausea back down.

I didn't know what to do with this information. I didn't know how to feel.

And I didn't know how to tell Mom or Trevor about it. What was I supposed to say? Dad really did have an affair?

I felt like I was standing on the edge of something, teetering between the girl I used to be and this… stranger who couldn't trust the man she called father.

The knot in my stomach tightened, and I pulled

my knees up to my chest.

I wanted answers. But the more I dug, the more I realized I might not want them after all.

It was almost 2 a.m. when I stared at my phone, thumb hovering over Ryan's contact. I didn't expect him to pick up. In fact, I hoped he wouldn't. But then again, I couldn't be sure of what I was hoping for anymore. I just knew that I needed him.

I swiped to FaceTime and hit the button, holding my breath as it rang. I sat there in the dark, watching the little circle spin, feeling the weight of the night pressing in around me.

When the screen finally lit up, I saw Ryan's face, eyes squinting in the dim light. His messy hair was flattened against his forehead, and he blinked a couple of times, clearly disoriented.

"What's going on, Nat?" His voice was thick with sleep, laced with confusion. "It's like, two in the morning. You okay?"

I almost laughed at how familiar the concern sounded, but it only made the knot in my stomach twist tighter. No. I wasn't okay. But how could I explain?

"Ryan," I said, my voice low and shaky. "I need your help."

He sat up a little more, frowning. "With what?"

"I… I need you to help me get into my dad's bank account."

His eyes went wide with alarm, his brows knitting together. "What?" He leaned closer to the screen, like he couldn't believe what I was saying. "Are you insane?"

"I—" I paused, biting my lip. I didn't know how to explain this without it sounding like a bad idea, but it was the only one I had. "I need to know where he's been sending money, Ryan. I need to know where he's been, who he's been talking to. Everything I've found is just… it doesn't make sense. And I can't stop now. Not when it feels like he's still hiding things from me."

His expression softened for a moment, but the skepticism was still there. He rubbed his face, letting out a frustrated sigh. "Nat, this is a terrible idea. You don't know what you're messing with. Hacking into someone's account—it's illegal."

"I'm not hacking anything. I just need access. Please." My voice was tight, and I could hear the desperation in it. I could feel it choking me. "You're the only one who can help me."

He stared at me for a long moment, and I could almost feel the weight of his hesitation. His eyes flicked down to the side, like he was considering something, his jaw clenched.

Then, just as I thought he was going to tell me to forget it, he sighed. A heavy, resigned sound that sank straight into my chest. "This is the dumbest thing I've ever agreed to," he muttered, but I could tell he was already mentally figuring out the logistics.

I swallowed, relieved but anxious all at once. "I know. But I can't do it alone."

There was a long pause, and I could hear the sound of his breath on the other end of the line. Then he muttered, "Fine. But if we get caught—"

"I know," I interrupted. "I know."

But it didn't matter. I was already in too deep.

Ryan let out a long breath. "Okay, let's just… let's see what we can find. But you owe me, big time, okay?"

"Deal."

I pulled the phone closer to my chest, closing my eyes for a second, trying to calm the storm inside me. This wasn't just about hacking into a bank account. This was about unearthing everything my dad had left behind. The lies, the secrets. I had to know.

But as I felt that familiar rush of adrenaline start to replace the anxiety, I couldn't ignore the unease gnawing at the back of my mind.

What if finding the answers only made everything

worse?

What if the truth was something I couldn't handle?

CHAPTER 6: THE DECISION

Ryan worked in silence, his fingers flying across the keys with an intensity that made me almost believe he could find something I missed. Maybe he could. Ryan was good at this—he'd hacked the school's system to change his grade once, just to see if he could. So I was sure he'd be able to uncover something, anything, that would explain why my dad disappeared without a trace.

But as the minutes ticked by, that sinking feeling in my stomach grew stronger. There was nothing. Nothing to explain why he'd left. Why he'd abandoned us.

Ryan paused and turned the laptop towards me. "Here," he said, his voice flat. "I pulled up the account statements."

I leaned in close, heart pounding as I scanned the screen. There were dozens of transactions, but nothing stood out. The joint account between my parents was untouched—no secret withdrawals, no payments to

France, nothing that could explain why he'd left.

"That's… weird," I muttered. "He had to have used it. He was always buying stuff online."

"It's not just weird," Ryan said, his tone hardening. "It's a dead end. Your dad didn't use this account for anything." He clicked through a few more pages of bank statements, but it didn't change anything. The silence between us grew, thick with the weight of unanswered questions.

My frustration boiled over. "There has to be something! I know there is. People don't just disappear. Not like this. Not without leaving a trace." My voice cracked, but I didn't care.

Ryan's expression shifted, becoming more serious, his eyes darker than usual. "Maybe he did, Nat. Maybe he wanted to."

I recoiled, as if he'd slapped me. The words hung in the air, sharp and bitter. I stood up, pushing the chair back so hard it scraped against the floor. "You don't get it," I said, my voice shaking. "You don't understand what this is like. You don't know what it feels like to be… this." I gestured vaguely at myself, at the mess of emotions swirling inside me.

"I get it more than you think." Ryan stood up too, his face strained. "You're not the only one who's lost someone, Nat. But you have to face the truth. Maybe your dad wanted to disappear. Maybe he just didn't care anymore."

His words felt like a punch to the gut. I opened my mouth, but the anger caught in my throat. How could he say that? How could he just give up on my dad like that?

"I can't just stop," I shot back, my voice trembling. "This is my dad we're talking about! I need to know why. I need to know where he went, and if there's a reason he left us."

Ryan's face softened, but the intensity remained in his eyes. "And I'm your best friend," he said, his voice much quieter now. "But I can't keep helping you chase ghosts, Nat. I can't keep doing this. It's not healthy. You have to stop."

The words hit me harder than any of his harsh ones. My chest tightened, the walls around me feeling like they were closing in. My best friend—the one person I thought would stand by me no matter what—was leaving me to face this alone.

"I don't need you to help me anymore, Ryan," I whispered, my voice hollow. "If you don't want to be a part of this, fine. I'll do it by myself."

He didn't say anything, but I saw the flash of hurt

in his eyes before he grabbed his jacket and walked out of the room without another word. The door slammed shut behind him, leaving me alone in the silence, with only the flickering glow of the laptop screen for company.

I stood there, frozen. The rage that had surged through me now morphed into something else—something darker, heavier. I felt small. Like I was losing control over everything. Even the one thing I thought I could control—the search for answers—was slipping through my fingers.

I sank back down onto the floor, the weight of it all crashing down on me. The guilt gnawed at me, but so did the anger. I couldn't stop. I wouldn't stop. But now… now I didn't know how to keep going. How could I keep searching for answers when the one person who had always been there for me had just walked out?

The laptop screen blinked in front of me, still showing the list of empty transactions, the silence screaming in my ears.

The days after Ryan walked out of my room felt like walking through water. I couldn't escape the weight of what had happened between us. At school, it was like we had become invisible to each other. We moved in separate worlds—his, a blur of quiet conversations with his other friends; mine, filled with a growing sense of isolation. I felt like a ghost, hovering at the edges of my own life, barely touching anything real.

I tried to keep it together. I focused on the dull hum of routine, going through the motions of schoolwork and pretending everything was fine. But every time I saw Ryan, I couldn't help but feel the silence between us stretch further, like a tightrope I couldn't walk across. He was mad. He had every right to be. But I wasn't sure how to fix what had happened. I couldn't undo the hurt, and it seemed like the distance between us only grew wider each time I tried.

By Friday, I couldn't take it anymore.

I grabbed my bike from the garage, a decision made out of pure impulse. I didn't know where I was going exactly, but I couldn't stay in the house. Not when it felt like it was closing in on me, suffocating me with the echoes of things unsaid.

I didn't ride fast. There was no need. The bike path to Grey Lake was familiar, the path I used to take when I needed to clear my head. It was quiet there, the kind of quiet where you can hear the distant calls of birds and the whisper of the wind through the trees.

But today, it wasn't enough. I needed more.

I reached the lake's edge and parked my bike against a nearby tree. The water was still, like glass, reflecting the pale gray sky above. I stood there, staring at it, trying to breathe, to pull together the pieces of myself that had been scattered by everything that had happened.

And then it hit me.

I didn't just miss my dad. I missed the idea of him—the dad I thought I knew, the man who promised me he would always be there. He wasn't there anymore. And it wasn't just his absence; it was the lie he'd built around it. He was gone, and I was left with nothing but questions that would never be answered.

I sank to my knees on the gravel, my hands shaking as I pressed them against my face. I couldn't stop the tears. They came in waves—silent at first, almost like a whisper, then harder, until I felt like I might drown in them. The grief was raw, exposed, and I couldn't control it. Not anymore. It had been like this ever since I found out what my dad had really done, and no matter how hard I tried to push it all down, the weight of it was unbearable.

The memories of him—of his laugh, his stories,

his promises—had turned into something darker, twisted into lies I couldn't undo. I thought I knew who my dad was. But now I wasn't even sure I knew who I was anymore.

I took a few shaky breaths, trying to steady myself, but it didn't work. The tears kept coming, unstoppable and relentless.

"Hey, are you okay?"

I jumped, wiping my face quickly as I turned around. There was a man standing a few feet away, holding a camera in one hand and a microphone dangling from the other. He was mid-forties, dressed in a slightly rumpled jacket, and his eyes held the kind of intensity that made me want to hide. He looked like one of those podcasters—the kind who think they can solve mysteries by digging into other people's pain. I hated them. At least the media had some boundaries. They wouldn't publish photos of minors or expose family secrets for the sake of a headline. But these people? They didn't care. To them, the truth was a commodity, and they'd sell anything to get it.

I wiped my face again, feeling the heat of embarrassment burning my cheeks. I didn't want him to see me like this. "Can I help you?" My voice came out hoarse, thick with the mess of everything I'd been holding in.

He stepped closer, that grin creeping onto his face like he was about to crack some big scoop. "I'm sorry to intrude. I'm working on a story about the man who faked his death last year—the one who was supposed to have drowned in the Grey River. You wouldn't happen to know anything about that, would you?"

My stomach twisted in a way I couldn't explain. The last thing I needed was some stranger digging into the wreckage of my life. It felt like he was poking at an open wound, and it made my skin crawl.

"I…" My throat tightened, and I had to swallow hard before I could say the next words. "I don't know anything." My voice was barely above a whisper, and I started backing away, instinctively wanting to flee, but my feet felt like they were glued to the ground.

The man didn't seem to hear me. He took another step forward, his eyes gleaming with the kind of eagerness that made me sick. "But you do, don't you? Your dad, it's all tied up in the story, right? He faked his death to escape the family. There's got to be some—"

I snapped. "No. I'm sorry, but you've got the wrong person." My hands trembled, and I turned away, heading toward my bike. But the man didn't stop. His footsteps were quick behind me, and I could hear the desperate pitch in his voice.

"Are you sure? This is a big story, and you might be able to help us—"

"Damn these podcasters," I muttered, my teeth gritted together. The words came out sharp, laced with frustration. I didn't even look back as I grabbed my bike, hopping on it as quickly as I could. But even as I pedaled away, I could feel his presence behind me, like an unwanted shadow. His questions lingered, heavy in the air, and I couldn't shake the feeling of being hunted.

Pedaling furiously, I pushed myself faster, desperate to outrun him, to outrun the invasion of my privacy, of my grief. I didn't stop until I reached the precinct, my legs aching from the effort. The cool air stung my face, and my heart was still pounding in my chest.

I wasn't sure what I expected, but I needed to know what had happened to my dad. Maybe Detective Maxwell could help me find some kind of closure, some explanation to make sense of the mess my life had become.

Inside the precinct, the buzz of activity around me seemed distant, like I was standing behind a glass wall.

The walls felt heavy, like they were closing in. I was still trying to calm my breathing, to steady myself, but it was hard to focus. All I could think about was the man, with his microphone, his camera, his probing questions that had pierced me in a way I wasn't prepared for.

I couldn't keep pretending it wasn't real. My dad had faked his death, and now the world—the people who had no right to invade my life—were poking and prodding at the wounds he'd left behind. Podcasters were worse than the media. At least with the media, there were some laws. There were things they couldn't do. But these people? They had no shame. No boundaries. They'd dig into every part of your life, every secret, just for a story. And that made them dangerous.

A part of me wanted to turn around and walk out of the precinct, just leave it all behind and pretend like it didn't matter. But I couldn't. There was too much left to uncover. Too much that didn't make sense, that I couldn't ignore.

I had to know what happened to my dad. I had to know why everything felt like it was falling apart.

"Can I help you?" a voice suddenly asked, pulling me from my thoughts.

I turned to find a uniformed officer standing at the

front desk, a warm, slightly tired smile on his face. He was young, maybe in his late twenties, his eyes kind but knowing, as if he'd seen more than he cared to. I swallowed, the words almost sticking in my throat.

"I… I need to talk to Detective Maxwell," I said, my voice barely above a whisper.

Maxwell was at his desk, hunched over a pile of papers, his usual stoic expression carved into his face like a mask. There was something comforting in the way he sat, absorbed in his work, his world of reports and files. I didn't know if he was tired of me showing up every time I needed answers or if he was just resigned to it, but when he saw me standing in his doorway, he didn't look surprised.

"Detective Maxwell," I started, my voice coming out rougher than I'd intended. I swallowed, trying to steady myself. "I need to know. What have you found out about my dad? You've been looking for him for months. You have to know something."

He set his pen down slowly, his eyes meeting mine. There was a flicker of something in them— maybe sympathy, maybe frustration—but it was gone before I could read it. He leaned back in his chair, sighing.

"We don't have much, Natalie," he said quietly.

"But we do have reason to believe your father is alive and well, somewhere in Europe. The evidence points to it. His passport hasn't been flagged in any of the countries we've checked, and there have been no signs of him trying to access any of his American accounts."

I felt a strange mixture of relief and dread in my chest. He was alive. That should have been the piece of information I'd been hoping for, but instead, it felt like a cruel reminder of everything that had fallen apart. He's alive… but that doesn't mean he's coming back.

"Do you think he'll come back?" I asked, my voice quieter than I intended, the question slipping out before I could stop it. There was a tiny part of me that still clung to the hope that he might—despite everything, despite how badly he'd left.

Maxwell hesitated, the weight of my question settling between us. "If he does, he'll be facing a restitution fine for the resources we've used to search for him—manpower, equipment. The cost is around three hundred thousand dollars."

The number hit me like a slap. I felt my face flush with a wave of heat, my stomach sinking as if the floor had dropped out from under me. "Three hundred thousand?" I echoed. "For what? For him running away?"

Maxwell didn't flinch. "That's the price, Natalie. And if he decides to come back, he'll have to pay it."

The words felt like a weight in my chest, like I was suffocating under them. Three hundred thousand dollars. For the cost of his disappearance. For all the damage he'd caused. For all the people he'd hurt. The idea of him returning, carrying the weight of that debt, felt like a cruel joke. It didn't feel real. It didn't feel fair.

I stood there for a moment, my mind racing, trying to make sense of it all. I was standing in a room full of cold, hard facts, but nothing about the situation felt concrete. I couldn't wrap my mind around the idea of my father, the man who had promised me he would always come back, this man who had left us to clean up the mess he'd made. How could I ever look him in the eye again knowing what he'd done? What would I even say to him?

I blinked, trying to focus, but the tears that had been threatening to spill earlier pushed their way to the surface. I swallowed, hard, forcing them back. This wasn't the resolution I'd hoped for. It wasn't the closure I needed.

It was nothing.

It was just more empty space.

I turned to leave, the weight of everything pressing

down on me. As I walked out of the precinct, I could feel the emptiness of it all—the questions with no answers, the endless, aching space where my dad's presence should have been. I stepped out into the cold air, feeling the sharp bite of winter against my skin, but it didn't make me feel any less cold inside. It was like I was holding onto nothing—just the echo of a life that had fallen apart, and no clear way of putting it back together.

The world felt too big, too much for me to navigate. I wasn't sure what I was supposed to do with this knowledge. Knowing that he was alive didn't change anything. It didn't make it easier.

The decisions had already been made for me, long before I even knew what they meant.

And all I could do was keep moving, even though I had no idea where I was going.

Soon, things started to shift, but slowly, almost imperceptibly.

Mom stopped drinking. It wasn't an overnight miracle, but it was something. There were fewer bottles in the recycling bin, fewer late nights where I could hear her moving around in the kitchen, her movements clumsy and distant. Sometimes, when I'd wake up, I'd catch her sitting at the kitchen table, her hands wrapped around a mug, staring out the window as if the world outside was a place she could still make sense of.

Trevor came out of his room for dinner one night. It was so ordinary it almost felt unreal—he walked in, sat down, grabbed a plate, and started eating without a word. Mom didn't blink. I didn't either. It was like some unsung miracle, one of those little things that people forget to mention when they talk about recovery.

"Pass the potatoes," Trevor muttered, his voice still hoarse from not using it much. His eyes were shadowed, but he was here. At the table. With us.

Mom slid the bowl toward him. "How was your day?"

"Fine."

It was the closest thing we'd had to normal in months, and it felt like a delicate thread, something to hold onto even if it was barely there. But still, it was something.

As for me? I was still frozen. I felt like I had been standing still for so long, my mind locked in place by the weight of everything that had happened. I was pretending to be okay, to hold it all together, but I knew deep down I wasn't. Not really. I was just...

surviving.

Senior year limped across the finish line, dragging me with it. I was too tired to care anymore. Too tired to hope. The days blurred together—tests, assignments, half-hearted attempts at friendships, all while my dad's disappearance haunted me like a ghost I couldn't shake.

And then it happened—the thing I had dreaded most. I didn't get into a single college. Not even the community college.

I had known deep down that it wasn't going to happen. It wasn't like I had the drive or the focus to really push for it. Every day had been like swimming through mud, and by the end, I was just too exhausted to put in the effort.

When the acceptance letters came, I only opened one before tossing it aside—another "Sorry, not this time" letter. The rest sat in a pile on my desk, untouched, waiting for the reality to settle in.

The truth was too heavy, but I couldn't hold onto it anymore. College wasn't my future. It was just another thing I couldn't have, like the family I used to know, like the life I thought I would have.

By some miracle—or maybe the school felt sorry for me—I passed all my classes. Just enough. The credits added up, and I had enough to walk across that stage, to wear that stupid cap and gown.

"Barely," Trevor teased the night before the ceremony. He leaned against my doorframe, his smirk just a flicker of the brother I used to know. His eyes were still heavy with the shadows of everything, but there was a spark there—maybe of something close to life again.

"Still counts," I said, shoving my tassel into the bag I'd laid out for the next morning. The weight of it was strange in my hands, like holding onto something that didn't belong to me.

"Are you gonna trip crossing the stage?" Trevor asked, raising an eyebrow.

I threw a pillow at him, and for a moment, we laughed—real laughter, like the world hadn't broken us. It was brief, but in that moment, it was everything.

But after the laughter died, I was still there, standing at the edge of something I didn't want to face. Graduation was just a ceremony. A piece of paper. But it wasn't going to fix anything. Not the hole in my heart, not the fact that my life was scattered, piecing itself together only when it felt like it.

I wasn't sure what I was supposed to feel. Relief? Joy? But all I felt was numb.

And so, I went to graduation. I walked across the stage, my heart pounding in my chest. But when I reached the end, when the principal handed me the diploma, it felt like nothing had changed. It was just a step. A marker.

I was still me. Still stuck. Still lost. And the future? It felt more uncertain than ever.

But in the midst of that uncertainty, I took a deep breath. I made it. Even if I didn't know where I was going, at least I was still moving.

The next day at school, the auditorium buzzed with energy—pomp and circumstance, cheesy speeches, and the sound of parents cheering a little too loudly. Everyone seemed to know exactly where they were headed next. But as I walked across the stage, diploma in hand, I felt... nothing. More hollow than triumphant. The applause from the crowd felt like white noise, an echo of a life I didn't feel connected to anymore.

Ryan Maxwell, valedictorian, stood at the podium in his crisp suit, looking more put-together than I'd ever felt in my life. His speech was polished, inspirational, and full of all the right words. He spoke about hope, about the future, about the endless possibilities ahead. But the words felt like something I could never quite reach. Every time he glanced out at the audience, his eyes never found mine. And I didn't look for his. Not because I didn't want to, but because I couldn't.

When it was my turn to walk offstage, the weight of that disconnect—the distance between us—settled in my chest like a stone.

Afterward, Mom gave me a hug that felt more obligatory than proud. She squeezed me tightly, but it was a hug that didn't quite reach her eyes, as if she was holding onto something more than just me. I didn't know if it was the stress of everything or just the quiet realization that we were falling further apart. Either way, I couldn't bring myself to feel good about it.

The three of us—Mom, Trevor, and me—went out to dinner afterward. It was a local place where most of the kids from school went to celebrate their graduation. The same restaurant that always smelled of fried food and nostalgia, where you could count on every corner booth to be filled with families taking photos they'd never look at again.

Trevor made fun of me when I got stuck with the "small" nachos as my order, and for the first time in a long while, it felt like he was back to himself, his teasing playful and easy. Mom actually laughed, and the sound of it was almost too much for me to handle—like it was a moment I wasn't supposed to let go of.

"You sure that's enough?" Trevor teased, eyeing my plate. "Those nachos are practically one bite away from being a snack."

"Shut up, Trevor. It's called portion control," I shot back with a grin, feeling light for the first time today.

Then dessert came—a warm chocolate lava cake—and for a moment, the world seemed a little bit less broken.

But, of course, the peace didn't last.

I took a deep breath, staring at the cake in front of me, and then I dropped the bombshell.

"I'm taking a gap year."

Mom blinked at me, her spoon frozen mid-air. "A gap year?"

"Yeah." I tried to sound casual, like I wasn't setting my life on a completely different course than anyone had expected. "I've been thinking about it for a while. I want to travel. See Europe."

Her hand gently set her fork down, and the silence between us grew heavier. "Natalie, we don't have the money for that kind of trip."

I forced a smile, trying to make it sound

convincing. "I've been saving," I lied. "And I'll work odd jobs while I'm there. People do it all the time."

She narrowed her eyes, studying me with an intensity I wasn't used to. "Why now? What about college?"

"I'll figure it out later." My voice wavered just a little, but I didn't let it show.

There was a long, suffocating silence, before she sighed and stood up. "You're eighteen. I can't stop you." Her words hit harder than I expected, and I could feel the weight of them settling like a storm cloud over me. She didn't even ask why.

I hadn't told her the real reason.

Dad's name was a ghost on her lips, but it still lived on mine. Europe wasn't about crepes by the Seine or backpacking through picturesque towns. It was about Margaux. It was about finding him.

Just as I was trying to steady my breathing, when I spotted him: Ryan, weaving through the tables toward us. He wasn't in a suit like earlier; now he was in a simple hoodie and jeans, his valedictorian medal stuffed haphazardly into his hoodie pocket. He looked tired, but then again, so did everyone else.

"Hey, Donovan," he said when he reached our table. His voice was light, but his eyes flicked between me, Mom, and Trevor, like he was taking the temperature of the situation. "Congrats. You made it."

"Thanks," I said, my heart skipping a beat when he looked at me—really looked at me—for the first time in months.

"Barely," Trevor quipped, earning a pointed glare from me. Ryan cracked a small smile.

"Congrats to you too, Mr. Valedictorian," my voice a little too even, like I was trying too hard to be cool about it.

"Thanks," he said, stuffing his hands into his pockets. His gaze lingered on mine for a second before he turned to Mom. "Mrs. Donovan, hi."

Mom smiled politely. "Ryan. It's good to see you. Are you two still…?" She trailed off, the question hanging in the air awkwardly.

Ryan cleared his throat. "Not really," he said. Then, almost as an afterthought, he added, "I leave for MIT in a week. Early admission."

My stomach twisted. Of course. I should've known. He'd been working toward it for years, while I couldn't even manage to figure out what I was supposed to do with my life.

"Congratulations," I said, the words coming out a little bitter even though I meant them.

My stomach sank, but I forced a smile. "That's great," I said, and I meant it. Ryan had worked harder than anyone I knew to get into MIT. He deserved it.

"Thanks," he said, but his gaze flicked back to me, sharp and knowing. He tilted his head, his tone deliberately casual as he asked, "What about you? Any big plans?"

Mom answered before I could. "Natalie's taking a gap year. She says she wants to travel, see Europe."

The moment she said "Europe," Ryan's posture stiffened slightly, and his eyebrows lifted, the surprise clear on his face. "Europe, huh?" His voice was careful, measured, like he was trying to read between the lines.

I shrugged, playing it off. "Yeah. Figured it's now or never."

Ryan nodded slowly, but his eyes didn't leave mine. "Well, I hope you have a good trip. Hope you find what you're looking for." His words were loaded, and we both knew it.

"Thanks," I said, my voice barely above a whisper. He gave a small nod to Mom and Trevor, then turned to leave.

"Congratulations again, Ryan," Mom called after him. He waved over his shoulder but didn't turn around.

With that he left me with the tension that hadn't existed until the moment he mentioned Europe. He knew. He knew exactly what I was after. And worse, I knew he thought I was making a mistake.

I stared at my half-empty plate, the weight of the conversation pressing in on me.

Trevor nudged me with his elbow. "That was weird."

I ignored him, staring at the spot where Ryan had been. Mom didn't say anything, but I could feel her eyes on me, waiting for me to explain. I didn't. And I could feel the space between us growing even wider. The silence was like a final acknowledgment that we were all moving in different directions.

Instead, I focused on the dessert that had just arrived, pretending everything was fine. But deep down, I knew the truth. Ryan's words would follow me all the way to Europe.

And me?

I was still standing at the edge of a decision I wasn't sure I could make. Was I ready to leave? Ready to walk away from everything that was left here, even if it meant chasing something that might not even exist?

I didn't know. But I was going.

And I was going to find my dad.

CHAPTER 7: DEPARTURE

The day after graduation, I sat cross-legged on my bedroom floor, surrounded by a mess of scraps of paper, old receipts, and a notepad covered in frantic calculations. The sun streamed in through my window, casting warm pools of light on the floor, but it only made the clutter around me seem more chaotic. My eyes darted from one number to the next, but nothing made sense. The costs of a one-way ticket to Paris—and whatever else I might need to survive for a month—were like a giant, insurmountable wall.

A flight to Paris was expensive, even if I booked the cheapest economy ticket. Then there was lodging—hostels were cheaper than hotels, but not by much, and I'd need to stay somewhere safe. Food costs, metro passes, emergency cabs, and who knew what else? Every number felt like it was mocking me. I scribbled out the calculations again, more desperately this time.

Flight: $700 round-trip, if I booked early.

Lodging: $40 a night for a month—$1,200 minimum.

Food: $20 a day—$600.

Transport: $100.

Emergency fund: At least $500.

The grand total stared back at me like a judge handing down a sentence: $3,100.

My stomach churned. I didn't even have half that. My "savings" from babysitting and part-time jobs over the years amounted to a laughable $900, maybe $1,000 if I skipped a few meals. And let's be honest, that was stretching it. I chewed on the end of my pen, heart thudding in my chest. If I wanted to find Dad—or whatever version of him was out there now—I'd need more money. A lot more.

I pushed the pile of papers aside and grabbed my phone, hoping for some divine intervention, or at least a hint of a miracle. I typed into Google: How to make money fast.

The search results were...not inspiring.

1. "Sell your old stuff!"

I glanced around the room. Most of my "old stuff" consisted of half-finished art projects from middle school, a pile of books I'd read once, and my dad's old leather jacket. I couldn't exactly sell the jacket. It was probably the only thing of his that hadn't been taken or packed away in a box in the attic.

2. "Take surveys for money!"

Yeah, that was going to make me $3,100 in the next three days. I rolled my eyes.

3. "Pet-sit for wealthy families!"

As if anyone would trust me with their prize poodle when I could barely keep a houseplant alive.

4. "Freelance on Fiverr!"

Maybe if I could draw or write or do anything that people actually wanted to pay for. But the only thing I was good at was being the girl who showed up to every party with the least embarrassing snack—bagged chips were a safe bet. I laughed bitterly, tapping the screen.

I flopped back on the floor and stared at the ceiling, groaning. This was ridiculous. My whole plan was a joke. My dad had faked his death—what was I even doing? Running after a man who didn't want to be found? A man who'd left without a single word? I could barely scrape together enough for the essentials of survival, and here I was, playing detective in a city I didn't know, with zero resources and a stack of unanswered questions.

I let out a long breath, feeling like I might burst from the tension coiling in my chest. This whole situation was too big. Too out of my control. And yet I couldn't stop myself from pushing forward. I had to know.

The truth was, if I didn't go, I'd never be able to move on. If I didn't find him—or whatever he'd become—then every moment would just be this empty space in my life that I couldn't fill. Every day would be a reminder of what I had lost and never fully understood. But how the hell was I supposed to pay for it?

I stared at the screen for a moment, my heart lightening just a little. It wasn't the solution, but it was a step in the right direction. Maybe I couldn't buy the whole damn trip right now, but if I worked hard enough, if I pushed through, I could at least get close.

I grabbed my pen again, scribbling a few more figures on the paper. It wasn't perfect. It wasn't ideal. But it was a plan. I closed my eyes for a second, letting the smallest bit of hope fill the empty spaces in my chest.

Tomorrow was another day. And if nothing else, I could keep fighting.

The garage smelled like mildew and motor oil. Dad's scent lingered there too, faint but unmistakable, tangled up with the memory of him tinkering on his old truck. I shoved those thoughts aside and focused on the task at hand.

Mom had given me a tired shrug when I asked if I could sell some of Dad's stuff. "It's just junk now," she said, not even looking up from the bills she was sorting. Trevor didn't care either; he barely glanced up from his phone.

Junk or not, it wasn't easy. I spent hours cleaning out the cobwebs and dusting off tools, old fishing gear, even a battered record player that still worked after some fiddling. I snapped photos, wrote detailed descriptions, and posted everything on Craigslist.

The first sale came two hours later: a retired carpenter bought Dad's toolbox for fifty bucks. The second sale, a set of vintage fishing lures, went to an enthusiastic collector for seventy-five.

By the end of the week, the garage was emptier, and my wallet was fuller. I'd raised $800—still not enough, but it was a start.

That night, I collapsed onto my bed, staring at the ceiling. I should've felt accomplished, but instead, a heavy weight settled in my chest. Selling off Dad's things felt like erasing pieces of him, even if I told myself they were just objects.

I hated how detached Mom and Trevor seemed.

It was like they'd already written him off, filed him under "Gone" in their minds and moved on. But I couldn't.

For me, Dad wasn't a ghost or a memory. He was still out there somewhere, laughing with Margaux, walking cobblestone streets I'd never seen, living a life I couldn't imagine.

I didn't care how much it cost or how impossible it seemed. I had to find him.

I was sitting on the cold garage floor, surrounded by piles of old stuff I'd sorted into categories: "sellable," "might sell," and "why did Dad even keep this?" when Jamie Garner wandered in.

Jamie was our next-door neighbor, a fifteen-year-old with a penchant for obscure facts and an uncanny ability to see patterns that most people missed. He'd always been quiet but sharp, with an attention to detail I admired.

"Hi, Jamie," I said, glancing up as he stood at the threshold, clutching a Rubik's Cube he'd probably solved a dozen times already.

"Hi, Natalie," he replied, his eyes scanning the room. "What are you doing?"

I gestured to the mess. "Trying to sell some of Dad's stuff online. Need to make money for a trip."

Jamie's brow furrowed as he stepped closer, his fingers twitching against the cube. "What kind of stuff?"

"Tools, fishing gear, random antiques," I said, holding up an old clock I hadn't figured out how to price.

Jamie crouched beside me, taking the clock carefully in his hands. "This is a vintage Seth Thomas mantel clock. Probably from the 1940s. It's missing a key to wind it, but people like these for parts. You could sell it for maybe seventy dollars."

I blinked at him, impressed. "How do you even know that?"

"I like clocks," he said simply.

For the next hour, Jamie combed through the piles with me, pointing out which items were worth more than I'd realized. He identified brands, explained quirks that collectors might care about, and even helped me clean some of the pieces to make them look more appealing.

"You're kind of amazing at this, you know that?" I said, grinning as he polished a brass compass.

Jamie's face stayed serious. "I like helping."

"Well, you're saving me from getting ripped off, so thanks."

He nodded, a small smile tugging at the corners of his mouth.

Later that evening, I was pricing out a set of antique wrenches when Trevor wandered into the garage. He'd been watching me work from a distance all week, his usual sarcastic comments replaced with quiet observation.

"Still selling Dad's junk?" he asked, leaning against the doorframe.

"It's not junk," I replied, holding up a wrench like a prize. "This is a collectible."

Trevor smirked but didn't argue. Instead, he reached into his hoodie pocket and pulled out his piggy bank. It was one of those ceramic dinosaurs we'd both had as kids, chipped and scuffed from years of handling.

"What's that for?" I asked, narrowing my eyes.

"For you," he said, setting it on the workbench.

"Trevor, no—"

"Shut up and take it," he interrupted, grabbing a hammer. Before I could protest, he smashed the bank open, sending coins and crumpled bills scattering across the table.

We spent the next few minutes counting. When we were done, I stared at the total in disbelief.

"Trevor, this is... over two thousand dollars."

He shrugged like it was no big deal, but his ears turned red. "It's for your trip. I was saving for a car, but you need it more."

My throat tightened, and I couldn't stop the tears from welling up. "I can't take this."

"You're taking it," he said firmly. Then he wrapped me in a rare, tight hug. "Just promise to text me every day. Even if it's just 'I'm alive.'"

I laughed through my tears, squeezing him back. "Deal."

For the first time in weeks, the weight on my chest felt a little lighter. Maybe, just maybe, this trip wasn't as impossible as I'd thought.

The night before my flight, Grandpa came over for dinner. He'd been a constant in our lives since Dad disappeared—a quiet but steady presence, always ready with a story or a dad joke. Tonight, he brought his signature apple pie, the one with the too-thick crust that Trevor and I loved to mock but secretly adored.

"Ah, Paris," Grandpa said, settling into his chair at the head of the table. "City of lights, art, and overpriced coffee. You'll love it, kiddo."

"Overpriced coffee sounds like Natalie's brand," Trevor teased, smirking as he passed the mashed potatoes.

I rolled my eyes. "Better than your gas station burrito aesthetic."

"Hey, don't knock convenience store cuisine," Trevor said, pointing his fork at me. "It's a lifestyle."

Grandpa chuckled, his laugh deep and warm. "Just don't come back with one of those berets. They'll never let you live it down."

Mom, quieter than usual, smiled softly as she refilled everyone's glasses. "Your uncles and aunts sent over some gifts for your trip," she said, gesturing to a pile of neatly wrapped packages on the counter.

One by one, I opened them: a guidebook from Uncle Ray, a fancy travel pillow from Aunt Lisa, and a tiny travel sewing kit from Aunt Cindy, who clearly thought I'd be mending ballgowns on cobblestone streets.

"They mean well," I said, holding up the sewing kit like a prized relic.

"Just don't sew your passport shut," Trevor quipped, earning a laugh from everyone, even Mom.

After dinner, I was packing the last of my things when the doorbell rang.

"I'll get it," I called, slipping past Trevor, who was eyeing the leftover pie.

When I opened the door, I found Ryan standing there, hands in his pockets, his eyes shifting between me and the porch floor.

"Hey," he said, leaning against the railing.

"Hey," I replied, unsure of what to say.

He held out a small envelope. "A going-away present."

I opened it to find a travel journal, the kind with a weathered leather cover and thick, blank pages that smelled faintly of ink and adventure.

"Thought you might want to write about all the people you meet," he said, his grin hesitant, almost sheepish.

"Ryan…" My voice caught, guilt pressing down on me like a weight.

"I was a jerk," he said, cutting me off. "I shouldn't have walked out like that. I just… I didn't know how to help you."

I studied him for a moment, the boy who'd been my anchor in a sea of chaos. "I wasn't fair to you either," I admitted, my voice soft.

"So…" he began, shifting his weight like he was bracing himself. "You're really going?"

I nodded. "First thing tomorrow."

He hesitated, then blurted out, "Let me come with

you."

I blinked, caught completely off guard. "What?"

"Let me come with you," he repeated, his voice steadier now.

"Ryan, you're supposed to start at MIT in, like, a week."

He shrugged. "Not exactly. They're advanced summer classes they offered me to sit in. Real college doesn't start for three months."

"You're going to give up MIT summer classes to backpack around Europe with me?"

He smirked. "You'd get lost in, like, Prague or wherever without me."

A laugh escaped me, surprising us both. "Ryan, you don't have to—"

"I know I don't," he said, cutting me off again. "But you're my best friend, Nat. And honestly? I don't think you should do this alone."

The words hung in the air between us, heavy with meaning.

I didn't say yes. But I didn't say no either.

The plane ride felt surreal, like stepping into a dream where nothing quite made sense. The hum of the engines blended with the soft chatter of passengers, the clinking of drink carts, and the occasional crying baby. Through the small, scratched window, the world was nothing but a sea of stars above and inky blackness below, both vast and unreachable.

Ryan, of course, didn't seem fazed. He spent most of the time scrolling through a playlist he'd made for the trip, occasionally jabbing me in the side to ask if I liked a song.

"Do you ever sit still?" I muttered, pulling my hoodie tighter around me as the plane rumbled softly.

"Not when I'm on my way to Paris," he said, grinning. "We're about to see the freaking Eiffel Tower, Nat. You can't just nap through that."

I rolled my eyes, but a small smile tugged at my lips. Ryan's enthusiasm was infectious, even if it felt like he was living a completely different experience than I was.

He nudged me again, more gently this time. "Okay, but seriously—'Wonderwall' or 'Boulevard of Broken Dreams'? Which one's more iconic?"

"You're asking me to rank sad guy anthems at midnight over the Atlantic Ocean?" I asked, raising an eyebrow.

"Hey, it's important," he said, eyes sparkling.

I laughed softly despite myself. "Wonderwall, obviously. But it's close."

He gave an exaggerated sigh of relief, crossing "Boulevard" off some imaginary list in his mind.

But when his attention turned to his screen, my mind wandered back to the weight sitting squarely on my chest. Every beat of my heart seemed to whisper a single word: Dad.

"I don't even know where to start," I blurted after a long stretch of silence.

Ryan pulled out an earbud, tilting his head. "What?"

"When we get there," I said, keeping my voice low so I wouldn't wake the sleeping woman in the next row. "What if I can't find him? Or worse, what if I do? What if he doesn't even want to see me?"

Ryan's face softened, and for once, he didn't have a quick comeback. "Nat, you're not doing this because it's easy. You're doing it because you need answers."

"Yeah, but what if I can't handle those answers?" I whispered, gripping the armrest as turbulence jostled the plane lightly.

"You will," he said simply, like it was the most obvious thing in the world. "And I'll be there, okay? Even if it means I have to run around Paris asking people in bad French if they've seen some guy with your dad's face."

That earned a laugh from me, though it was shaky. "Your French is definitely bad."

He grinned. "Terrible, actually. But seriously, Nat. Whatever happens, you don't have to figure it all out in one day. One step at a time, okay?"

I nodded, even though my chest still felt tight. It wasn't a solution, but it was something to hold onto, and for now, that was enough.

The cabin lights dimmed as the plane cruised into the night, and Ryan finally settled down, his head lolling against the back of the seat as his breathing evened out. But sleep didn't come for me, not with the questions ricocheting inside my head.

The flight attendant passed by, offering water, and I took a cup, staring into it like it might hold the clarity I was desperate for.

Somewhere out there, across the black expanse of ocean, was Paris. And maybe—just maybe—there was Dad, too.

The flight attendant served our in-flight dinner on trays that smelled faintly of microwaved mystery. Ryan poked at his chicken with a plastic fork, his face contorted in an expression of theatrical dread.

"Are you sure this isn't some kind of scientific experiment?" he whispered, holding up a limp green bean for inspection.

"Pretty sure," I replied, chewing cautiously on a piece of bread that had the texture of a stress ball.

Ryan leaned closer, lowering his voice. "You think if I fake food poisoning, they'll let me off this plane?"

"Stop being dramatic," I said, though I couldn't help laughing as he made a show of recoiling from his tray.

Later, when the cabin lights dimmed and most passengers were trying to sleep, Ryan's restlessness peaked. "I can't do this, Nat. I'm losing my mind," he whispered, staring at his darkened phone screen like it had betrayed him.

"What are you even talking about?" I mumbled, my head propped awkwardly against the window.

"No internet. No Wi-Fi. No memes." He shook his phone as if that would bring it back to life. "I need something."

"You could just sleep like a normal person," I suggested.

"Or," he said, pointing dramatically, "I could pay for an hour of Wi-Fi and stay sane."

"Ryan, it's like twenty bucks for thirty minutes," I said, eyebrows raising.

"Extortion," he declared. "But desperate

times…"

I watched as he wrestled with the decision, finally caving and grumbling the entire time as he entered his credit card information. Five minutes later, he groaned again.

"What now?"

"The Wi-Fi's slower than dial-up. It's like being mocked by the internet gods."

I rolled my eyes, pulling my blanket tighter around me. "You're hopeless."

By the time breakfast arrived—watery eggs and a half-frozen croissant—we were bleary-eyed and aching, but Ryan managed to scarf his down in record time. "Fuel for Paris," he said around a mouthful of croissant crumbs.

"More like fuel for complaining," I teased.

At immigration, the officer stared at us with the kind of stoicism that made me question my life choices.

"Purpose of your visit?" she asked, her accent sharp.

Ryan opened his mouth, but I shot him a look, silently begging him not to say anything stupid.

"Vacation," I said quickly, my voice cracking slightly.

The officer's eyes narrowed. "And how long will

you stay?"

"A couple of weeks," I answered, but Ryan decided to chime in.

"Maybe longer if she finds her—"

I kicked his shin, hard, and his words dissolved into a yelp.

The officer raised an eyebrow but stamped our passports without further comment. As we walked away, Ryan whispered, "You didn't have to maim me."

"Yes, I did," I hissed.

When we landed, Paris unfolded like a storybook. The air smelled like fresh bread and car exhaust, an odd but intoxicating mix that immediately filled my lungs with possibilities. Every corner seemed like a photograph waiting to happen—flower-strewn balconies, winding cobblestone streets, and the lazy curve of the Seine glittering under the summer sun.

"Where do we even start?" Ryan asked, spinning in a slow circle as we stood outside the airport, surrounded by suitcases and taxi drivers shouting rapid-fire French.

One driver, an older man in a scuffed leather jacket, grabbed at my suitcase, his rapid French catching me off guard.

"Non, merci!" Ryan said, stepping in front of me.

Once the driver backed off, he leaned closer and whispered, "I saw a TikTok about this. Never take taxis at the airport. It's a scam."

I sighed. "Then what do you suggest, TikTok guru?"

"Public transit," he said, grinning. "We're going full local."

I pulled out my crumpled itinerary, already regretting bringing him along.

"I have a plan," I said, unfolding the paper.

Ryan snatched it out of my hands, squinting at the scribbled addresses and time stamps. "This is just locations. Where's the fun stuff?"

I shrugged. "We'll get to it later."

He muttered, "Classic Natalie," under his breath, but there was a small smile on his face as he handed it back.

As we walked toward the train station, I couldn't help but feel a spark of something unfamiliar—maybe excitement, maybe dread, or maybe both.

Paris had never felt so close, and yet, I had never felt so far from certainty.

CHAPTER 8: CLUES IN PARIS

Our first day in Paris was exactly what you'd expect for two clueless Americans. Within an hour, we'd managed to get lost on the Metro, ending up in a quiet neighborhood far from anything remotely resembling my carefully planned itinerary.

"You sure this is where our hotel is?" Ryan teased, squinting at a faded street sign that looked like it hadn't been updated since the 1960s.

"No," I said flatly, dragging my suitcase over a cobblestone street that felt designed to destroy wheels and hopes alike.

"Good," he replied, gesturing dramatically to the sleepy corner bakery and shuttered shop windows. "Because this looks like the set of Emily in Paris after they cut the budget."

We must've looked ridiculous—two barely adults, one dragging a suitcase with a broken wheel, the other trying to balance a backpack and a map that might as well have been written in hieroglyphics. My feet ached, my patience was threadbare, and the romance of Paris felt like a cruel joke.

"This doesn't even look like the hotel district," Ryan said, glancing at a street lined with small shops and graffiti-covered walls.

"No kidding," I muttered, staring at the map on my phone like it might spontaneously develop the power to guide us.

"Are you sure you put in the right address?" he asked, peering over my shoulder.

"Yes, Ryan. I know how to type an address," I snapped.

"Well, apparently not in French."

I shot him a glare, dragging my suitcase behind me as it rattled loudly over uneven cobblestones. The wheels caught on every crack, and it felt like the universe was mocking me with each lurch forward.

The longer we wandered, the crankier we got.

"This is your fault," Ryan muttered after the third wrong turn.

"How is this my fault?" I snapped. "You said you could read the map!"

"I said I could try to read the map. It's in French, Natalie!"

I huffed, slamming my suitcase down for emphasis. "Then why didn't you let me handle it?"

"Because you're a control freak!"

"At least I'd be in control of where we're going!"

We stood there, glaring at each other, while an older French woman passed us with an amused smile, shaking her head as if to say, tourists.

Eventually, hunger forced a truce. We stumbled into a tiny café that smelled like butter and coffee, its faded awning promising authenticity, or at least a chance to sit down.

"I'm going to ask for directions," I said, already making my way to the counter.

Ryan followed, his hands shoved in his pockets. When it was his turn to order, he squared his shoulders like he was preparing for battle. "Bonjour," he said, overly enunciating every syllable. "Uh… croissant. And… coffee?"

The waiter stared at him with the kind of disdain that only a Parisian could master. "Espresso?" he said in flawless English.

"Yeah, that," Ryan mumbled, his confidence deflating like a popped balloon.

I tried to keep a straight face but failed miserably, laughing into my scarf. I added my own order, and soon we were sitting at a wobbly table with steaming cups of espresso and buttery croissants that almost made up for the disaster of our morning.

Ryan took a bite and sighed dramatically. "This? This is why people romanticize Paris."

"And here I thought it was the Eiffel Tower," I said, smiling despite myself.

The croissants were heavenly, the kind that flaked apart in perfect golden layers with every bite. We sat at a wobbly table near the window, sipping espresso that was so strong it made my head buzz.

Ryan leaned back in his chair, stretching out his legs. "Okay, I'll admit it. Paris might have its moments."

I smirked. "Glad to see your faith restored."

He glanced out the window, watching as an old man shuffled by with a baguette tucked under one arm. "So, what's the plan, oh fearless leader?"

I pulled out my crumpled itinerary, smoothing it against the table. "We find the hotel first. Then we figure out where to start looking."

"Looking for what, exactly?" Ryan asked, his voice careful.

I hesitated, staring at the scribbled notes in the margins of my notebook. "Anything. Something."

He didn't push, just nodded and stood up, grabbing his bag. "Alright then. Lead the way."

Dragging our luggage through the streets of Paris felt like the beginning of a very bad comedy sketch. Ryan tripped over his suitcase twice, and I nearly rolled mine into a parked scooter.

"Why didn't we just call a cab?" Ryan grumbled.

"Because," I said through gritted teeth, "the driver at the airport was definitely going to scam us. You even said so yourself—remember the TikTok?"

"Oh, great," he said, throwing his hands in the air. "We're taking life advice from TikTok now. Fantastic."

When we finally made it to the hotel, we were too tired to argue anymore. Instead, we stood in stunned silence, staring at the peeling paint and the neon sign that flickered ominously.

The website had promised "charming vintage charm" and "authentic Parisian flair." The hotel was…not what I'd expected.

Ryan stood in the doorway, staring in disbelief. "Are we on a reality show right now? Is someone going to pop out with a camera crew and tell us we've been pranked?"

"It's not that bad," I said weakly, though even I didn't believe it.

He pointed at the sagging couch in the corner. "That thing looks like it's seen more wars than Napoleon."

Despite everything, I couldn't help laughing. "Come on. Let's check in and see if the rooms are any better."

They weren't.

The bed was lumpy, the window barely opened, and there was a mysterious stain on the carpet that I decided not to investigate.

"This is…quaint," Ryan said, his tone dripping with sarcasm.

"It's not that bad," I said, though the lumpy mattress in the corner of our room and the faint smell of mildew suggested otherwise.

Ryan flopped onto the bed with a groan. "You seriously booked this online?"

"The pictures looked better," I muttered, yanking the window open for some air.

"Better as in they hired a professional liar to take them?"

Despite everything, I laughed, and for the first time that day, the tension between us eased.

Ryan flopped like a fish on the mattress with a dramatic groan. "I don't know about you, but I'm feeling very Parisian right now."

I threw a pillow at him, shaking my head. "Get some sleep. Tomorrow, we start for real."

He caught the pillow and smirked. "And by real adventure, you mean more walking, more getting lost, and more tiny coffees?"

"Exactly."

As I lay in bed that night, listening to the muffled sounds of the city outside, I felt the weight of what lay ahead pressing against my chest. This wasn't a vacation. This was a mission, and every moment mattered.

But for now, at least, I could let the city hold its secrets for one more night.

We woke up to the jarring sound of garbage trucks outside, their metallic clanging echoing up through the narrow streets. I groaned, burying my face in the pillow as the morning sun filtered through the thin curtains.

"This is not the Paris I imagined," Ryan mumbled from the other bed, his hair sticking out in every direction.

"It's authentic," I muttered.

Authentic, I discovered, also meant no hot water. I turned the shower knob experimentally, waiting for the icy stream to turn warm. It didn't.

"Ryan," I called, poking my head out of the bathroom.

"Don't even say it," he groaned.

We went down to the front desk, where the clerk greeted us with a disinterested expression and rapid-fire French.

"I don't think he understands us," I whispered to Ryan.

"No kidding," Ryan replied. "Let me try." He leaned on the counter and said loudly, "No hot water!" miming a shower.

The clerk stared at him, unimpressed. "Non," he said simply, waving us away.

"Great," Ryan said, throwing up his hands as we trudged back upstairs. "Now I know what mime school dropouts do for a living."

Once we'd freshened up as much as cold water and questionable soap allowed, I sat on the windowsill of our room, pulling my knees to my chest. The view wasn't much—just a narrow alley and the side of another building—but it felt like Paris anyway.

I snapped a quick picture and sent it to my mom and Trevor.

Mom: First morning in Paris! You look so grown up, sweetie. I'm proud of you.

Trevor: You better bring me back something cool, or I'm raiding your room when you get home.

I smiled, tucking my phone away as Ryan tapped impatiently on the door. "Ready yet?"

We stepped outside into the crisp morning air, the city already buzzing with life.

"Okay," Ryan said, squinting at the map on his phone. "Where to first?"

"Where else?" I said with a grin. "The Eiffel Tower."

As we debated the best way to get there, I suggested hailing a cab.

"Why would we do that?" Ryan asked, appalled. "We can walk."

"Because it's faster?" I countered. "And I'm not exactly in the mood for another Parisian death march."

"It's part of the experience!" he insisted.

"Getting blisters is not an experience."

He sighed dramatically. "Fine. But when we pass some amazing bakery that you wouldn't have seen from a cab, don't come crying to me."

By the time we made it to the Eiffel Tower, my feet were aching, but I had to admit the sight was worth it. The sun was setting, casting the entire structure in a warm golden glow that made it look like something out of a dream.

We sat on the grass in Champ de Mars, a bag of overpriced macarons between us. I pulled out my dad's snow globe, turning it over in my hands as the tiny flakes swirled around the miniature Eiffel Tower inside.

Ryan watched me carefully. "You really think he's here?"

"I don't know," I admitted, my voice quiet. "But this… this is the closest I've felt to him in years."

Ryan didn't say anything, just reached over and plucked the snow globe from my hands. He turned it over, studying it from every angle.

"What are you doing?" I asked.

"Looking for clues," he said, his tone only half-joking.

"Ryan, it's a snow globe, not a treasure map."

But then his finger brushed against something on the base, and his brow furrowed. "Hey, there's an inscription here."

"What?"

He held it up, squinting. "It's tiny, but it says... 'Boutique Lumière.'"

My heart leapt. "That must be the shop where he bought it!"

Ryan handed it back to me, his excitement infectious. "It's a long shot, but we should try to find it."

I clutched the snow globe tightly, hope flickering to life in my chest. "Let's do it."

As the Eiffel Tower began to twinkle against the darkening sky, I felt something I hadn't in a long time—a sense of direction, of purpose.

The small wooden sign outside read Boutique Lumière, its paint faded and peeling, but still managing to exude charm. The shop was tucked away on a quiet side street, its window display filled with delicate trinkets: Eiffel Tower keychains, miniature paintings, and a rainbow of Parisian snow globes.

"This is it," I said, gripping the snow globe tightly in my hand.

Ryan pushed open the door, setting off a little bell overhead. Inside, the shop smelled faintly of lavender and old wood. Shelves lined every wall, each one crammed with souvenirs that sparkled under the warm light.

"Wow," Ryan said, spinning slowly to take it all in. "If kitsch had a capital, it'd be this place."

"Shh," I hissed, elbowing him in the ribs.

At the counter, an elderly man with a neatly trimmed beard and wire-rimmed glasses looked up from a book he was reading. His expression was kind but tired, as though he'd been running this place for decades.

"Bonjour," I began nervously, pulling out my phone and opening a translation app. "I… need help?"

The man tilted his head, watching me curiously but didn't respond.

"Great start," Ryan muttered.

"Excuse me," a lilting voice interrupted. A young woman emerged from behind a curtain in the back, her dark hair pulled into a loose braid. She was probably around our age, wearing an effortlessly chic outfit that screamed Parisian cool. "You need translation, yes?"

"Yes!" I said, relieved.

The girl smiled, leaning on the counter. "I am Amélie, his granddaughter. What can we do for you?"

I placed the snow globe carefully on the counter. "This. My dad bought it here years ago. I'm trying to find out if the owner—your grandfather—remembers anything about it."

Amélie translated rapidly, her words spilling out in a stream of French that made the old man nod slowly. He picked up the snow globe, turning it over in his hands.

After a moment, Amélie spoke again. "He says he remembers these. They are from his older collection, but he does not make them anymore. Too delicate, he says."

I swallowed hard. "Does he... remember who might have bought it?" I pulled out my phone, showing a picture of my dad. "Him?"

Amélie asked her grandfather, who shook his head apologetically. He said something in French, which she relayed. "He says he sees many tourists. It is hard to remember faces."

My heart sank. I tried to muster a smile. "Thank you anyway."

As I turned to leave, I caught Amélie giving Ryan a lingering look.

"You are very... how do you say... mignon," she said, her accent thick but undeniably flirtatious.

Ryan blinked. "Uh, thanks?"

She leaned across the counter, holding out her phone. "If you like to party while in Paris, call me. I will show you the city."

Ryan flushed as she airdropped her number to him. "Uh, sure."

I clenched my jaw, an uncomfortable heat rising in my chest. "We should go," I said tersely.

Amélie smiled sweetly at Ryan. "Goodbye, beau garçon."

As we stepped outside, Ryan glanced at me, clearly amused. "What's with the face?"

"Nothing," I said flatly.

"Oh, come on," he teased, nudging my arm. "Are you mad that French girls find me irresistible?"

"No," I snapped. "I'm mad that we're wasting time while my dad is out there somewhere."

Ryan's smile faded, and he shoved his hands in his pockets. "Sorry," he muttered.

We walked in silence after that, the weight of disappointment settling over me. The snow globe felt heavier in my bag, like it had absorbed all my dashed hopes.

But there was a flicker of something else too—a strange, gnawing sensation I didn't want to name. It wasn't just about my dad or the wasted lead.

I hated that she'd flirted with him.

The argument started small, like a crack in a windshield, but it spread fast.

Ryan and I were walking back to the hotel after the fruitless visit to Boutique Lumière, my hand clenched around the snow globe like it might crack open and reveal something more—something I could understand. Something I could hold onto.

"I don't get why you're so obsessed with this," Ryan muttered, his voice tinged with frustration. "You're in freaking Paris, Nat. You're here to have an adventure, not just dig around in the past."

"I'm not obsessed!" I snapped, glaring at the cobblestone street beneath my feet. "I'm just trying to find answers. This trip was supposed to mean something, and I—"

"And what? You thought you'd just walk into a shop and they'd hand you some magical key to all your dad's secrets?"

I stopped walking, turning to face him. "You don't get it. I need this. I need something that makes sense." My voice cracked.

Ryan sighed, rubbing his face in that way he always did when he was trying to figure out what to say. "I know, Nat. I know. But you can't just keep looking for your dad in every shadow. You need to—" He paused, searching for the right words. "Look around. You're in Paris. This is your moment. You can't just keep your head in the clouds."

I felt a sharp pang in my chest, the familiar weight of grief pulling me down again. "I'm not wasting it, okay?" I muttered. "I'm doing the best I can."

"Then do something different," Ryan said, his voice softer now. "Take a chance. See Paris. Really see it." He dropped his hands into his pockets, his face serious. "You can't find answers in a shop. You have to go out there and live the experience, Nat. Don't waste your gap year. Don't waste this."

The words stung, but beneath them was a truth I didn't want to hear. I didn't know how to live without constantly searching. Without doing something that might lead me to my dad.

I opened my mouth to argue, but he held up a hand, stopping me. "Trust me. There's more to you than this mystery. More to Paris than whatever you're looking for."

I didn't reply. I couldn't. The truth of it hit me harder than I wanted to admit.

The next day, Ryan tried a different approach.

He dragged me out of bed earlier than I would've liked, insisted on breakfast at some tiny café, and then led me to a bridge I'd never even heard of before.

"We're going to Pont des Arts," he announced,

grinning like he'd just won some sort of personal victory.

"Pont des Arts? What's that?" I asked, still half-dazed from the lack of sleep.

He gave me an exasperated look. "You've never heard of it? It's the lock bridge, Nat. The one where couples put locks with their names on it and throw away the key. It's pretty damn iconic, if you ask me."

I couldn't help the small laugh that slipped out. "You sound like a tourist brochure."

Ryan shot me a look, but didn't respond. He was too busy, already leading me to the bridge, where the whole structure shimmered with a rainbow of locks.

"You can't just keep your head in the clouds," he said as we leaned over the railing, the Seine glinting below us. "Paris is literally right here. Don't waste it."

I scanned the water below, wondering what I was looking for. Was there something in the ripples that would give me an answer? Some hidden clue to the puzzle of my dad?

"I'm not wasting it," I said, a little too sharp. "I just…" I trailed off, unsure how to explain the weight I carried.

Ryan's tone softened, but it was still firm. "Nat, you're not going to find your dad under a bridge."

The words hit me harder than I'd expected. I wanted to argue, to say that everything had to lead somewhere, but I couldn't. He was right. I had to stop searching for him in every corner of Paris. I had to let go.

I stared at the locks for a moment before sighing. "Fine," I muttered. "But I'm not doing the lock thing."

Ryan raised an eyebrow and grinned. "We'll see about that."

A few minutes later, he was holding up a lock, a huge grin on his face. "I got one," he said, twisting it in his fingers. He produced a pen and scribbled something on the surface. "There. Done."

"What did you write?" I asked, intrigued despite myself.

He showed me the lock. "Just something random." He raised an eyebrow. "It's for good luck, anyway."

I leaned in closer to see the inscription. Ryan + Nat = Best friends forever. Don't forget it.

I blinked, a laugh bubbling up despite myself. "You're such a nerd."

"You know it," he said, winking.

He handed me the lock, and we clicked it onto the bridge. I watched the key drop into the river below. It was silly, but something about it made the weight on my chest feel a little lighter.

We snapped a few selfies with the locks and the bridge in the background. I hated how cheesy it felt, but Ryan's laughter was contagious.

"Okay," I said, wiping tears from my eyes after our fourth attempt at a selfie. "You win. This is kind of fun."

Ryan grinned. "I knew you'd come around."

Afterwards, I let him drag me through the winding streets, taking me to a street market filled with the scent of fresh bread and sizzling crepes.

We ate Nutella crepes that were far too big for any normal human to eat, and Ryan tried to haggle with the vendor in what I could only describe as extremely made-up French.

"Vous voulez… ah, no," he said, his eyes darting between me and the vendor. "Uhh, une baguette, s'il vous plaît!" He grinned as the vendor gave him a confused look. "Come on, that's got to be worth a discount."

I was already laughing too hard to translate what he'd just said. Ryan's bad French, combined with his unshakable confidence, was making me feel lighter than I had in days.

"Can you stop trying to bribe the vendor with bad French?" I said, trying to catch my breath. "You're embarrassing yourself."

"Hey, I was this close to getting us a free baguette," he argued, pulling a Nutella-streaked finger from his mouth.

I smiled, feeling something I hadn't in a long time—like maybe, just maybe, things were going to be okay.

As the sun dipped below the horizon, casting the streets of Paris in a golden glow, I finally felt like I was here—really here—and not just clinging to the past.

Maybe I didn't have all the answers yet, but I had time. And for the first time in days, I wasn't afraid of that.

CHAPTER 9: THE SCAM

The morning started with a croissant that tasted like heaven and a coffee that could've powered an entire city. Paris had a way of making even the simplest things extraordinary.

Ryan insisted we rent bikes to explore Montmartre. "It's the best way to see the city," he declared, already fumbling with the lock on one of the rental bikes.

"You mean the best way to die in traffic," I muttered, eyeing the crowded streets.

"Where's your sense of adventure?" he shot back, hopping onto his bike with an exaggerated wobble. "Come on, Nat. Paris waits for no one."

Despite my reservations, I followed.

We pedaled our way up the steep hill to Sacré-Cœur, my legs burning but my heart strangely light. The climb was worth it. At the top, the basilica glowed in the early sunlight, its domes framed against a clear blue sky.

We snapped a few blurry selfies, Ryan sticking his tongue out in most of them while I tried to look somewhat composed.

"Okay, now one where you actually look like a human," I said, laughing as I adjusted the angle.

"This is my human face," Ryan replied, making an even more ridiculous expression.

We laughed so hard a group of tourists gave us side-eyes, but I didn't care. For the first time in days, the weight in my chest felt just a little lighter.

Afterwards, we coasted downhill, weaving through narrow streets lined with cafés and art galleries. That's when it happened.

Ryan veered into the wrong lane, narrowly missing an oncoming taxi.

"American idiot!" the driver yelled in heavily accented English, leaning on his horn.

Ryan, unbothered, threw up a peace sign and shouted back, "I'm global now, baby!"

I couldn't stop laughing, even as I scolded him. "You're going to get us killed, you moron!"

"Worth it," he said with a grin, pedaling ahead.

By the time we reached the Louvre, my meticulously planned itinerary was forgotten. I'd stopped caring about checking off boxes and started actually seeing the city.

Inside, the museum was everything I expected—breathtaking, overwhelming, and just a little too crowded.

"Okay," Ryan said, stopping in front of the Mona Lisa. "What's the verdict?"

I tilted my head, studying the famous painting. "It's…small."

"Right?" he said, gesturing wildly. "I thought it'd be, like, life-sized or something. She's just sitting there, all smug and tiny."

We spent the next hour wandering through the endless halls, making up backstories for random statues.

"That guy?" Ryan said, pointing at a marble figure missing an arm. "Definitely a part-time DJ. Goes by the name 'DJ Limbless.'"

I snorted, shaking my head. "You're ridiculous."

"And that guy," he continued, pointing at another statue, "was totally dumped at the altar. Look at his face. That's heartbreak if I've ever seen it."

"Or he's constipated," I added, grinning.

Ryan clutched his stomach, laughing so hard a museum guard gave us a stern look.

"Shh," I hissed, dragging him into another room.

"You're going to get us kicked out."

"Worth it," he said again, his smile infectious.

For a little while, I let myself forget why I'd come. I wasn't the girl with a missing dad and a suitcase full of questions. I was just Natalie Donovan, laughing with her best friend in the middle of Paris.

But as we left the museum, the lightness began to fade. The reality of my search crept back in, gnawing at the edges of my thoughts.

I glanced at Ryan, who was still grinning, probably planning our next ridiculous adventure. He caught me looking and raised an eyebrow.

"What?" he asked.

"Nothing," I said quickly, forcing a smile.

But inside, I felt torn. For the first time, I wondered if Ryan was right—if maybe I needed to stop searching so hard and just let myself be here. But how could I, when every step I took felt like it might lead me closer to the truth?

As we biked back, the Seine sparkling in the afternoon sun, I couldn't shake the thought: What if I was looking in all the wrong places?

The restaurant Ryan had picked was tucked away in a narrow alley, the kind you'd miss if you blinked. Strings of fairy lights crisscrossed above the cobblestone street, casting a warm glow that made everything look like it was straight out of a postcard. A guitarist played softly near the entrance, his music blending with the gentle murmur of conversations. It should have been perfect, but the knot in my stomach wouldn't let me enjoy it.

Ryan had insisted on ordering escargot, much to my horror.

"You have to try it," he said, holding up a fork with one of the slimy little creatures perched precariously at the end.

"I absolutely do not," I replied, pushing the plate away and grabbing another piece of bread. "This is as French as I'm getting."

"Your loss," he said, popping the snail into his mouth with exaggerated relish.

I made a gagging noise, which earned me a scandalized look from the elderly couple at the next table. Ryan just grinned.

As the meal went on, his usual chatter faded, replaced by a thoughtful silence that made me uneasy.

"You've been quiet," he said finally, breaking the stillness.

I stabbed at my salad, more for something to do than because I was hungry. "I'm just thinking."

"Big shock there," he said, though his smile was softer this time, less teasing.

I looked up, meeting his gaze. "You don't have to be here, you know."

"Nat, come on——"

"No, really," I interrupted, setting my fork down with a clink. "I dragged you halfway across the world for something that might not even matter. And you're…"

"Still here," he finished for me, his voice steady. "Because you're my best friend. And yeah, this whole thing is insane, but so are you. Maybe that's why I like you."

My heart skipped, but before I could say anything, he plowed ahead.

"I just want you to find what you're looking for," he said. "But, Nat… you have to let yourself live a little too. You can't keep chasing ghosts."

His words hit me like a punch to the gut, and for a moment, I couldn't speak. He was right—of course he was—but that didn't make it easier to hear.

The hum of nearby conversations filled the silence between us, a buffer against the weight of what had just been said. I looked away, focusing on the flickering candle between us.

"Thanks," I said finally, my voice barely above a whisper.

He smiled, and for the first time in days, the knot in my stomach loosened just a little.

Back at the hotel room, Ryan's optimism took a hit.

"This is it," he groaned dramatically from the tiny bathroom, his voice echoing off the tiled walls. "This is how I die."

"Death by croissant?" I called back, unable to suppress a laugh.

"It's not funny, Nat!" he shouted, though the strain in his voice made it clear he was… preoccupied. "Do you know how much butter is in those things? My digestive system is staging a full-scale revolt."

"Maybe don't eat five of them in one sitting next time," I said, trying to sound sympathetic but failing miserably.

"You're enjoying this way too much," he muttered.

"Little bit," I admitted, grinning at the sound of him groaning again.

Despite myself, I felt a flicker of amusement break through the heaviness that had settled over me. It was such a Ryan thing, turning even the most mundane crisis into a spectacle.

That night, as I lay in bed listening to the city outside, Ryan's words replayed in my head.

You have to let yourself live a little too.

I hated how much they resonated. How much they reminded me of everything I'd been avoiding since the moment I stepped off the plane.

But he was right. I couldn't spend every second searching for answers that might not even exist.

As I drifted off to sleep, I promised myself I'd try to take his advice—if only for a little while.

That night, sleep was restless, my dreams fragmented and vivid. In one, I was sitting with my dad at our old kitchen table, a mug of coffee in his hands and a travel book between us. He was talking about Paris the way only he could—like it was more than a place, like it was magic itself.

"Paris," he said, his voice curling around the word the way a French person would, soft and melodic. "Not Par-iss like Americans say. You have to feel it, Natalie. Say it with me. Pah-ree."

I'd giggled then, rolling my eyes but secretly loving how much he lit up when he talked about his favorite city. "Okay, Dad. Pah-ree."

He'd grinned at me, a proud look in his eyes that

I hadn't seen in so long it hurt to remember.

When I woke, his voice still echoed in my mind, and for a brief second, I thought I could smell his aftershave, warm and familiar. But it was just the faint scent of bread wafting up from the bakery downstairs, mingling with the crisp Parisian air leaking through our cracked window.

I'd barely drifted back to sleep when Ryan nudged me awake.

"Nat, wake up," he whispered, his face lit by the eerie blue glow of his laptop screen.

"What?" I groaned, pulling the scratchy hostel blanket over my head.

"Got it," he said, his voice brimming with excitement.

"Got what?" I mumbled, my words muffled by the blanket.

"Your dad's email login."

That got my attention. I pushed the blanket away and sat up, blinking against the dim light of the room. Ryan was perched at the tiny desk in the corner, his laptop open and a triumphant grin on his face.

"What are you talking about?" I asked, shuffling over to him.

"Remember the shopping account you found?" he

said, turning the screen toward me. "The one with the password, Fishing4Days?"

"Yeah," I said slowly, my heart starting to race.

"Well, I was poking around—don't ask how, it's better if you don't know—and I found the IP logins."

"You hacked it?" I asked, equal parts impressed and horrified.

"Let's not label things," he said, waving me off. "The point is, there was another login. After the one you found from Margaux."

"From where?"

"Here," he said, leaning closer, his voice dropping like we were part of some grand conspiracy. "In Paris. At a café."

I blinked, his words taking a moment to sink in. "Are you serious?"

"Dead serious," he said, his tone solemn but his eyes alight with triumph.

"And it wasn't just a random login," he continued. "He was looking at maps."

"Maps for what?"

Ryan shrugged. "That's what we're gonna find out."

As I stared at the screen, the weight of what Ryan was saying pressed down on me. My dad had been here—recently enough for it to matter. He'd been searching for something, planning something.

A mix of emotions churned in my chest: hope, fear, and something I couldn't quite name. I wanted to feel relief, but instead, I felt the stakes rising all over again.

"What if it's nothing?" I whispered, my voice barely audible.

Ryan turned to me, his expression softening. "And what if it's not?"

It was such a simple answer, but it hit me like a tidal wave. What if it wasn't nothing? What if this was the thread I'd been looking for, the one that could unravel the whole tangled mess of my dad's disappearance?

I didn't know whether to cry or laugh or throw myself out the window just to release the overwhelming mix of emotions.

Ryan gave me a small nudge. "Get some sleep, Nat. Tomorrow, we'll figure it out."

But as I crawled back under the blanket, I knew sleep wouldn't come. My dad's voice was still in my head, whispering Pah-ree, and for the first time since we'd arrived, it felt like maybe—just maybe—I was getting closer to him.

The café was tucked into a bustling corner of Montmartre, where cobblestones gleamed faintly under the weak morning sunlight. Its weathered red-and-white awning flapped gently in the breeze, inviting both locals and wandering tourists. Inside, the smell of espresso and fresh pastries hit me like a warm embrace. A chalkboard menu hung lopsidedly behind the bar, and tiny marble-topped tables were crammed into every available space, each one occupied by someone engrossed in a book or deep conversation.

We slid onto stools at the bar, the cool metal pressing against my legs. Ryan shifted uncomfortably beside me, muttering something about the heat, his ongoing "croissant problem," and the lack of air conditioning.

"What can I get for you?" asked the bartender, a wiry man with salt-and-pepper hair and an easy smile that creased the corners of his eyes.

"Iced teas," Ryan blurted before I could say a word. "Two of them. Extra ice."

The bartender smirked. "Ah, you're American. Ice, always."

"Guilty," Ryan admitted, raising a hand like he was being arrested.

We sipped our drinks in relative silence until Ryan

leaned forward on his stool, adopting the kind of casual demeanor that immediately screamed I'm about to ask for something weird.

"So," he began, "we're looking for someone who might've been here recently. An American guy. Dark hair, early forties. Probably looked stressed or, I don't know, mysterious?"

The bartender raised an eyebrow, his expression one part amusement and two parts skepticism. "Many Americans come through here. You'll have to be more specific."

Ryan drummed his fingers on the counter, then grinned. "What if I sweeten the deal?" He reached into his pocket, pulled out a crumpled ten-euro note, and slid it across the bar.

The bartender laughed outright, a deep, hearty sound that made a few patrons glance our way. "Monsieur, that will buy you another iced tea, not information."

I rolled my eyes. "Ryan, seriously?"

"Hey, it was worth a shot," he muttered, shoving the money back into his pocket.

As if on cue, Ryan winced and pressed a hand to his stomach. "Uh, can I use your restroom?"

The bartender's eyes lit with recognition. "Ah, I

see the problem now." He pulled a small bottle from beneath the counter and poured a splash of something green and viscous into a glass. "Americans with weak stomachs. Always the same."

Ryan eyed the concoction suspiciously. "What is that?"

"A cure," the bartender said simply, sliding it toward him.

Ryan hesitated before taking a tentative sip. His face twisted like he'd bitten into a lemon. "Oh my God, that's horrible!"

"It will help," the bartender assured him, chuckling as he watched Ryan run to the restroom. "Trust me."

When Ryan returned from the restroom, looking marginally less pained, I decided to take over.

"He was probably meeting a woman," I said, pulling my phone from my bag. "French, elegant, maybe in her thirties?"

The bartender's expression remained neutral until I pulled up a photo of my dad and held it out to him.

"Do you remember him?" I asked, my voice tight.

Recognition flickered in his eyes. "Ah, oui. I remember now. He was here many… many months ago. Met with a beautiful woman." He paused, searching for the right words. "She seemed… how do you say? Distant."

"Distant?" Ryan asked, leaning forward again, his curiosity renewed.

The bartender nodded. "At first, she acted like she didn't know him. But they talked for a long time. Very intense."

My heart thudded painfully against my ribs. "Do you remember anything else?"

The bartender hesitated, his brow furrowing as if he was trying to pluck details from the recesses of his memory. "Not much. But she was here again just yesterday."

"Yesterday?" I repeated, my voice catching.

He nodded. "Alone. She sat at the same table. Did not stay long."

A storm of emotions churned inside me. Excitement, dread, and frustration all swirled together, leaving me feeling hollow and restless.

"He was here," I said finally, breaking the silence. "He was actually here."

"And so was she," Ryan added.

"But we're no closer to knowing who she is or why they met."

Ryan bumped my shoulder lightly as we talked.

"We'll figure it out, Nat. You're not exactly the kind of person who gives up."

I managed a weak smile, but the truth was, I wasn't sure what to feel anymore. The pieces of the puzzle were starting to come together, but the picture they were forming was still maddeningly out of reach.

Ryan sighed heavily, running a hand through his hair. "Well, that's a dead end. Thanks, anyway."

We were halfway to the door when the bartender's voice stopped us cold.

"Wait."

Ryan and I turned back in unison, his expression puzzled while my pulse quickened. The bartender tilted his head toward the door, his voice low and measured.

"She just walked in."

I spun around so fast I nearly knocked into Ryan. My breath caught in my throat.

There she was. Dark hair pulled into a sleek twist, red lipstick so vivid it seemed to glow against her pale skin. She wore a trench coat cinched tightly at her waist, the kind of outfit that screamed effortless sophistication. The café seemed to shift around her as though her mere presence dimmed everything else.

"Nat," Ryan whispered, his voice tight. "What do we do now?"

I didn't answer. Couldn't. My eyes were locked on her as she strode toward the counter, completely oblivious that she'd just walked straight into the center of our search.

The bartender's words hung in the air like a neon sign, glaring and impossible to ignore. She just walked in.

The woman exchanged a few words with the bartender, her voice low and melodic, before settling into a corner booth. She ordered a drink, crossed her legs, and pulled out her phone, scrolling with one hand while absently stirring her coffee with the other.

Ryan shifted beside me, his movements stiff and uncertain. "Okay, seriously," he muttered. "What now?"

I swallowed hard, trying to steady my racing heart. "We wait."

His eyebrows shot up. "Wait? What does that even mean? What are we waiting for, her to finish her drink and waltz over here to confess everything?"

"Keep your voice down," I hissed, nudging him with my elbow.

We retreated to the bar, pretending to sip our cappuccinos while keeping her firmly in our line of sight. She seemed completely at ease, her posture relaxed, her expression unreadable. Meanwhile, I felt like my insides were made of static electricity, every nerve ending on high alert.

I couldn't tear my eyes away from her. Was she the woman my dad had met here? What had they talked about? Was she lying when she acted like she didn't know him?

A dozen questions swirled in my mind, each one more urgent than the last. But beneath the curiosity and adrenaline was something else—a flicker of fear.

Because what if she wasn't just some random woman? What if she knew exactly who I was?

Ryan leaned closer, his voice barely above a whisper. "You sure she doesn't know we're watching her? We're not exactly blending in here."

I glanced down at our cups, realizing too late that we hadn't even bothered to stir the foam. The bartender, catching my eye, gave me a small, knowing smile.

I exhaled slowly, trying to rein in my nerves. "She doesn't know."

"You're a terrible liar."

I glared at him. "Just… let me think."

For the next ten minutes, we sat there in tense silence, the café's chatter and clinking dishes a dull hum in the background. Ryan fidgeted with his phone, occasionally glancing over his shoulder to check on her.

"What's the plan?" he asked finally, his tone edged with impatience.

"I don't have one," I admitted, my voice softer than I intended.

He frowned but didn't say anything, his expression surprisingly gentle.

I felt a knot of frustration tighten in my chest. I was supposed to have answers, to know what to do next. Instead, I was frozen, caught somewhere between fear and hope.

After what felt like an eternity of stolen glances and second-guessing, Ryan nudged me, breaking the spell of my spiraling thoughts.

"Your move," he whispered, though his voice lacked its usual bravado.

My stomach churned as I stood, each step toward her table feeling heavier than the last. The woman glanced up as I approached, her dark eyes sharp and unyielding. Up close, she was more striking than I'd realized, her beauty edged with something cold and unreachable.

"Excuse me," I said, my voice wavering despite

my best efforts to steady it.

Her brows arched delicately. "Yes?"

"I'm Natalie Donovan," I began, the words tasting foreign in my mouth. "I think you knew my father. John Donovan."

For a fleeting second, something flickered across her face—recognition, maybe? But it was gone so fast I couldn't be sure. Her expression settled into a cool, unreadable mask.

"I'm sorry," she said, her voice low and deliberate, her accent carving each word with precision. "I don't know who that is."

I didn't leave. I couldn't. Instead, I pulled out the chair across from her and sat down.

"The bartender said you met him here," I pressed, keeping my voice calm.

Her lips curved into the faintest trace of a sigh as she set her phone down on the table. "I suppose there's no point in denying it. Yes, I met him. But it was not what you think."

My pulse quickened. "What do you mean?"

Her gaze flickered toward Ryan, who had abandoned any pretense of subtlety and was blatantly staring at us while pretending to text. She gave him a once-over before turning her attention back to me.

"Your father was… desperate," she said, her words careful, as if she were afraid of how they might land. "He thought I was someone I wasn't."

I frowned, the pieces not fitting together in my mind. "Someone you weren't?"

She tilted her head slightly, studying me as if deciding how much to say. Finally, she leaned back in her seat.

"He believed I was Margaux," she said. "A woman he'd been speaking to online. But I wasn't. I had no idea who he was until he approached me here."

My head swam. Margaux. The name from his emails. The mysterious connection that had driven me across the ocean.

Ryan, apparently unable to contain himself any longer, slid into the chair beside me. "So why did you talk to him?" he asked, his tone somewhere between accusatory and curious.

Her lips pressed into a thin line. "Because I felt sorry for him," she admitted, her gaze dropping briefly to her hands. "He looked so… lost. Like he needed someone to listen."

Something in her voice made my chest tighten. My dad, always so sure of himself, reduced to a man searching for answers in the wrong places.

"What happened?" I asked, my voice smaller now.

She straightened her posture, brushing an invisible speck off her sleeve as if distancing herself from the emotion she'd just shown.

"I told him the truth," she said simply. "That whoever he thought he was meeting wasn't real. It's a common scam."

"A scam?" Ryan repeated, his brow furrowed deeply.

"Yes," she said, her voice steady but tinged with disdain. "Men are lured into relationships online, convinced to send money or make promises. But the person they're speaking to doesn't exist. It's cruel, but it happens all the time."

Her words hung in the air, heavy and unyielding.

I felt the blood drain from my face, my mind racing to make sense of what she was saying. A scam. My dad had been conned. Had he known? Or had he been so desperate to believe in something—someone—that he'd ignored the signs?

"He wasn't stupid," I said, the words escaping before I could stop them. My voice cracked slightly, and I hated how vulnerable it sounded.

She didn't respond right away. Instead, her gaze softened, just a fraction. "No," she said at last. "He wasn't stupid. Just… hopeful."

Hopeful. The word cut deeper than I expected, slicing through the anger and confusion to land somewhere raw and tender.

Ryan shifted beside me, clearly uncomfortable. "So… what now?" he muttered under his breath, like we weren't sitting in front of the person who had just unraveled everything we thought we knew.

I didn't answer. My thoughts were a whirlwind of anger, shame, and something I couldn't quite name—grief, maybe, for a man who had been chasing something he could never catch.

The woman glanced between us, then stood, smoothing her coat with a practiced motion. "I'm sorry," she said, her voice devoid of warmth but not unkind. "But that's all I know."

Finally, the woman stood, pulling on her trench coat and slinging a leather bag over her shoulder. My breath hitched as she made her way to the door, heels clicking softly against the tiled floor. Leaving us sitting in the crowded café with nothing but questions—and a silence so loud it felt deafening.

"Nat," Ryan said urgently.

"I know," I whispered.

We watched her step out onto the cobblestone

street, her silhouette vanishing into the crowded square.

I felt a sharp pang of disappointment, followed by an even sharper sense of resolve.

"We have to follow her," I said, standing abruptly.

Ryan's eyes widened. "Follow her? Like, spy on her?"

"Yes, exactly."

"Do you hear yourself right now? This isn't a movie, Nat. People get arrested for this kind of stuff!"

"Then don't come," I snapped, grabbing my bag.

For a moment, he just stared at me, his expression torn between disbelief and exasperation. Then he sighed, shaking his head.

"You're insane," he muttered, grabbing his jacket. "Let's go."

CHAPTER 10: THE CHASE BEGINS

We followed her out of the café, careful to keep a reasonable distance. The streets of Montmartre were busy, filled with tourists snapping photos and locals weaving through the chaos with practiced ease. She walked quickly, her heels clicking against the cobblestones like the ticking of a clock, and I couldn't shake the feeling that every step was pulling us closer to something big—or dragging us deeper into confusion.

"Do you think she knows we're following her?" I whispered to Ryan, who was trailing slightly behind me.

"If she does, she's got a great poker face," he replied, though his voice sounded strained.

I glanced back at him. His face was pale, beads of sweat forming on his forehead.

"Are you okay?" I asked.

"I'm fine," he said, but the way he winced told a

different story.

"She's turning," I hissed, pulling his attention back to the chase. We hurried around the corner, just in time to see her enter a narrow alleyway.

"Should we follow her in there?" Ryan asked, clearly torn between curiosity and the obvious urgency of his current predicament.

"Yes," I said, grabbing his arm. "Come on."

But by the time we reached the alley, she was gone.

"What the—" Ryan muttered, scanning the empty space. A door slammed somewhere nearby, the echo bouncing off the walls.

"She must've gone inside," I said, frustrated. "But which door?"

Ryan groaned, doubling over slightly. "Can we call it a day? Seriously, I'm at DEFCON 1 over here."

I blinked at him, momentarily forgetting my annoyance. "DEFCON 1?"

He waved a hand toward his stomach. "The croissants. They're staging a rebellion."

I sighed, torn between laughing and smacking him. "Fine. Hotel it is. But you're not off the hook for abandoning this lead."

Back at the hotel, Ryan bolted for the bathroom the second we walked through the door. I dropped onto the bed, staring at the ceiling as the events of the day played on a loop in my head. The café. The woman. My father's name on her lips, and the sharp edges of her words cutting deeper than I wanted to admit.

By the time Ryan emerged, looking both relieved and slightly sheepish, I was pacing the room.

"You're going to wear a hole in the carpet," he said, dropping onto the chair by the desk.

I ignored him, my thoughts spinning too fast to keep up with. "How could he fall for something like that?" I muttered, more to myself than to him. "He was always so careful. So—"

"Human," Ryan interrupted, opening his laptop.

I stopped mid-step, turning to glare at him. "What?"

He didn't look up. "Your dad's just a person, Nat. People make mistakes. Even big ones. Doesn't mean he wasn't careful most of the time."

His words hit harder than I wanted them to. I sank onto the bed, my head in my hands.

The image I'd held onto of my dad—steady, reliable, infallible—was crumbling faster than I could piece it back together. He wasn't the hero I'd built up in my mind; he was just a man, flawed and vulnerable like everyone else.

"He always seemed so… invincible," I admitted quietly. "Like he had it all figured out."

Ryan glanced at me, his expression softening. "Maybe that's what he wanted you to see. But trust me, nobody's got it all figured out. Not even parents."

I stared at him, torn between gratitude and frustration. "Why do you have to be right all the time?"

"Someone's gotta keep you grounded," he said with a small smile.

I managed a weak laugh, but the knot in my chest didn't loosen. My dad's mistakes weren't just his—they felt like mine, too. And I couldn't shake the feeling that every answer we found only raised more questions.

The tension in the room hung heavy, broken only by the soft clicks of Ryan's laptop keyboard. I sat cross-legged on the bed, arms wrapped around my knees, replaying the events of the day in my head. Losing her on the crowded streets of Montmartre had felt like a sucker punch, and my frustration simmered just below the surface.

"I can't believe we let her slip away," I muttered.

Ryan, perched on the desk chair with his laptop balanced precariously, didn't look up. "I said I was sorry, Nat. You wanna stick me in the stocks or something?"

I rolled my eyes but didn't respond.

Then suddenly, he sat up straighter, a triumphant grin breaking across his face. "Got it!"

"Got what?" I asked, my voice tinged with suspicion.

He spun the laptop to face me. The screen showed a grainy photo of the French woman, her expression frozen mid-sentence as she spoke to us at the bar.

"You... took a picture of her?"

"Don't look at me like that," he said defensively. "It's not creepy. It's resourceful. Anyway, I ran it through a reverse image search for known scammers."

"And?"

Ryan's grin faded slightly, replaced by a grim expression. "She wasn't lying. Her face is tied to dozens of fake accounts. She's part of a network."

My stomach twisted. "Okay, but what does this have to do with my dad?"

"Hold on," he said, his fingers flying across the keyboard. After a moment, he pulled up an Instagram profile. The account was filled with pristine travel shots—sun-drenched beaches, quaint cobblestone streets, perfectly plated meals. It all looked a little too curated, like the kind of life that existed more in hashtags than reality.

"This is one of the accounts linked to the scam," Ryan explained.

I leaned closer. "And?"

"Here." He scrolled to a post of a brightly colored street, the kind that felt ripped straight from a postcard. In the comments, nestled between heart emojis and generic compliments, was a single cryptic message: "Never too late to start over."

It was from my dad's account.

My chest tightened, my breath catching. "No way."

Ryan glanced at me, his face serious now. "It gets better. Check the geotag."

With a few more clicks, the screen displayed the location of the photo. Barcelona.

I stared at the name as if it might vanish if I blinked too hard. My dad had been there—been involved in this mess. And now, somehow, Barcelona felt like a thread that might unravel everything.

"Nat," Ryan said softly, breaking into my thoughts. "You okay?"

I nodded, but my voice was shaky. "I just... I don't get it. Why would he comment something like that? What was he doing there?"

Ryan hesitated, then leaned back in his chair.

"Maybe he was trying to tell someone something. Or himself."

The words hit harder than I expected. My dad wasn't just part of this mess; he'd left breadcrumbs. And now it was up to me to follow them.

But beneath the determination stirring in my chest, a deeper, more painful realization was taking root: whatever answers I found in Barcelona, they might not be the ones I wanted.

Saying goodbye to Paris felt like leaving behind the middle of a story, the kind that didn't wrap up neatly but left loose threads dangling in the air. The train to Barcelona was a silver streak slicing through the countryside, promising new answers—or maybe just more questions.

As we settled into our seats, the world outside turned to a blur of green hills, golden fields, and small villages that felt like something out of a painting. Ryan stretched out beside me, already half-asleep, while I stared out the window, clutching my phone like it might provide some kind of reassurance.

When Ryan's soft snores filled the compartment, I pulled out my notebook and flipped to the back page, where I'd been quietly tracking my expenses. A twinge of anxiety curled in my stomach as I added up the numbers. Train tickets, cheap hostels, meals we couldn't really afford but justified anyway—it was all adding up fast. At this rate, I wasn't sure I could afford to get back home.

But I wasn't going to tell Ryan that.

Instead, I scrolled through travel blogs on my phone, searching for ideas. There were plenty of tourists who picked up gigs while traveling—teaching English, working at hostels, selling handmade jewelry on street corners. Could I do that? The thought made me queasy, but I pushed it aside. If it came to that, I'd figure it out.

Ryan shifted in his sleep, mumbling something about churros, and I stifled a laugh. At least one of us was relaxed.

Barcelona hit us like a jolt of electricity the moment we stepped off the train. The scent of churros frying in oil mixed with the saltiness of the nearby sea, and the warm breeze carried the strum of a street performer's guitar. The sun was blinding, reflecting off the intricate tiles that adorned buildings like mosaic masterpieces.

"This," Ryan said, spinning in place as we exited the station, arms spread wide, "is what I'm talking about. Paris was cool, but Barcelona? This is where the magic happens."

Despite the weight in my chest, I couldn't help but smile. His energy was contagious, and for a fleeting moment, I let myself feel the thrill of being somewhere new.

But then reality settled back in.

"We need to head to the hotel," I said, pulling out my phone to double-check the geotag.

Ryan groaned dramatically. "And there it is. Classic Natalie."

"What?" I asked, raising an eyebrow.

"You're like a bloodhound with a mission," he teased. "No time for churros, no time for fun, just sniff, sniff, sniff."

I rolled my eyes and gave him a light shove. "Let's just get this over with."

He laughed but followed my lead as we navigated the winding streets, the sound of his suitcase wheels bumping along the uneven pavement behind us.

Finding the hotel was easier than I'd expected, though maybe I was just too tired to question how fate had made it so simple. It was tucked in the heart of the Gothic Quarter, where ancient stone buildings loomed over narrow, cobbled streets like quiet witnesses to centuries of history. The hotel's façade was a strange blend of old-world charm and modern sleekness, with glass windows that reflected the sun in a way that made everything feel surreal, like we'd stepped into some kind of movie.

We walked in, luggage clattering behind us, and immediately the atmosphere shifted. The lobby was cool and quiet, a stark contrast to the noisy pulse of the streets outside. The hum of traffic, the chatter of tourists—it all seemed so far away as we entered this oasis of calm.

A woman behind the desk smiled, her expression polite but reserved. "Can I help you?" she asked in accented English, her gaze flicking over us, taking in the backpacks and rolling suitcases.

I cleared my throat, pushing aside the tightness in my chest. "Yes," I said, forcing the words to come out steady despite how much I wanted to flee. "I'm looking for someone who may have stayed here recently. John Donovan?"

Her smile didn't falter, but something in her eyes shifted, just enough to make my heart skip a beat. "I'm sorry," she said, voice soft but firm. "We can't share information about our guests."

I swallowed hard, biting back the frustration that rose like bile in my throat. "Please. It's important. He's my dad." My voice was thin, too quiet, but I pushed on. "He is missing. Maybe you can just check?"

She hesitated, her eyes flicking to something I couldn't see, maybe a security camera, maybe an internal protocol. "I understand, but it's against our policy," she said gently.

I stared at her, willing her to understand. But there was no magic word, no special plea that would change her mind. "Is there anything you can tell me?" I asked again, voice sharper now. "Anything, even if—"

Ryan's hand landed on my shoulder, warm and grounding, cutting me off before I could say more. "Thank you for your time," he said smoothly, his voice calm and authoritative as he gently steered me toward the door.

I didn't fight him. I couldn't. As we stepped back into the sunlight, the weight of everything—every question, every dead end—pressed down on me like a heavy coat that I couldn't take off.

I paced in front of the building, my heart pounding in my chest. I wanted to scream, to punch the air, to do something—anything—that would make this all feel like it was worth it. But there was nothing. Just a long stretch of quiet and frustration that had become my life.

"That's it. Dead end. Again," I muttered to myself, rubbing my face with my hands.

Ryan stepped in front of me, blocking my path with a gentle but insistent hand on my arm. "Nat—"

"No, Ryan," I snapped, cutting him off before he could finish. "I've been chasing breadcrumbs for days, and I'm just—" My voice cracked, and suddenly, everything came rushing up—every emotion, every fear. "I'm so tired."

He didn't say anything at first, just stood there watching me, his eyes softening, the quiet understanding in them that I couldn't bear to meet. I hated this—hated how vulnerable I felt, hated that my anger and my exhaustion were wearing me down in front of him.

"I know you are," he said quietly, his voice a low, steady thing that seemed to hold the weight of my frustration. "But we're getting closer. Every time, we're closer."

I looked up at him, my throat tight. "Closer? How? Because nothing's happening. I'm just chasing ghosts."

His expression softened further, and for a second, he almost looked like he was about to say something else. But then he just nodded, his voice still steady.

"We're doing this together, okay? That counts for something."

I didn't say anything, but the lump in my throat didn't go away. Maybe it wasn't about the answers. Maybe it was about the people I was with, the ones who stuck by me even when everything felt like it was falling apart. And maybe, just maybe, that was enough to keep going.

But I wasn't sure how much longer I could keep pretending everything was okay. Every time we took a step forward, the ground felt more unstable, and the weight of my dad's absence pressed harder. My heart ached with the fear that I was chasing a version of him that never existed, that my search was just a way to distract myself from a truth I wasn't ready to face.

I ran a hand through my hair, taking a deep breath to steady myself. I had to keep going. For him. For me.

"Okay," I said finally, swallowing down the lump in my throat. "Let's find the next lead."

Ryan didn't respond, just gave a small nod and a half-smile, the same one he always gave when he thought I needed it. And for a moment, I let myself believe that maybe this wasn't the end.

Maybe we weren't out of options after all.

Ryan was all about the experience. The real

experience, not the polished version you saw in brochures or online travel guides. So, when we left the upscale hotel behind, he suggested we stay at a hostel. "Budget-friendly, international flair. It'll be fun, trust me," he said, eyes practically glowing with excitement as he threw his backpack over his shoulder.

I couldn't help but roll my eyes. "A hostel?" I repeated, half-laughing. "Are you trying to turn us into one of those backpacking clichés?"

He shrugged, looking far too pleased with himself. "What's wrong with being a cliché? Plus, you'll see, it'll be worth it. Think of it as a chance to, I don't know, live a little."

In the back of my mind, I was already calculating. I had a tight budget, no doubt about it, and the thought of a pricey hotel had never seemed more out of reach. But with Ryan? I didn't even have to mention it. He just knew. Maybe he was just that observant, or maybe he was just smart enough to see the way I hesitated before making any purchases. Whatever it was, it felt like we were synced in a way I hadn't expected.

I never had to tell him. It was like he knew, without saying a word, how to navigate the tightrope of my finances. There was an ease between us, a rhythm I hadn't realized we'd developed.

And so, off we went—backpacks heavy, energy lighter.

The hostel we checked into was a far cry from the polished glamour of the hotel we'd left behind. It had that gritty charm only places that thrive on backpackers can muster—bare concrete floors, mismatched furniture, and a few strands of colorful, eccentric décor scattered around like someone had just tossed them in on a whim.

But despite the mess, there was a hum of excitement in the air—people mingling, languages mixing, laughter spilling out from every corner. It was the kind of place where you could be anyone, anyone at all.

When we checked in, the receptionist—an overly cheerful woman in her twenties with dreadlocks and a nose ring—handed us our keycards and then recited the hostel rules like she was reading from a manual.

"Check-in time ends at 10 p.m., no exceptions," she said, smiling like she was in on a secret. "Lights out at 1 a.m. sharp. Keep your noise level reasonable, and respect others, yeah? If you're out past curfew, no worries, just make sure you've got your keycard with you."

I couldn't help but glance around. The hostel was

buzzing with life—travelers huddled together, speaking in different languages, sharing stories, or typing away on their laptops. It felt like the entire world was in one place, and it made me a little dizzy, like the whole world was suddenly open to me.

We made our way to our room, and the exhaustion hit me like a truck. The moment I stepped inside, I just wanted to collapse. The room was basic— a pair of bunks, a tiny window that overlooked an alley, and a narrow dresser. But it was clean, and it had character. It was a far cry from the luxury of the hotel, but I didn't mind.

I dropped my bag onto the lower bunk, the metal frame creaking under the weight. It was everything I could do to sit on the edge of the bed, my eyes heavy, my body demanding rest.

Ryan, however, was already in full research mode, his fingers flying over the keys of his laptop as he clicked through different tabs. I watched him for a second, wondering how he could just keep going, keep pushing forward like he did.

"Do you ever just... take a minute to breathe?" he asked, glancing over at me.

I shifted uncomfortably, feeling the weight of his words before he'd even finished speaking. I pulled my phone out, pretending to focus on a text message from my mom, trying to ignore the sudden heat creeping up my neck.

"I breathe," I said, my voice a little too sharp. "I just don't have time to stop."

Ryan smirked, his eyes twinkling with amusement, but there was something deeper in them too—something that made me uncomfortable, like he could see more than I wanted him to. "Uh-huh," he said, his voice dripping with gentle teasing. "Sure you do. You're just so busy trying to solve everything that you forget to exist."

The words stung more than I wanted to admit. The truth of them hit me harder than I'd thought it would. My breath caught in my throat, and I looked away, pretending to scroll through my phone even though I wasn't really reading anything.

Ryan seemed to notice. He softened, his voice quieter when he spoke again. "Look," he said, his tone serious now, "I get it. This is important. But so are you, okay? Don't burn yourself out before we even get to the good stuff."

I let his words linger, letting them twist through my thoughts like vines. It was easy to forget that I was running on fumes, that I was throwing myself into this search with everything I had because I was scared, because I didn't know what would happen if I stopped. But what if he was right? What if I was losing myself in all of this?

I glanced over at Ryan. His fingers were still moving on the keyboard, his focus unwavering. There was something about the way he lost himself in the task at hand, how he could dive headfirst into something and still be present for the people around him, that made me want to learn how to do the same.

I sat up, trying to shake off the weight of the exhaustion pressing down on me. There was a city outside the window, a world to explore, but more than that—there was a mystery waiting for me, just like always. I wasn't about to let it slip through my fingers, even if I had to do it alone. But maybe—just maybe—I didn't have to.

With a sigh, I leaned back against the pillow, closing my eyes for a second. But before I could even slip into sleep, I felt something in the pit of my stomach, a reminder that no matter how many dead ends we ran into, I couldn't stop searching.

Somewhere, out there, was the key to everything. And I was going to find it.

CHAPTER 11: ROMANTIC TENSIONS

The hostel became our makeshift home for the next few days. It wasn't much—barely more than a bed and a place to shower—but it had a certain charm. The walls were thin, and at night, we could hear muffled laughter and foreign conversations drifting through the corridors. The air smelled like coffee and toothpaste, and I'd gotten used to the constant buzz of people coming and going, of languages I didn't understand weaving in and out of my thoughts.

Ryan, as usual, threw himself into his research. He barely noticed the chaos around him—just laptop in hand, headphones on, working through the night like it was the most natural thing in the world. I, on the other hand, found it hard to concentrate with the hostel so alive, so unpredictable. Every time I glanced up, I could see someone new—someone with a story I could never know.

I tried not to mind, but I couldn't help feeling like

I was the only one really invested in finding answers. It wasn't just about the case anymore—it was about proving to myself that I could do this, that I could face whatever truths came with it.

In the meantime, there was always a small part of me that wished Ryan would pause, just for a second, and take in the world around him. But he was always moving, always looking for the next piece of the puzzle. And it was contagious. Every time I tried to take a break or even think about the possibility of relaxing, he'd shoot me a look that silently said, Let's keep going.

I needed to talk to my mom.

Pulling out my phone one evening, I tapped out a quick message to her: In Barcelona. I'm okay. I'll update you soon.

She'd been texting me constantly, checking in, asking if I was safe, which was sweet, but also a little overwhelming. She didn't know the full extent of what I was doing, and I wasn't sure how to tell her. Would she understand? Would she freak out? I didn't want to deal with her anxiety on top of everything else, so I kept things short, offering only the bare minimum of details.

When the message sent, I turned to Ryan, who

was scribbling furiously in his notebook, his brow furrowed with concentration.

"Hey," I said, hesitating for a moment. "Have you talked to your family yet?"

He froze for a fraction of a second before looking up at me, his eyes flicking to the side.

"No," he said quickly, too quickly. "Not yet. It's... it's been kind of hectic, you know? With everything going on."

I wasn't sure why, but the way he said it didn't sit right with me. It felt rehearsed, like he was dodging something. I didn't push him, but the question lingered in the air, heavy and unresolved. What was he hiding?

We didn't have time to dwell on it. There was no time for anything but the chase.

The next few days were a blur of faces. Every morning, we'd grab breakfast from a corner café, then hit the streets, asking everyone we could find, Have you seen this man? I showed them the photo of my dad, the one that had come up on the reverse image search, and no one seemed to recognize him. Some were polite enough to smile and shake their heads, others just shrugged and walked away. The further we ventured into the city, the more hopeless it all felt.

At times, I wondered if I was losing myself in the

search, if maybe I was grasping at something that wasn't there. But then I'd look at Ryan, and the way his eyes lit up when someone gave us a new lead—however small—and I knew there was no turning back.

By the time we realized we hadn't stopped for lunch, the sun was dipping low, casting long shadows over the cobbled streets. My stomach grumbled in protest, but I ignored it. We'd walked for hours, covering entire districts in search of someone who might have seen my dad, someone who might remember his face.

Ryan finally stopped at a food cart, grabbing a sandwich and tossing me one of those pre-packaged salads that looked like it had been sitting out for hours. We ate quickly, standing on the side of the street, not bothering to find a place to sit.

"You good?" he asked, his voice muffled by a mouthful of food.

I nodded, wiping my hands on my jeans. "Yeah. Just... I don't know. Maybe we're chasing shadows."

He swallowed, eyes narrowing as he considered my words. "Maybe. But that doesn't mean we stop looking."

We didn't stop.

The day ended, and the night settled over

Barcelona with a soft hum, the lights of the city glittering in the distance. We'd walked so much my legs ached, my feet felt blistered, and the exhaustion hung like a heavy blanket over me.

But it wasn't just physical fatigue. It was the weight of everything I was uncovering—the small truths, the half-lies, the feeling that we were only scratching the surface of something much bigger than we realized.

Ryan and I didn't talk much that night. We both knew the silence was our way of recharging, preparing for whatever tomorrow might bring.

Back at the hostel, I tossed my bag onto the bed and collapsed beside it, my head in my hands, as if somehow the weight of the world had settled there. I'd been holding it together—barely—but the exhaustion finally hit, both physical and emotional. The questions, the uncertainty, the frantic search that felt more like a marathon than a mystery—everything was piling up, and I was about to crack.

Ryan sat on the edge of the bed, watching me carefully. His gaze was soft, but there was that underlying intensity that never seemed to fade, no matter what we were doing. "You're not a quitter, Natalie."

I glared at him, the words I wanted to say jamming up in my throat. "Maybe I am now."

"You're not," he insisted, his voice steady and sure. It was the kind of certainty I couldn't ignore, even when I wanted to.

I lifted my head, meeting his eyes. "I just feel like we're... chasing nothing. Like we're in circles, getting nowhere. And I can't keep doing this."

He didn't say anything for a moment, just let the silence sit between us, thick and heavy, like a storm waiting to break. Then he leaned forward, his elbows resting on his knees. "Look, I get it. This sucks. But you've got two options: sit here and mope, or get out there and live a little while we're figuring it out."

I scoffed. "So your grand plan is churros and Gaudí?"

He grinned. "Exactly."

I blinked at him, completely thrown off by the sudden lightness in his tone. Churros and Gaudí. I couldn't help but laugh, just a little, despite myself. He always seemed to have this way of turning everything into some kind of adventure. Even if I didn't believe it, his insistence on making something fun out of the mess was contagious.

"You're unbelievable," I muttered, but the smile

tugging at my lips betrayed me.

"Come on," he said, standing up. "I promise you'll thank me later. Who else gets to solve mysteries and eat churros at the same time?"

I rolled my eyes, but he was already pulling me toward the door.

The next day, Ryan's plan won out. We wandered through Park Güell, its vibrant mosaics shimmering under the sun, each tile a riot of color and whimsy that seemed to echo the surreal beauty of the city. The steep hills nearly killed me—my legs were on fire—but the views of the city stretching toward the sea were worth it. Barcelona looked like a painting, alive and messy and impossible to take in all at once.

Ryan, ever the showman, insisted on taking a selfie with me. His phone camera flashed as he held it up between us, and for a moment, I let go of the tension in my chest, smiling at the ridiculousness of it all.

"See?" he said, his voice full of mock triumph. "Not so bad, right?"

I rolled my eyes but let him snap the picture anyway. The sun was warm, and there was a light breeze that carried the scent of fresh flowers and street food through the air. For a moment, I forgot about everything—the case, the unknowns, the constant pressure to find something, anything. I forgot about the ache of wanting answers I wasn't sure I'd ever get.

"You're so cheesy," I said, but I couldn't keep the laughter out of my voice.

"I'm just a man of many talents," Ryan replied with a wink, making a dramatic show of putting his phone away.

We spent the rest of the afternoon meandering through the park, taking our time to enjoy the beauty of the place. Every so often, Ryan would pull out his phone and check something for the case—an address, a location, a new lead—but mostly, he just let me take it all in. And, I realized, I didn't mind. There was something grounding about him, something that made the frantic pace of the search feel less consuming, more like part of a larger picture I couldn't yet see.

By the time we hit La Rambla that evening, I was starting to feel the effects of taking a breather. I hadn't even realized how tightly I'd been wound until I finally allowed myself to breathe.

We sat on a bench with gelato in hand, watching the street performers draw crowds. One was playing an acoustic guitar, his voice soft and melodic, carrying with the rhythm of the city. The sweet, sugary taste of the gelato balanced out the heat of the day, and for a second, I could almost pretend everything was normal.

"I get it now," I admitted quietly, my eyes tracing the motion of a couple walking hand in hand across the street.

"Get what?" Ryan asked, turning toward me with a quizzical expression.

"Why you said I should live a little. I've been so focused on the next clue, the next step, that I forgot to… see what's right in front of me."

He studied me for a second, a thoughtful look in his eyes before the corners of his mouth lifted into a soft smile. The kind that made his dimples appear. "Told you I was a genius."

I laughed, the sound feeling unfamiliar but not unwelcome. It was the first real laugh I'd had in days, maybe even longer. "You're impossible," I said, shaking my head, but I didn't mean it.

The city around us hummed with life, a chorus of voices, footsteps, and distant music blending together like a song. For the first time in days, I felt something shift. Maybe it was the gelato or the warmth of the late afternoon sun, or maybe it was just Ryan's effortless ability to make everything feel just a little bit lighter. But in that moment, I didn't feel so alone in this search. And I didn't feel so overwhelmed either.

I felt... human again.

I wasn't sure what I was expecting when I woke up the next morning—whether the weight of the case would be back on my shoulders, suffocating and insistent, or if I'd carry a new kind of lightness into the day.

But when I looked at Ryan across the room, already sitting with his laptop and earbuds in place, the answer was clear. The chase wasn't over. But for the first time in a long time, I was starting to understand that maybe I didn't have to lose myself in it.

And maybe, just maybe, I didn't have to face it alone.

Barcelona pulsed with energy even at night, its streets alive with music, laughter, and the clatter of dishes from late-night diners. It was one of those cities that felt awake 24/7, where the buzz of life never really settled down. I slumped on a bench overlooking the Magic Fountain of Montjuïc, its colorful lights casting shimmering reflections across the plaza. The water shot up in rhythmic bursts, timed perfectly with the orchestral music blaring from the speakers hidden in the trees.

Ryan plopped down beside me, his sneakers squeaking on the stone bench as he held out a churro dipped in chocolate sauce, the warm, cinnamon-sugar smell reaching me before he even spoke. "Here. Comfort food."

I took it without a word, nibbling the end while the fountain sprayed arcs of water into the air. The music swelled, rising up around us like a symphony for the night. I wasn't sure what I expected, but this wasn't it. I'd hoped for answers, for some sign that we were getting closer to the truth. But instead, I was sitting in a plaza, eating churros and watching water dance.

"This is a pretty great sulking spot," Ryan said, leaning back and stretching his legs out in front of him. "Top ten, easily."

I shot him a look. "I'm not sulking."

"Sure you're not," he teased, his grin widening. "You're just 'resting your face in a broody manner while eating sad churros.'"

I let out a breath of laughter, quiet enough to almost get lost in the hum of the crowd. Despite everything, I couldn't help but smile at him, at how easily he could make me forget—at least for a moment—the weight of the search. "Not sulking," I muttered, though it wasn't quite as convincing as I wanted it to be.

"I just thought we'd find something," I admitted

after a moment, staring at the fountain. The lights shifted from blue to purple, casting an almost eerie glow over the plaza. "Anything."

Ryan's tone softened, the teasing dropping away as he looked at me with something unreadable in his eyes. "We will, Nat. You don't have to do this alone, remember?"

I nodded, grateful for him in a way I couldn't quite put into words. He was here, right beside me, always with that steady presence that seemed to anchor me when I started to drift. I didn't know what I would have done without him, though I wasn't sure I had the courage to admit that to him just yet.

Back at the hostel, the night had already turned chilly, and the common room was buzzing with the usual sounds of late-night travelers—voices in different languages, the clink of beer bottles, the tap of laptops. Ryan had made a few friends, all fellow tech nerds who seemed to share his obsession with gadgets. I watched them from the corner of the room, surrounded by an array of screens and wires. I couldn't help but smile at how easily he fit in, how naturally he'd found a group of people who spoke his language. They were deep in conversation about some new software update, their hands moving in animated gestures as they debated which app was the best for tracking hidden messages on social media.

It was endearing, really, how Ryan could shift so easily between the worlds of serious investigation and moments like this. But as I watched him laughing with his new friends, I couldn't help but feel something tighten in my chest. It was a strange feeling, one I couldn't quite name. He was becoming more and more... comfortable. In the group, in the city, in our case. He was sliding into places where I had yet to fit.

I shook my head, trying to shake off the thought. Maybe it was just that I was tired, or maybe I was reading too much into things. I glanced around the room at the other travelers, the other faces. Everyone was here, doing their thing, living their stories, and I was trying to figure out the ending of mine. Maybe that was what it was. Maybe I was just jealous of Ryan's ease.

But still, there was that small, nagging sensation that I couldn't quite shake.

Later that night, I found myself alone in our shared room, staring out the window at the lights of Barcelona, reflecting off the buildings like tiny stars in a sea of gray. The cool air filtered in through the cracked window, carrying with it the faint sounds of the city—voices, laughter, the hum of traffic.

I didn't even realize that I had been thinking about Ryan until I heard him knock lightly on the doorframe. I turned and saw him standing there, leaning against the door, a mischievous smile on his face. "You good?" he asked, raising an eyebrow. "I figured you could use a distraction."

I closed the window, my heart picking up speed for no reason at all. "Yeah, just... thinking."

He grinned, stepping into the room and sitting on the edge of my bunk. "What about?"

I hesitated, not quite sure how to explain it. I was never one to dive too deeply into feelings, especially not when they involved someone I was working with. Or someone like Ryan—someone who could still make me feel like the world was larger than the narrow view I often gave it.

"I don't know," I admitted finally. "It's just... weird, you know? This whole thing. Sometimes it feels like we're doing everything together, but then... I don't know. There's this distance, like we're both just... floating around it."

Ryan was quiet for a moment, his eyes thoughtful as he looked at me, his hand absentmindedly tracing the seam of his sleeve. And then, almost too casually, he asked, "You ever think about what happens after this? When the case is solved and we go back to... I don't know, wherever we're supposed to go?"

It caught me off guard. I opened my mouth to answer but couldn't find the words.

Ryan smiled, leaning back with a hint of playfulness in his eyes. "I'm just saying. We've got this... vibe going, right? Maybe it's just me, but it's kind of hard to ignore."

For a moment, the silence between us stretched. The words felt heavy in the air, but the distance, the tension, was thick enough that I couldn't tell if he was serious or just teasing.

But then again, why did it matter? I didn't know how I felt about him—about us, if there even was an "us." So why was my heart racing?

"You're impossible," I said finally, looking away to hide the flush creeping up my neck. But I wasn't sure if I meant it or not.

His grin deepened, dimples flashing. "I get that a lot."

I couldn't stop thinking about it. Every glance, every quiet moment between us felt charged with something new, something I wasn't sure how to handle. And it scared me. It scared me because this—

whatever this was—wasn't part of the plan. We weren't supposed to get distracted, not with so much still hanging in the balance.

But when I look at Ryan, standing there with his usual easy grin and infectious confidence, I realized I didn't want to walk away from it, whatever it was. And that terrified me more than anything else.

CHAPTER 12: A DANGEROUS ENCOUNTER

The night stretched on, and the streets grew livelier. Barcelona had a way of staying awake, like it was a city that never needed to sleep. The sounds of chatter, laughter, and clinking glasses spilled out of bars, mixing with the pulse of music that seemed to seep from every corner. Ryan, as usual, couldn't resist pulling me toward the next distraction. I knew what was coming, but I didn't mind. A part of me was ready for a break from the constant tension of the case, from the endless questions that crowded my mind.

"This is Barcelona," he declared, his voice lively as he tugged at my sleeve, his eyes lit with that same spark of mischief I had come to expect. "And there's only one cure for a bad mood here."

I raised an eyebrow, already half-laughing before I even knew what he was going to say. "Let me guess—food?"

Ryan's grin widened, flashing his dimples. "Close.

Dancing."

I stared at him for a moment, half amused, half exasperated. "You know, I'm not much of a dancer."

"Well, good thing I am," he said, pulling me along as if I had no say in the matter.

We ended up at a nightclub tucked into the corner of a plaza, its entrance nearly hidden behind a pair of tall, wooden doors adorned with a vibrant mural. The thumping bass vibrated through the floor before we even stepped inside, the music vibrating against my chest. Inside, the air felt thick with heat, sweat, cologne, and the occasional spill of sangria. The lights flashed in wild colors, cutting through the haze of smoke and bodies. It felt like a place where time didn't matter, where the hours slipped away without anyone noticing.

Ryan's enthusiasm was contagious, and I couldn't help but feel a flutter of excitement in my chest. I followed him through the crowd, my movements tentative at first, but the energy of the room was enough to pull me in. We found a small table near the back, tucked into a shadowy corner. The flickering candlelight on the table cast jagged shadows on the wall, giving the room an intimate, almost secretive feel.

"I don't dance," I protested, though my voice was

more playful than I meant it to be. I knew what was coming. He was not going to let me off the hook so easily.

"Liar," Ryan shot back, his smirk widening as he reached out to grab my wrist. He spun me around before I could protest, and suddenly, I was facing him, caught in the momentum of his movement. "You danced at Homecoming sophomore year. I remember because I spilled punch all over your dress."

"That wasn't dancing," I said with a laugh, trying to maintain my sense of control, but failing miserably. "That was flailing."

"Whatever it was," he said with a laugh, his hand still on mine, "you're doing it again."

Before I could say anything else, the music shifted, a Latin beat filling the room with its pulse. The rhythm was infectious, and somehow—before I knew it—I found myself swaying with the beat. Ryan didn't let go, pulling me deeper into the crowd, where the bodies moved in sync with the music like a wave, undulating through the space.

At first, I felt clumsy, unsure, but Ryan was a good lead—fluid and confident—and somehow, in the rhythm of it all, I started to forget. I forgot about the weight on my shoulders, the search for answers that never seemed to come. I forgot about the tightness in my chest, the fear of what might be hiding in the dark corners of the city.

Ryan spun me again, and I laughed, feeling the energy of the crowd lift me, as if for a moment, nothing else mattered. We bumped into strangers who smiled at us, caught in the same joy, the same abandon. It felt so... freeing. The world outside this nightclub disappeared, and for the first time in days, I let myself enjoy being here, in this moment.

A group of locals joined us, their enthusiasm contagious. One of them, a tall guy with a thick accent, offered Ryan a drink, and before I knew it, he had twirled me around as if we were all longtime friends, as if we'd known each other for years. His hands were warm, his grip steady, and I couldn't help but laugh as he led me through the steps, the beat carrying us faster than I could keep up.

Ryan was laughing too, dancing beside me, his eyes never leaving mine, a look that seemed to hold something I couldn't quite place. Maybe it was just the mood, the music, the place—who knew? But for a moment, it felt like we weren't just two people caught in the middle of a messy investigation. It felt like we were two people who had found something, some kind of connection, amid the chaos.

The music surged, pulling us deeper into the moment. My breath came faster, a mix of exertion and exhilaration, and for the first time in a long while, I wasn't thinking about the case, about my dad, or about what we might or might not find.

And that scared me.

But then, just as quickly as the music had swept me up, the night started to turn. The fun that had been so infectious, so intoxicating, began to unravel in the way only nightlife in a foreign city could.

Ryan and I had wandered toward the bar to get a quick drink when something caught my eye. A man stood in the corner of the room, watching us with an unsettling intensity. He wasn't the type of person you'd expect to stand out in a crowd like this—nothing about him was extraordinary. But there was something in the way he held his gaze, as if he knew something I didn't.

I turned back to Ryan, but he was already facing me, the same curious expression on his face. "What is it?" he asked, his voice low.

"I think I just saw someone," I said, my voice tight, my eyes never leaving the figure.

"Who?" Ryan asked, glancing toward the corner, but the man was already gone, swallowed by the crowd.

I shook my head, uncertain. "I don't know. I just… I felt like he was watching us."

Ryan studied me for a moment, his lips pressed together in thought. He didn't say anything, but I could feel the shift in the air between us, a new tension creeping in. Something about that moment, about the strange feeling that had settled in my chest, told me we weren't as safe as we thought.

It felt like a warning. And I couldn't shake it.

I excused myself from the table, my heart racing now, unsure if it was from the dance or from the unsettling feeling that had latched onto me.

Ryan followed me, his face creased with concern. "What's going on?"

"I don't know," I said, my voice a little more frantic than I meant it to be. "I just... felt like we were being watched."

Ryan reached out, his hand on my arm. "Hey, it's probably nothing. We've been working a lot, and you're running on fumes. Let's get some air, clear your head."

But even as he said the words, I could feel the weight of something else—something darker—settling between us.

I didn't know what it meant, but I knew one thing

for sure. That moment in the bar wasn't just a coincidence. Something was happening, and I wasn't sure if I was ready for it.

The air in the nightclub was thick with the mingling of sweat, cologne, and a thousand stories woven into the night. The music pulsed like a living thing, beating in my chest, making my thoughts swirl. I hadn't realized until that moment how much I needed this distraction, how much I'd been holding my breath since we landed in Barcelona. But now, as Ryan pulled me through the crowded dance floor, I felt that old weight settle back into my bones, uninvited and unwelcome.

We had danced for hours, laughed until our sides ached, and let the world blur into the background. But something was shifting, something had been creeping at the edges of my mind, and it wasn't just the adrenaline of the music or the strange energy of the night. I could feel it, the tension thickening between us. The way Ryan kept looking at me, his attention a little too focused, his hand brushing against mine in a way that was just enough to make my heart flutter and my pulse quicken. But I couldn't dwell on it, not now—not with everything else hanging over us.

It was when we decided to step away for a breather

that it happened.

I saw him first. The man. His presence cut through the noise and movement of the club like a sharp edge. He stood against the bar, his wiry frame leaning casually, his dark eyes fixed directly on me. For a moment, I froze. My skin prickled with an uneasy recognition, the same feeling I had when I noticed someone watching me from across the room—unseen, unnoticed, until you realize you're the target of their stare.

He wasn't just staring; he was watching me.

Ryan noticed me stiffen and followed my gaze. "What is it?" he asked, his voice low, a frown pulling at his mouth.

Before I could say anything, the man stepped toward us, moving with the grace of someone who knew exactly where he was going. His leather jacket was too pristine for the gritty atmosphere of the club, and his hair, slicked back, looked like it had never been mussed by a breeze. There was something off about him—something that didn't belong.

"You're looking for someone," he said, his English smooth but laced with an accent I couldn't quite place. The words slid from his mouth like he'd rehearsed them a thousand times.

My heart thudded harder in my chest, a sudden spike of adrenaline shooting through my veins. I nodded, trying to stay composed. "My dad. John Donovan. We think he might have been in Barcelona."

The man didn't flinch, didn't blink. Instead, he leaned in closer, his eyes glinting with something dark—something I couldn't quite place but that made me want to take a step back.

"I've heard of him," he said, his voice quieter now, as if he was sharing a secret with me. "An American man, yes? There are whispers."

I felt a wave of heat wash over me, my hands trembling slightly as I gripped the edge of the table. This was it—the moment we had been waiting for. But it didn't feel like the relief I had hoped for. It felt more like a trap.

The man's gaze flickered to Ryan, who had his arms crossed, his posture tense. I could feel him ready to react to whatever came next.

"Information is not free," the man added, his eyes flicking back to me, reading me in a way I wasn't sure I wanted to be read.

Ryan shifted beside me, the tension in his shoulders palpable. "How much?"

The man smiled, his lips curling into something

that wasn't quite a smile. It was more like a warning. He rubbed his thumb and forefinger together, the sound of it slicing through the air like a knife. "Two hundred euros."

Ryan's face immediately hardened, his jaw tightening as he glanced at me. He didn't say anything, but his expression said it all: This is sketchy. We're better off walking away. But something inside me—something I couldn't control—urged me to keep going.

I pulled out my wallet, my fingers feeling clumsy, my hands shaking as I slid the cash across the table. Two hundred euros. The exchange felt too easy, too quick, and yet it was the only option I had. My eyes didn't leave the man's face as he took the money, his fingers swift and sure as he pocketed it, his dark eyes never leaving mine.

His smile faded then, replaced by something more dangerous. "Your father…" he started, but the words caught in his throat, his voice lowering, like he was about to tell me something I shouldn't hear. "He was involved with dangerous people. He—"

Suddenly, without warning, he shot to his feet. The chair screeched loudly as he bolted for the door, the sound of his movements slicing through the hum of the room like an alarm. My breath hitched, panic setting in before I could process what was happening.

"Hey!" I shouted, standing up quickly, my legs unsteady. But he was already gone, disappearing into the crowd with a speed that left no room for hesitation.

Ryan was on his feet in an instant, his hand gripping my wrist as he yanked me toward the door. "Come on!" he shouted, urgency in his voice as he pulled me through the chaos of the club, our footsteps echoing against the walls as we raced after him.

I barely registered the people we bumped into as we pushed through the crowd, the heat and noise fading into the background. My focus was on the door, on the man who had just disappeared. What did he know about my father? And why did it feel like he was warning me instead of helping us?

I felt a knot form in my stomach, the weight of it settling deep within me. I wasn't sure if I was more afraid of what we were about to find or what had already been uncovered.

As we stepped outside, the cool night air hit my skin, sharp and fresh, but it did nothing to ease the suffocating tension in my chest. I turned to Ryan, my breath coming faster than I wanted it to.

"What just happened?" I whispered, my voice

shaking, but I couldn't stop it. I couldn't stop the fear that was creeping up my spine.

Ryan didn't answer immediately. His eyes were scanning the street, watching for any sign of movement. He was already alert, already in detective mode, and for a moment, I envied his composure. But all I could think about was that fleeting moment when the man's dark eyes met mine. His words echoed in my mind, twisting into something sinister.

Your father was involved with dangerous people.

I had no idea what that meant, but suddenly, everything about this trip—the case, the search for answers—felt like it was leading us into something far darker than I'd ever expected. Something that wasn't just dangerous, but personal. And that made my heart race in a way I didn't know how to stop.

I swallowed hard, my voice barely a whisper. "Ryan, do you think… do you think we're in over our heads?"

Ryan's eyes softened, but his expression remained focused. "No. We're not giving up. We're getting closer."

But his voice held a note of uncertainty that I didn't want to acknowledge. I wanted to believe him, but that nagging feeling in my gut—the one that had been with me all along—wasn't so sure.

I wasn't so sure. But then we saw him in the crowd.

The cobblestones beneath my feet felt jagged, unforgiving, as I sprinted through the narrow alleyways of Barcelona, the cool night air stinging my cheeks. My heart thudded in my chest, faster than the rhythm of my steps, and my breath came in quick, shallow bursts. The man ahead of us was a blur of dark leather and slicked-back hair, weaving in and out of the crowd like he knew these streets better than we did. A smirk twisted on his face, as if he was playing some kind of game—one he was determined to win.

"Ryan!" I gasped, my voice strained as I tried to catch up. "He's getting away!"

Ryan's pace didn't falter. He was a few steps behind me, but his long strides made him close the gap between us with ease. His jaw was set in determination, his eyes narrowed in a way that said nothing could stop him from getting what we came for.

"Not a chance," Ryan growled, his voice low and steady, like this was all just another puzzle for him to solve. The guy ahead of us glanced back, his smirk widening. I swear he was enjoying this—leading us on, testing our resolve.

We rounded another corner, and I nearly collided with a woman carrying a tray of drinks. I barely managed to dodge her, heart racing as I pushed forward, nearly stumbling in my hurry to stay close to Ryan. Every moment felt like it could be the one where I lost him—where I lost the only lead we had.

The man ahead of us veered into a crowded square, shoving through a group of tourists. The sounds of chattering voices and the clang of a street performer's tambourine filled the air, but I couldn't focus on any of it. My focus was entirely on him, on catching him before he disappeared into the dark night.

Ryan lunged forward, arms outstretched. The man's eyes widened as Ryan grabbed his jacket and they both crashed to the ground in a tangle of limbs. My feet faltered for a moment as I caught up, skidding to a stop beside them. The crowd was thick now, but I was too focused to care about the people around me. This was it. We couldn't let him slip away again.

"Give it back!" Ryan shouted, his voice rough with exertion, as he wrestled with the man. There was a flash of silver—coins or a knife, I wasn't sure—but I didn't have time to figure it out.

The man twisted, his foot catching Ryan in the chest, but not before Ryan yanked the wad of euros from his pocket. He pulled back, just as the man twisted free and darted into the crowd.

"Shit!" Ryan swore, scrambling to his feet. I watched, breathless, as he held up the money with a triumphant grin. "Got it," he said, his chest heaving with the force of his breath.

I stood there for a moment, unable to do anything but stare at the small pile of euros clutched in Ryan's hand. The adrenaline buzzed in my veins, leaving me dizzy and unsteady. Part of me wanted to collapse onto the ground, to breathe and let the tension slip away. But another part of me was still caught in the chaos of the chase, the pounding rhythm of my heart, the feeling that I'd just been part of something much bigger than I'd ever imagined.

I finally let out a shaky laugh, the sound coming out higher than I expected, almost breathless. The tension was slipping away now, but in its place was something else—something I couldn't quite name.

"That was insane," I said, still trying to catch my breath. My legs felt like jelly, and my knees were threatening to buckle. "We actually caught him."

Ryan was still grinning, though his expression was a little softer now, the edge of intensity slipping away. He nodded. "Yeah, but it's not over yet. We've got the money, but we still don't have answers."

I nodded, but my mind was still buzzing. There was a strange feeling in the pit of my stomach—excitement, relief, and something else, something a little more unsettling. The man's warning still echoed in my head. My father had been involved with dangerous people. That wasn't just a passing comment. It was a clue. And now we had a piece of the puzzle. But where did it fit? And what did it mean for us?

As we walked back through the square, the pulse of the music and the chatter of the crowd seemed muted in comparison to the storm raging inside me. The city felt both distant and near, its lights blurring into streaks of neon and shadow. I glanced over at Ryan, wondering what he was thinking, but his face was unreadable, his focus on the road ahead.

"You okay?" Ryan asked after a long silence, his voice suddenly softer, gentler than before.

I nodded, but my mind was still tangled in a thousand different thoughts. "Yeah. I think so. It's just… this is all so much, you know? I mean, it's one thing to hear stories about my dad, but it's another to actually be this close to finding him. To finding out what really happened."

Ryan's gaze softened, and he reached over, giving

my shoulder a light squeeze. "We'll figure it out," he said quietly. "One step at a time."

I swallowed, trying to calm the jittery feeling that was crawling up my spine. It wasn't just the mystery anymore. It was something else. Something about Ryan's presence, the way he always seemed to have everything under control, even when everything around us was falling apart. And I wasn't sure if I was grateful for that or scared of it.

"Thanks," I said, my voice a little quieter than I meant it to be.

"For what?" Ryan asked, his eyebrow cocking in that way that always made him seem too damn charming when he didn't mean to be.

"For... being here," I said, trying to make the words sound casual, like it wasn't a bigger deal than it was. "For not leaving me to do this alone."

He flashed me a small, almost shy grin. "I wouldn't dream of it."

I glanced at him quickly, the warmth in his expression stirring something in my chest. But I pushed it down, focusing instead on the path ahead of us, on the dark alleyways and hidden corners of this city that were now starting to feel more like a labyrinth than an adventure.

I wasn't sure where this journey would take us, but one thing was certain—I was already too deep to turn back.

CHAPTER 13: A GLIMPSE OF THE TRUTH

Ryan walked beside me, his hands buried deep in the pockets of his jacket, the faint glow of the streetlights catching the sharp planes of his face. A small smile tugged at the corners of his mouth, the kind that felt private, like it was meant just for me. I didn't know if I should look at him or away, but I couldn't seem to help myself.

"Admit it," he said, glancing sideways at me. "You had fun."

I rolled my eyes, fighting the smile that threatened to break free. "It was… okay," I said, even though a part of me was still caught up in the rhythm of the music, in the way my body had moved to the beat without thinking about it. It was the first time in days that I hadn't felt weighed down by the mystery, the questions that had been pressing into my chest like a stone.

"Okay?" Ryan repeated, feigning offense, and I

could hear the teasing edge in his voice. "I'll take it. For now."

I shot him a look, trying to suppress the grin, but the smile that crept onto my face was too genuine to hide. "You're impossible."

"You love it," he shot back, a playful glint in his eyes.

There was a quiet moment between us as we continued walking, the sounds of the city drifting around us—the low hum of conversation from nearby cafés, the occasional clink of a bicycle bell, the distant honk of a car horn. It wasn't uncomfortable, this silence, but it wasn't easy either. There was a tension to it, something unspoken hanging in the air, just out of reach.

I could feel it. Ryan's teasing had softened, his smile lingered a little longer than usual, and his gaze seemed to hold more than it had before. I caught him looking at me out of the corner of my eye, his expression unreadable for a moment before he glanced away.

I knew what it meant. I wasn't blind, and I wasn't naive. He was looking at me differently now. The jokes weren't just jokes anymore, and the smiles weren't just friendly. I could feel it in the way he moved, in the quiet way he stayed close without needing to say anything.

And I wasn't sure how to handle it.

I wanted to lean into that. To let him be more than just my best friend—the one who knew all my secrets, the one who had been there through every stupid decision, every heartbreak. But then I would remember the weight of the mystery, the unanswered questions about my dad, about who he really was and why he'd vanished. I couldn't let myself forget why I was here in the first place, chasing ghosts across Barcelona. Not yet.

As we walked in silence, my mind drifted back to the man at the bar, the one who had given us the lead. I could still see his dark eyes glinting, still feel the sting of his words: "Your father was involved with dangerous people." It felt like a weight on my chest, something pressing down with every step.

Ryan, sensing the shift, slowed his pace. "You okay?" he asked, his voice soft, as if afraid to break the fragile space between us.

I nodded, though I wasn't sure I was. "Yeah. Just... a lot to think about."

"You don't have to do it alone," he said quietly, his words laced with something more than simple reassurance. It was something deeper, something that made my chest tighten in a way I didn't know how to handle.

"I know," I whispered, the words barely escaping.

And that was the problem. I did know. Ryan was always there. He always had been. But was that enough? Could it be enough? My heart wavered between the two worlds—the one where I was still chasing after answers, still untangling the mess of my father's life, and the one where Ryan stood beside me, not just as a friend, but as someone who made my pulse quicken, my thoughts scatter.

I wasn't sure how to navigate that space between us.

As we neared the hostel, I couldn't help but glance at him again, this time catching the faintest flicker of something in his eyes. But before I could say anything, the sound of laughter in the distance pulled me back to the present.

The night felt different now. The weight of the city seemed to settle into my bones, but it wasn't just the city that felt heavy. It was the way I was starting to see Ryan, and the way he was starting to see me. We had crossed a line, even if neither of us wanted to admit it.

But there was no going back now.

And for the first time in a long while, I wasn't sure if that was a good thing or not.

Back at the hostel, the chase still lingered in my veins, like a fever dream I couldn't shake. My legs were sore, and my heart hammered in my chest, not from the run but from everything that had happened—and everything that was still unanswered. I collapsed onto the bed, letting my body sink into the soft mattress as I stared up at the bunk. The world felt both too loud and too quiet, like everything around me was pulsing with a hum I couldn't tune out.

Ryan flopped down beside me, his breath still coming fast. His hair was wild, and his face flushed from the adrenaline, but he had this grin on his face, like the whole thing had been some sort of joke, and I had a feeling he didn't mind being in the middle of it. "Well, that was... something."

I turned my head to look at him, and despite everything—the man running, the chase, the euros—I couldn't help it. A laugh bubbled up in my chest, almost against my will. "We're idiots."

"Definitely," Ryan agreed, his grin widening, and there was something in his eyes that made it feel like we were the only two people in the world for a moment.

We were quiet for a while after that, the air between us shifting, softening. The tension from the night, the breathless chase, started to fade, and what was left was... different. There was something heavier now, something lingering in the way Ryan was looking at me, in the way I could feel his presence next to me without needing to glance over.

Then, without warning, his smile faltered, his gaze growing more serious. He shifted closer, his shoulders brushing mine. "Nat…" His voice was quiet, almost uncertain, like he wasn't sure if he should even say it.

I didn't move, didn't speak. Just let him find whatever it was he needed to say. The moment felt fragile, like we were teetering on the edge of something, and I wasn't sure if I was ready to fall.

But before I could think too hard about it, he leaned in, his breath warm against my cheek, and everything else faded out of focus. The kiss was sudden, like it had been waiting in the air between us for too long. Warm and steady, like a grounding force, it pulled me out of my whirlwind of doubts and fears, and for the first time in what felt like forever, I didn't think. I just... was.

His lips were soft but sure against mine, and I didn't pull away. I didn't even want to. Everything I'd been holding back—every fear, every hesitation, every worry about why we were here, about what was happening—just melted away in that moment. It was just him and me, and for once, I wasn't alone in the middle of all of it.

When we finally pulled apart, my chest felt tight, my breath coming faster than before. I couldn't look at him right away, unsure of what to say, what to feel.

Ryan broke the silence first, his voice light but his eyes serious. "Guess I owe you churros after that." He smiled, but it didn't quite reach his eyes, not in the way it usually did. It was a smile that didn't quite fit the moment.

I smiled softly, even though there was a twist in my stomach I couldn't quite explain. "You're never going to let that go, are you?"

"Never," he replied, his voice teasing, but there was an undercurrent to it, something unsaid hanging between us.

I leaned my head against his shoulder, feeling the warmth of him against me, but even with him so close, something inside of me felt distant. It wasn't anything he had done—Ryan was always the same, always there in ways I could count on. But I couldn't shake the feeling that this was a turning point, that something was shifting in a way I wasn't ready for. In a way I didn't understand yet.

But it wasn't about understanding right now. It was about the weight of the moment. The way his arm wrapped around me, how the air between us felt charged with something new, something uncertain. Maybe it was the chase, the danger, the kiss... or maybe it was just me, trying to piece together everything that was happening, trying to make sense of what it all meant.

I closed my eyes for a moment, taking a deep breath, feeling the thrum of the city outside our window, its lights still flickering like tiny stars in the distance. But for once, it didn't feel like everything was pulling me in different directions. For once, it felt like maybe I could just... be. Be with him. Be here.

But even as I let myself sink into that feeling, a part of me—deep down—wondered if I was about to lose myself in something I wasn't ready for.

The morning after the chase, the air felt too still, like the calm before a storm. I could still feel the echo of the chase in my limbs—the quick, frantic pulse of adrenaline that had fueled my every step. But now, everything felt heavier, more uncertain.

Ryan sat hunched over his laptop at the small desk

by the window, the soft glow of the screen casting an eerie light over his face. His brow was furrowed, his fingers tapping furiously on the keys. I sat cross-legged on the bottom bunk of our hostel room, staring at the crumpled receipts and scribbled notes scattered around me, as if I might find something, anything, to piece together the puzzle of my father's disappearance. But with every passing second, the hope of discovering something useful seemed to slip farther away. The weight of unanswered questions was starting to crush me.

I reached over and absentmindedly fiddled with a scrap of paper, my mind a fog of exhaustion and frustration. Then Ryan's voice pierced through the quiet.

"Wait," he said, his tone sharper than I'd heard it all morning.

I straightened up instantly, my heart skipping a beat. "What is it?" I asked, my voice tense.

He turned the laptop screen toward me, his eyes still locked on the words that had caught his attention. There, in the middle of an otherwise mundane inbox, was an email—one we hadn't seen before. It stood out like a red flag, buried deep in my dad's old account, as if someone didn't want us to find it.

It was short and to the point. No greeting, no signature—just a cryptic message:

"Florence. I'll be waiting."

The timestamp was from a week before Dad had disappeared. My breath caught in my throat as I reread the words, my mind spinning. Florence. Was it a place? Florence, Italy? Or was it something else? A name? A woman?

I turned to Ryan, my hands shaking. "Do you think it's real?" The words felt like they were stuck in my throat, heavy and hard to say.

Ryan didn't look at me at first. His eyes were locked on the screen, tracing the letters like they were the key to something he hadn't quite figured out. "I don't know," he murmured, his voice low and distant. "But it matches the timeline. If he sent this... he's following some kind of plan."

Plan. The word hit me like a punch to the gut. A plan meant intention. It meant my dad had left on purpose. He hadn't just vanished. He had chosen to go, to follow something—or someone—else. The thought twisted in my chest, made me feel both nauseous and helpless. What had he gotten himself involved in? What kind of plan could be worth disappearing for?

I blinked rapidly, trying to push back the rising panic. "A plan…" I repeated, but the words didn't comfort me like they should have. They felt hollow, empty.

Ryan's gaze softened, and he closed the laptop, though the weight of the words still hung between us. "We'll figure it out, Nat. We have to." His voice was steady, but there was an undercurrent to it, a tension I could feel deep in my bones.

I nodded, but it didn't make anything clearer. My dad had left a trail, sure, but it was a trail full of holes, one that led me to more questions than answers.

I swallowed hard, trying to push down the feeling of being utterly lost. "I don't know if I'm ready for this," I whispered, more to myself than to Ryan.

But before I could finish, the weight of the night's events crept back in—the chase, the fear, the desperation to find something, anything, to explain why my father was gone. The weight settled on me like a thick, suffocating blanket.

Ryan was quiet for a moment, watching me with a look in his eyes that made my stomach tighten. Then he stood up, his movements slow but deliberate. "You don't have to do this alone, you know. I'm here. I always will be."

The simple words should have been comforting, but they hit me harder than I expected. I swallowed the lump in my throat, fighting back the tears that threatened to break free. "I know," I whispered, barely able to speak. "I just… I don't know if I can handle this. If I can handle the truth."

Ryan reached over, his hand gentle on my shoulder, offering me a brief touch of reassurance. I wanted to believe him. I wanted to believe that everything would be okay, that we would find answers and piece together this shattered puzzle. But there was a gnawing feeling in my gut, something I couldn't shake—the feeling that whatever I was about to uncover, it would change everything.

I tried to force a smile, but it came out as a sad half-curve of my lips. "Thanks," I said softly. "I don't know what I'd do without you."

Ryan didn't respond right away. Instead, he gave me a small smile, one that seemed to say more than words could. Then he left me to sit there, alone with the weight of what we had just uncovered.

I let out a slow, shaky breath and sank back onto the bed, my mind spinning, the uncertainty settling deep in my chest. I needed answers. But I wasn't sure I was ready to face whatever truths they might hold.

The train station in Barcelona was a blur of faces, luggage, and hasty goodbyes as we stood in front of the massive, scrolling departure board. I was scanning it, trying to focus, but my thoughts kept drifting. The train to Florence, or a flight? I hadn't even thought about the logistics until now, when the weight of it all—money, travel, my dad's disappearance—pressed in on me.

Ryan was standing beside me, his fingers drumming lightly against his thigh. He looked at the board too, but I could tell his mind wasn't on the train times. His gaze flicked toward me every few seconds, his eyes searching, almost as if he could sense I wasn't okay.

I knew I should say something. I knew I couldn't hide this from him anymore.

"Ryan…" I started, my voice barely audible against the cacophony of the station. He turned to me, waiting. I swallowed hard, trying to steady the wave of anxiety. "I… I don't know if I can afford this. The train, the flight, everything." I looked down at the cracked pavement beneath my boots, feeling my cheeks flush. "I mean, the whole trip… I wasn't sure about how I'd pay for it in the first place, and now… I don't even know how I'll get back home after this. I don't want to be a burden."

Ryan blinked, his expression softening. I could see the muscles in his jaw tense as he processed what I was saying. He stepped closer, lowering his voice.

"Natalie, listen to me. Don't worry about the money. I've got it covered. Okay?"

I shook my head, not entirely able to process his words. "No, Ryan. I can't just let you—"

"I'm not asking," he cut me off, his tone firm but not harsh. "You're my best friend. I told you before, I'm here. And if this means getting you to Florence, then that's what I'm gonna do."

I felt a lump form in my throat, a mix of gratitude and guilt. "I… I don't know what to say."

"Then don't say anything," Ryan said with a half-smile. He shrugged. "We've come this far. Let's just get on the damn train."

But as we stood there in the growing tension of the moment, something else gnawed at me, something I'd been trying to ignore. The kiss. The night we'd danced in the club, laughing and spinning with no care for what was happening in the world outside. It had felt natural in the moment. Like it was just another step, another layer of our friendship. But then, the aftermath. The awkwardness. The shift in the air between us.

I turned to him, my voice dropping. "Ryan," I started, my words a little too sharp, a little too quick. "About the kiss… I just—" I cut myself off, the words tangled in my mouth. "It was a mistake. Okay? You're my best friend. It wasn't supposed to happen."

The air between us seemed to freeze for a second. Ryan's brow furrowed, and he stared at me for a long beat. His lips parted like he was about to say something, but then he closed them again, exhaling through his nose. His eyes were unreadable.

"Okay," he said finally, his voice quiet, but not angry. "I just want to make sure we're on the same page."

"Yeah," I said quickly, nodding. "We are. I just… I don't want things to change."

For a moment, we just stood there, not saying anything, but the weight of it still hung in the air, thick and unspoken. Finally, Ryan sighed and ran a hand through his hair.

"Let's go to Florence and get this over with," he said, his voice steady. "That's the last stop. After that, we can figure everything else out."

I nodded, relief flooding through me, and we moved toward the platform together. The tension between us was still there, but there was a quiet understanding now, a mutual acknowledgment that sometimes things just happen, and we had to move forward.

The train ride felt endless. The click-clack of the wheels on the tracks became a rhythm, something to hold onto as we sped through the Italian countryside. The hills were a blur of green and gold, the sunflowers stretching endlessly toward the horizon, their faces following the sun. I leaned against the window, my breath fogging up the glass as I watched the landscape blur by.

I tried to shut out the overwhelming rush of thoughts that kept threatening to break through, the weight of everything pressing in. My dad, the mystery, the secrets, the betrayal that seemed to be woven into every memory I had of him.

The man who had been my anchor, the steady, reliable presence in my life. And now I was watching the illusion of who he was shatter before me, piece by piece.

I didn't know if I could trust the man in the pictures anymore. The dad who made pancakes shaped like smiley faces. Who knew my favorite ice cream. Who always had the right words when I was scared.

The more I uncovered, the more it felt like the version of him I'd always known was slipping through my fingers.

"Did I ever really know him?" I whispered aloud, the words slipping out before I could stop them.

Ryan looked up from the train schedule he had been studying, his eyes meeting mine, a frown tugging at his lips. "What?"

I shook my head, my voice barely audible over the hum of the train. "Nothing."

But it wasn't nothing.

Every memory I had of Dad—the good ones, the ones that had felt so solid, so real—now felt like they belonged to someone else. Someone who wasn't quite as perfect as I'd imagined him to be. The man I thought I knew had secrets. Dark ones. And now I was chasing those secrets across the world.

I let out a shaky breath, trying to steady myself. Trying to hold on to the pieces of him that still felt real. But with each passing mile, the truth seemed to grow more elusive, slipping further and further out of reach.

CHAPTER 14: FINDING JOHN

Florence unfolded before us like a painting come to life, its terracotta rooftops glowing under the golden afternoon sun. The narrow, cobbled streets wound like threads through a tapestry of pastel-colored buildings, their balconies bursting with flowers—vibrant reds, purples, and yellows. The air was thick with the scent of freshly baked bread and the bitter warmth of roasted espresso, curling into my senses and filling me with an unexpected sense of peace.

I lifted my phone, snapping a picture of the scene before us. The sunlit piazza was alive with energy—tourists snapping photos, couples strolling hand in hand, and street vendors calling out to passersby. I sent the picture to my mom and Trevor with a quick text: Florence. We're here. A part of me wanted them to feel the magic of this place too, to share in the small victories of this trip, even if they weren't physically here with me.

Ryan gave me a sideways glance as I tucked my

phone back into my jacket pocket. He was already studying the map on his phone, his brow furrowed in concentration.

"Okay," he said, voice low but steady. "The email didn't give us much to go on, so where do we start?"

I felt my heart race in my chest. This moment, right here, felt pivotal. We were standing in the heart of a city that was steeped in history, beauty, and secrets—and my dad's name echoed somewhere in its winding streets. Could this be it? Was I really close to finding him?

Taking a deep breath, I surveyed the area, my mind racing. My dad had always been drawn to places that thrived with energy, with movement. He liked to be where the action was, where the people were. Florence was alive with people—tourists, locals, all rushing about their business. I could feel the weight of something starting to settle inside me—a tiny flicker of hope that maybe, just maybe, we were getting closer.

"Let's try the center of town," I said, the words leaving my mouth before I had time to second-guess them. "He'd want to be near the action."

Ryan glanced up from the map, a quiet nod of agreement. "Sounds good. Lead the way."

We started walking, slipping through the narrow

streets like we were part of the rhythm of Florence itself. There was an energy here—something intangible and electric that made everything seem just a little more possible, just a little more alive. I could almost hear my dad's voice in my head, telling me that this was what he wanted: to be somewhere full of life, where every corner held a new secret, a new opportunity.

I quickened my pace slightly, driven by that tiny flicker of hope that had started to bloom in my chest. It felt like I was on the edge of something big—like I was standing at the edge of a cliff, staring out at the vast unknown below, waiting for the right moment to take the leap.

As we passed a corner, I stopped in front of a café, its tables spilling out onto the sidewalk. The chatter of people eating lunch, the clinking of glasses, the sound of baristas preparing coffee—it was a world so full of life it almost felt like a dream. The warm sunlight bathed everything in a soft, golden glow. For a moment, I let myself be caught in it.

Ryan nudged me, his voice teasing. "You're getting distracted. We have a mystery to solve."

I shot him a smile, but the ache in my chest didn't go away. The weight of it all, the years of wondering, of waiting, of wishing—was it possible that the answers were just up ahead?

I nodded, my voice steadying. "I know. But sometimes it helps to take a second and breathe it all in."

Ryan didn't argue. He just nodded, glancing around the square. "Let's find somewhere to sit and figure out our next move."

We found a small bench in the shade of a stone wall, and I pulled out my notes, my eyes skimming the pages I'd written in the last few days. The scribbled thoughts, the theories—none of it made sense, not really. But I knew this: I was close. Every step, every clue, was leading me here.

"Do you think we'll actually find him?" Ryan asked, breaking the silence between us. His voice was quiet, but there was an edge of uncertainty there.

I turned to look at him, the question hanging in the air between us. I didn't know how to answer. I wanted to say yes, I wanted to be sure. But the truth was, I wasn't. Not completely.

"I don't know," I admitted, my voice barely above a whisper. "But I have to try. I have to know."

Ryan's eyes softened. He leaned back against the stone wall, folding his arms across his chest. "Then let's do it. Let's figure this out together."

Something about the way he said it made the weight in my chest lift, just a little. In that moment, I wasn't alone. Not completely. And that meant more than I could say.

As we sat there, watching the world move around us, the sound of church bells ringing in the distance, I realized that Florence wasn't just a city. It wasn't just the place where my dad might be. It was a turning point. For me. For all of us.

I didn't know where this journey would end, or if I would find my dad—or if I would find the answers I was looking for. But I knew one thing for sure: I was ready to take the next step.

And somehow, with Ryan by my side, I knew I could keep going.

The day in Florence had been one long string of disappointments, one person after another shrugging their shoulders as we asked around about my dad. Each conversation, though polite, was met with confusion or a quick "no" before the person we spoke to hurried off, as if they didn't want to get involved. I couldn't blame them, really. This wasn't their mystery to solve.

The language barrier didn't help. Even with the translation app on my phone, it was hard to fully communicate what we were looking for. It was like we were trying to navigate a foreign world, not just in the literal sense, but in the way we were speaking about my dad—this man who had so many versions of himself, each one harder to grasp than the last.

Ryan was patient, though. He always was. Still, I could tell the tension was starting to wear on him too. It was hard to hide the frustration in the way he tugged at his shirt collar or the deep sighs he let slip when the translation app would misfire.

Finally, by late afternoon, we decided to take the train out of the city, heading to a smaller town further south that matched the details in the email. I wasn't sure what I was expecting—maybe something clearer, something that would help me understand my dad, the man he was, the man he had been when he left.

The small town didn't look like much from the train station—a few winding streets, whitewashed buildings with terracotta roofs, and a single square where old men sat playing chess beneath the shade of olive trees. The air smelled of lemons and dust, and the silence was almost deafening after the buzz of Florence. It felt so different here, quieter in a way that made my heart ache with the weight of uncertainty. Was this the place? Was my dad here?

We spent hours wandering the streets, asking

people who seemed just as uninterested in our questions as the ones in Florence. Nobody had seen him, the man who had once been my dad. I wanted to scream, to demand answers, but I couldn't. I couldn't risk blowing this, not when we were this close.

The whole day felt like it was slipping away, and with it, my hope. By the time we stopped for a quick dinner in a small café, I was beyond exhausted, both physically and emotionally.

But then, as we passed the grocery store near the town's main square, I saw him.

A tall man, bald, moving quickly out of the store with a bag of groceries tucked under his arm. The back of his neck, the way he walked—something about him felt too familiar. My heart skipped a beat.

"It's him," I said, my voice almost a whisper, but Ryan heard it. He didn't hesitate, he just grabbed my arm and we followed, staying a few paces behind as the man moved down the street.

I felt every step in my legs, the urgency and adrenaline pushing me forward. It was like something in me had snapped into focus, and I couldn't pull away even if I wanted to.

We followed him to a rundown apartment building on the outskirts of town. The building was a mess—paint peeling off the walls, shutters hanging crookedly, as though the place had given up on ever being beautiful again. My chest tightened, and I had to swallow down the nausea that rose in my throat.

Ryan pulled out his phone, checking the address once more, his brows furrowing.

"This is it?" he asked, squinting at the screen.

I nodded, but the tightness in my throat made it hard to speak. This was it. The man who barely even looked like my dad anymore, the man who seemed to be a ghost of the person I had known, was leading us here. To this place. To this moment.

My legs felt like lead as we climbed the narrow staircase to the second floor, each step echoing in the quiet of the building, the sound bouncing off cracked, peeling walls. The air in the stairwell was damp and smelled faintly of mildew. Every step felt like it was pushing me further into an unknown.

When we reached the second floor, I stopped in front of a door. The number "2B" was scrawled in faded black paint on the wooden door. It didn't look like a place where anyone had lived recently, much less a place where the man I was searching for had stayed.

I felt my pulse racing in my ears, my heartbeat thudding like a drum. This was it. This was where my dad had been.

"Are you ready?" Ryan asked softly, his voice cutting through the thick silence.

I turned to look at him, and for a moment, I saw the uncertainty in his eyes. He had been with me through all of this, through the endless questions, the unanswered calls, and the dead ends. He wasn't just my friend anymore, not in the way he used to be. There was something else between us, something I didn't know how to name.

"No," I whispered. "But we have to do this."

I raised my hand and knocked on the door, my knuckles barely making a sound against the weathered wood.

And then I waited.

The minutes stretched on forever, each one heavier than the last. I was afraid to turn around, afraid to face the truth that might or might not lie behind this door. I wasn't sure if I was ready for what I might find.

But this was the moment. The door was about to open, and whatever was on the other side of it would change everything.

The door creaked open with a groan that seemed to echo down the hallway. I froze for a second, my breath catching in my throat, my whole body stiffening. There he was.

My father.

His face was thinner than I remembered, the once sharp jawline now hollow, like someone had carved out pieces of him without his permission. His skin looked tired, almost gray, and the shock of hair that had always been neatly combed was now bald, leaving him exposed in a way I couldn't quite explain.

We stood there for what felt like an eternity, just staring at each other. The silence between us wasn't just heavy; it was suffocating. It was as if the space between us was filled with all the years of unanswered questions, of the anger, the hurt, the confusion. I could feel it, pressing down on me, making it hard to breathe.

"Peanut?" His voice cracked on the word, the name he used to call me when I was younger, when I was small and innocent, before I had any idea what it meant to be abandoned, to be left with no explanation.

A jagged edge of fury sliced through me. "You don't get to call me like that," I snapped, the words sharp and unforgiving. I pushed past him into the apartment, not giving him a chance to explain or to even ask me to come in. "You don't get to act surprised after what you put us through."

I could feel Ryan behind me, staying silent, but I

knew he was there, a presence that somehow made the weight of this moment a little less unbearable. He was my anchor now, more than my dad ever had been.

But my dad? He wasn't standing strong. His shoulders hunched, and he looked smaller than I had imagined. The man who had been my hero, the man who I'd once thought could do no wrong, was a shadow of himself. I couldn't decide if I wanted to scream at him or cry.

"Natalie, wait—" His voice was hoarse, like it hadn't been used in years, like he was out of practice at trying to make things right.

"No!" I spun around to face him, my hands trembling with frustration, my chest tight. "Do you have any idea what you've done? Mom's a wreck, Trevor's falling apart, and I've spent the entire summer chasing you halfway across Europe like some stupid game of hide-and-seek!"

The words came out in a rush, each one more painful than the last, each one cutting into him. He didn't deserve my anger, I knew that. But I didn't care. I needed him to feel this, to understand the mess he had left behind.

He sank onto the worn-out couch behind him, his head falling into his hands, as though the weight of his own guilt was too much to bear. His whole body seemed to deflate, like a balloon losing all its air in an instant.

"I never wanted you to find me," he said, his voice barely above a whisper, as if speaking those words out loud made them somehow less true, less painful.

"Well, congratulations," I shot back, unable to hold back the bitterness that laced my voice. "You failed."

There was a long pause as he sat there, and I could hear the raggedness of his breathing, the slight shake in his hands. I wanted him to get up, to try, to do something that showed me he wasn't just a shell of the man I used to know. But he didn't. He just sat there, small, broken, and utterly lost.

For a moment, I stood there, my heart beating in my ears, wondering if I should just walk out, turn my back on him and pretend none of this had happened. Maybe that would have been easier. But no. I couldn't. Not when the truth was hanging right in front of me.

He finally lifted his head, his eyes bloodshot and rimmed with exhaustion, but there was something else in them too—something that made my stomach turn. Regret. Fear. And maybe, just maybe, a little bit of love. But I wasn't ready to see that. Not yet.

I had so many questions, so many things I needed him to explain, to answer. But the words wouldn't come. It was like I was choking on the weight of everything I'd carried—the pain, the years of wondering why he left, why he didn't say goodbye. Why he couldn't be the man I thought he was.

Ryan stepped forward then, his voice quiet but steady, as if he were trying to ground me in this moment.

"Natalie, you don't have to do this now," he said, his eyes flicking between me and my dad. "You've found him. That's enough for today."

I shook my head, barely hearing him over the rush of emotions. He was right, of course. I didn't have to do this. But I didn't know how to stop.

I turned back to my dad, my heart aching with a kind of raw pain I didn't know how to process. I didn't know how to feel anymore. I wanted answers, but I didn't know if I could handle what those answers might be.

"Why?" I whispered, my voice trembling, as I took a step toward him. "Why did you leave us?"

For a moment, he didn't answer. But then, he lifted his eyes to meet mine, and for the first time, I saw something real.

"I thought I was doing the right thing," he said softly, the words heavy with regret. "I thought I was protecting you."

But from what? From him? From the man he had become? From the secrets he was keeping?

I didn't know what to say to that.

The silence stretched between us again, thick and suffocating, and I realized something. I had been searching for answers, for closure, but maybe… maybe there was no neat, tidy ending to this. Maybe there was just this—broken pieces, messy emotions, and an uncertain future.

But that didn't mean I wasn't going to try.

I wasn't going to walk away this time.

Not yet. Not until I knew everything.

Ryan stood by the door, awkwardly shifting his weight from foot to foot, his gaze flitting between me and my dad. The silence felt heavy, suffocating, like it was pressing in from all sides, making it impossible to think. My hands trembled at my sides, the urge to lash out still buzzing under my skin. My dad sat there, shoulders slumped, head lowered, like he couldn't bear to meet my eyes. For a long moment, neither of us said anything.

Finally, he broke the silence, lifting his gaze to

mine. His eyes were rimmed red, and his voice cracked when he spoke.

"I messed up," he admitted, the words falling out in a rush. "I don't even know where to start."

I crossed my arms tightly over my chest, heart hammering in my throat. "How about the truth?" I demanded, my voice sharp, bitter. "You've been hiding from us for how long, and now you want to act like it's all just some mistake?"

He let out a heavy sigh, leaning back against the couch as though the weight of his confession had already drained all his energy. His eyes closed for a moment, his hands rubbing his temples like he was trying to push the thoughts away. "It started small," he said, his voice barely above a whisper, as though the words were hard to form. "Just messages, a little harmless flirting. She seemed real. Margaux seemed real." He swallowed hard, eyes darting toward the floor. "And then she started asking for things. Money for her 'visa,' plane tickets, a place to stay."

"You gave her money?" I asked, incredulous. It didn't make sense. How could he have been so... blind?

He nodded, his eyes glassy. "All of it. Our savings, the emergency fund. I thought... I thought I was helping someone who cared about me. I thought I was… I don't know, doing the right thing." He let out a bitter laugh, but it wasn't funny. "By the time I realized it was a scam, it was too late."

I took a step back, the gravity of his words pressing down on me. My mind was reeling, my chest tightening. "And that's why you ran?" I asked, my voice tight with disbelief. "Because of a scam?"

His gaze dropped to the floor, like he couldn't bear to face me anymore. "I ran because I didn't know how to face you. Or your mom. Or myself. I felt…" He paused, searching for the words. "I felt trapped. By the mess I'd made. By the life I'd been living."

"What's that supposed to mean?" I asked, my voice rising, a thread of anger weaving through the shock.

He rubbed a hand over his face, his fingers pressing against his temples like he was trying to hold himself together. "I felt like I was drowning, Nat," he said, his voice hoarse. "Your mom and I, we've been pretending for years. Pretending we were happy, pretending I was enough. And I couldn't do it anymore."

The words slammed into me, and I staggered back, my legs feeling weak under me. My whole body seemed to crumple under the weight of it. "So, what?" I choked out, my voice breaking. "You just decided to disappear? Start over?"

"I didn't know what else to do," he said, his voice hollow, distant.

I took a step forward, my chest tightening with the pressure of everything I was feeling, everything I needed to say. "Do you even care about us?" I asked, the question tumbling out before I could stop it, the sting of betrayal sharp on my tongue. "Or were we just part of the life you wanted to escape?"

His head snapped up, his eyes wide, and for the first time since I'd walked in, I saw something raw in his gaze. Something like panic, like the reality of what he'd done was finally crashing down on him. "Of course I care about you," he said, his voice cracking. "I love you, Natalie. That's why I didn't want you to find me. You deserve better than this mess."

The words hung in the air between us, and for a moment, I almost believed him. Almost. But then my mind twisted, and the anger bubbled up again, a fire that burned too hot to ignore.

"You don't get to decide what I deserve," I said, the words quieter this time, but no less fierce. "I get to decide that for myself."

He didn't respond. Instead, he just sank deeper into the couch, his shoulders hunched as though the weight of my words had crushed him. The room felt like it was closing in on me, and for the first time, I realized how much this—all of this—had taken from me. Not just the time, not just the money, not just the emotional toll. But everything. The way I saw my father. The way I saw myself.

I wanted to feel angry. I wanted to scream at him and demand more answers, more reasons. But the anger drained out of me slowly, replaced by a hollow ache, a pit in my stomach that I couldn't fill with anything. Not even the truth.

My gaze flicked to Ryan, standing silently by the door, his expression unreadable. He hadn't said a word this whole time, but I could feel the weight of his support, the way he was waiting, holding space for me. I wanted to say something to him, to thank him, but the words wouldn't come. Not now. Maybe later.

For now, all I could do was stand there, my heart torn between the person I used to be and the person I had to become to move past all this.

The silence stretched between us, suffocating and thick, and I felt something inside me break. Maybe it was the last thread of hope I had, the one where I still believed things could go back to normal, where my dad could come back and we could be a family again. But that wasn't the truth. Not anymore.

I closed my eyes, trying to swallow the ache in my throat, but it wasn't enough. It never would be.

CHAPTER 15: BROKEN BONDS

The air in the apartment felt thick, heavy, like it had absorbed every harsh word, every unspoken truth. My footsteps echoed in the small space as I paced, unable to sit still, unable to stop the anger bubbling over. The flickering light from the overhead bulb cast long shadows on the cracked walls, and the smell of stale coffee mixed with the lingering scent of something else I couldn't quite place—regret, maybe. Or fear.

"You don't understand," Dad said, his voice low and strained, almost pleading.

I stopped pacing and turned to face him, my hands balled into fists at my sides. "Oh, spare me," I snapped, my voice sharp, cutting through the silence. "You didn't have a choice? You had a family, Dad. A wife, two kids, a life you just—what? Walked away from?"

His eyes darkened, and he stood from the couch, gripping the back of it like it was the only thing holding him upright. His knuckles whitened as he clenched his hands. "I know I hurt you. All of you. But you don't know what it was like. I was—" He trailed off, his voice faltering.

I stepped closer, the words spilling out before I could stop them. "You were what?" I demanded. "Lonely? Tired? Bored? Do you have any idea what it was like for us? For me? While you were off playing house with some woman who didn't even exist?"

His face crumpled at my words, like I had physically struck him, but I didn't stop. I couldn't. The frustration, the hurt—it all rushed to the surface in a flood, and I was drowning in it. "Do you know what it's like to lose someone and not even know why? To think they're dead, only to find out they left because they were too much of a coward to face their mistakes?"

My breath came in sharp gasps as the final sentence tumbled out. It felt like a confession, like something I'd been holding inside for too long. My heart thudded painfully in my chest, and my throat tightened with the weight of everything I'd never said until now.

Ryan stepped closer to me, his hand hovering near my shoulder, but I shook him off. I didn't want comfort. Not now.

"Nat," he said gently, his voice soft and steady. "You don't have to do this."

But I did. I had to.

"No," Dad said quietly, his voice barely audible, the words cracking under the strain of the moment. "She's right."

I froze, my heart skipping a beat. My dad, the man who had run from us, the man who had left without a word, was admitting it. He was saying it out loud. "I am a coward."

The words hung in the air, thick and suffocating. The admission felt like a blade cutting through the silence, leaving raw, exposed truth in its wake. I didn't know how to react. I didn't know what to do with it.

I could feel Ryan's presence beside me, a quiet support, but I couldn't look at him. Not now. Not when everything I thought I knew about my family was crashing down around me.

The room seemed to shrink with every breath I took, each one heavier than the last. I had spent so many months, so many days, trying to figure out what had happened, why my dad had disappeared, why everything had gone wrong. And now, here he was, standing in front of me, confessing his weakness, his mistakes, like it was supposed to make everything better.

But it didn't. It didn't fix anything.

My thoughts were jumbled, a mess of confusion and anger. I didn't know how to forgive him. I didn't know if I ever could. But what terrified me the most was how much I still wanted to.

"You think that changes anything?" I finally managed, my voice quieter now, but no less bitter. "You think saying you're a coward makes it okay? You think that makes up for the fact that we've been living in this broken shell of a family for years?"

Dad's head drooped, the weight of my words pressing down on him. I wanted him to say something else, something that would make all the pain go away. But he didn't. He just stood there, silent, broken.

I could feel the space between us growing, widening, like an abyss I couldn't cross.

"I didn't want to hurt you," he said, his voice hoarse now, almost pleading. "I never wanted to hurt you."

"But you did," I whispered, the words barely leaving my lips. "You hurt all of us, every single day."

I didn't know if it was the finality in my voice or the exhaustion from everything I'd just unleashed, but something inside me snapped. All the anger, all the hurt, the months of chasing him across Europe, of trying to find answers—it just… stopped. There was nothing left. Not for him. Not for us.

I couldn't fix this. And I wasn't sure I even wanted to anymore.

Ryan reached out to me again, his hand steady, but this time, I didn't pull away. I let myself sink into him, the weight of everything pressing down on my chest like it was too much for my body to bear. The anger, the hurt, the betrayal—it all came crashing down in waves. But with Ryan's arms around me, for a fleeting moment, the storm inside me calmed.

His warmth enveloped me, and for the first time in what felt like ages, I wasn't alone. I didn't have to carry the burden of it all by myself. Maybe that was enough, even if I didn't have the answers or a clear path ahead.

I closed my eyes, letting the quiet settle around us. Ryan's hand slid gently up and down my back, grounding me, offering me a kind of peace I didn't know I needed until that moment.

When I opened my eyes again, he had pulled away, stepping into the small kitchen. The clink of the kettle was a soft, almost comforting sound. The apartment was so quiet, so empty, that every little noise seemed amplified.

I sank down onto the couch, the cushions sagging beneath me. The apartment felt like it had been forgotten, like it was just a shell of a place someone used to live. There was no life here—no pictures on the walls, no signs of someone actually calling it home. It was sterile, like a waiting room for something that was never going to happen. The bare walls, the faded curtains hanging loosely by the windows, all of it made the room feel smaller, like it was closing in on me.

I took in a shaky breath, staring at the chipped paint on the ceiling, my mind still spinning. How could a person who once filled our house with so much life— my dad, the man who had been everything to me— become this shadow? This stranger who couldn't even look me in the eye anymore.

Ryan returned with two steaming cups of tea. His calm presence felt like a barrier against the storm I couldn't seem to outrun. He placed one cup on the coffee table in front of me, the other beside him as he sat down, his knees brushing mine. I took a slow sip, feeling the warmth slide down my throat, but it didn't settle the ache in my chest.

"Okay," Ryan said, his voice steady, the kind of calm that seemed to make everything else feel unimportant. "Everyone needs to take a breath."

I opened my mouth to argue, to ask how we could all breathe when everything was falling apart, but he stopped me with a glance, holding my gaze long enough to make me swallow my words.

"Ryan—"

"No," he said firmly, his gaze shifting to Dad. "Just listen for a second."

I looked at him, unsure of where this was going, but I stayed silent. Ryan's gaze turned back to Dad. "You're not helping her understand anything by just saying you're sorry. Tell her. Tell her everything, no filters."

Dad stiffened, his shoulders tense as if the suggestion physically pained him. His eyes flicked to me briefly, like he was looking for permission to speak, but I had nothing left to give. His silence felt like a slap in the face.

"She doesn't want to hear it," he murmured, his voice barely audible.

"She does," Ryan said, glancing at me, his eyes soft but persistent. "Even if she doesn't know it yet."

I crossed my arms tightly, the motion defensive, almost instinctual. I didn't want to hear it. I didn't want to know why he left. I didn't want to understand the reasoning behind all of it. Not when everything I'd known felt like it had been stripped away piece by piece. But Ryan was right. I did want to know. Even if it hurt. Even if it tore everything I thought I understood apart.

I just wasn't ready to admit that to myself.

My eyes remained fixed on the table, my heart thudding in my chest, a mix of rage and disbelief clouding my thoughts. It felt like every part of me was warring against itself—wanting to shut down, wanting to yell, wanting to scream at the man who had broken us all and left without a second glance.

But still, I stayed silent.

Dad let out a long breath, his fingers tapping against the edge of his cup, his hands fidgeting like he couldn't keep still. He wasn't looking at me now, his gaze fixed on the floor, like he couldn't bear the weight of my stare.

"I messed up," he said quietly, his voice raw. "But there's more. I never... I never wanted to leave. I thought I could fix it, thought I could fix things with her. But I was wrong."

The words were slow, heavy, each one dragging itself into the space between us. He wasn't looking at me, but the way his words hung in the air felt like he was giving up something—something I had wanted from him for so long.

My breath caught in my throat, but I didn't move. My mind was still spinning, piecing everything together. This man—this person who I used to call my dad—had walked away from us, not because of a simple mistake, but because he was too wrapped up in his own mess to see the damage he was causing. I had always blamed the situation, the circumstances. But now, looking at him, I realized it wasn't just that. It was him. It was his choices.

I didn't know what I was supposed to feel anymore.

"You could've come back," I finally whispered, my voice quiet, hoarse from all the shouting I hadn't done yet. "You could've fixed it. But you didn't."

He flinched, the words stinging more than I had meant them to. But it was too late for apologies now. He was here, and we were here, and nothing could change that.

"I... I couldn't," Dad admitted, his voice cracking. "I was scared. Scared of everything I had broken, scared of you, of her... of facing what I had done. I thought if I stayed away long enough, it would get easier. But it never did."

The silence that followed hung between us like a weight I couldn't escape. It wasn't just the years of hurt, the betrayal, or the fact that I had spent so many sleepless nights trying to fill in the gaps of my dad's absence. It was the undeniable truth that nothing would ever go back to what it had been. We were no longer the family I had known, no longer the people who shared small moments and unspoken promises. That was gone, and there was no getting it back.

Dad's breathing was labored, shaky, like he had been holding it all in for far too long, and now that the dam had cracked, everything came flooding out. He ran his hands through his thinning hair, his eyes wide but distant as he spoke, as if recounting the moments to himself as much as to us. "It started small. Just a few messages. She was funny, sweet… She listened in a way I hadn't felt in years."

"Dad…" My voice faltered, but I couldn't stop him. I had to hear it.

"Let me finish," he said, his tone raw, like it was a struggle to get the words out. "I thought it was harmless. A distraction. But then it got serious. She said she wanted to meet, that she felt the same way I did. And I believed her."

His voice broke on the last words. The bitterness

in it—self-loathing, regret, maybe even self-pity—wrapped around me like a blanket, suffocating in its heaviness.

"I fell for it completely," he continued, his laugh more of a sound of disgust than anything else. "Sent her money for a plane ticket. Then for her 'visa.' Then for... other things."

I was frozen in place, my thoughts tangled, my stomach twisting. It was so hard to wrap my mind around it, so much harder than it should've been to accept that the man I had looked up to for so long—my dad, the one who taught me right from wrong—had let himself get tangled in something this dark, this dangerous.

Ryan didn't look at me. He didn't have to. His attention was fixed on my dad, as if he were waiting for something that would give him more of an answer. "How much money?"

"All of it," Dad admitted, his voice low, like each word he spoke was a crack in the foundation of everything we had built. "The savings, the emergency fund. Every dollar I had."

I could feel the weight of those words in my chest, a painful squeeze that made my heart ache, even though I didn't know how to feel about it. My mind was struggling to make sense of this mess, and I couldn't find a clear path out of it.

Ryan was silent, processing, and I could feel the unspoken tension that had always existed between us—the way he was here, grounding me in this moment, and yet, I still wasn't sure how to lean on him without cracking. He looked back at Dad, his voice steady, but with an edge. "And then?"

Dad's gaze dropped to the floor, his face twisting with shame, as if the weight of this confession was enough to break him. "Then she asked for photos. Intimate ones. And I sent them."

My breath caught in my throat, and the room seemed to tilt for a moment, as if the gravity had shifted and everything around me was a blur. My hands went clammy. "Oh my God," I whispered, horrified by what he was admitting.

Dad's voice trembled, raw with self-hatred, and he looked at me for the first time in what felt like forever. "I didn't realize what was happening until it was too late. She—whoever was behind it—started threatening to send them to your mom. To you. To everyone."

I wanted to scream at him, ask how he could have let this happen, how he could've been so careless. But the words caught in my throat. There was something more, something darker hanging in the air that made it feel impossible to speak.

"So, what?" I asked, my voice quieter than I intended, as though hearing the answer would make it somehow more real. "You just… ran?"

His eyes were wide with panic now, his hands shaking as he rubbed them over his face, like he was trying to erase the guilt that was seeping into every inch of him. "I thought if I gave her what she wanted, she'd leave us alone," he said, the words coming out jagged. "But it never stopped. She kept asking for more, and I couldn't—I didn't know how to make it stop."

The finality in his voice hit me harder than anything else he had said. It wasn't just the lies. It wasn't just the betrayal. It was the resignation. The defeat.

I felt like I couldn't breathe. My heart was thumping so loudly I thought it might burst from my chest. Every muscle in my body was tense, and yet I couldn't move. It was like the world had turned into a series of disjointed images—my father, a man who had once been the solid ground beneath me, falling apart in front of me. His confession was a punch to the gut, leaving me with nothing but the bitter taste of betrayal and confusion.

I wanted to ask more. I wanted to scream at him, demand answers, ask how he could've been so selfish, so blind. But I couldn't. My throat was dry, my voice nothing but a hoarse rasp. I felt sick, like I might choke on everything I was holding inside.

Ryan's hand brushed against mine, his touch warm and steady, but it did little to ease the storm raging inside of me. I pulled away, instinctively, like it was too much to feel anything right now—too much to process.

The room was heavy with silence again, and I realized, with a sinking feeling, that it wasn't just my dad who was lost. We were all lost. The pieces that had once fit so neatly together were scattered now, irreparably broken.

And there was nothing left to do but stare at the fragments.

"So you left us to deal with the fallout?" My voice cracked as I demanded the answer I'd been waiting for—waiting for far too long, though I hadn't known it until now.

Dad's eyes shimmered with the sheen of tears, but his voice was rough when he responded. "I thought if I disappeared, she'd stop coming after me. I thought I was protecting you."

I didn't even know how to react to that. "By abandoning us?" I snapped, the words sharp, as though each one was its own accusation. "By leaving Mom to clean up your mess?"

His face twisted, and the guilt was evident in his eyes. I almost expected him to apologize, to try and explain away the years of absence, the hurt that had been left behind. But the silence that followed was like a thick fog—suffocating, filled with things unsaid, things that could never be said.

Ryan stepped in before I could rip into him again, his voice calm but unwavering. "Nat, he's not saying he was right. He's saying he was scared. And maybe he was stupid, but he thought he was doing the best thing for you."

I shot him a glare that could've set him on fire. I didn't want his calm right now, didn't want any more words that tried to make sense of what had been done. "I'm not asking for excuses. I'm asking why," I said, the heat of anger still burning in me. But there was something else, too—a growing coldness, something empty that spread through me with each passing second.

Ryan didn't back down, but he didn't say more. Instead, he let the silence fall between us, giving me space to think. To stew. And all I could do was stare at Dad, who couldn't look me in the eye anymore.

"You weren't thinking about us at all," I finally said, my voice shaking with a raw mix of anger and pain. "You were thinking about yourself. You let yourself get conned, and then you ran because you didn't want to face the consequences. That's not protecting us, Dad. That's selfish."

I expected him to argue, to defend himself. But he didn't. His head dropped, his shoulders hunching as though the weight of the world had settled there. He didn't argue, didn't try to shift the blame. He just sat there, a man who had been shattered by his own mistakes, his own weakness.

For the first time, I didn't see the man I had put on a pedestal for years—the dad I thought could do no wrong. The dad who was supposed to protect me, take care of me, be the constant in my life. Instead, I saw a man who had made mistake after mistake, a man who didn't know how to fix what he had broken.

"You're right," he said quietly, the words like a confession. "I was dumb. And selfish. And I don't know how to fix it."

His voice was a whisper now, heavy with regret. And yet, it didn't change anything. I didn't feel the weight of forgiveness stirring inside me. I didn't feel the relief that maybe I thought I would. No, the only thing I felt was an aching emptiness, a hole that was left where my father used to be.

I looked away, unable to meet his eyes anymore. The man I had grown up with—the man who was supposed to be invincible, untouchable—had crumbled in front of me, leaving nothing but dust. Nothing but shattered pieces of what could have been.

I didn't know how to respond to that. Didn't know how to accept his apology, if it could even be called that. It didn't feel like enough. It didn't feel like anything, really.

I wasn't ready to forgive him. Not yet. Maybe I never would be.

Ryan's hand brushed against mine once more, a small, grounding gesture. His presence was steady, and for a brief moment, I let myself lean into it, hoping it could fill the gap that had widened between my father and me. But even Ryan couldn't heal what had been broken.

I closed my eyes, squeezing them shut to hold back the tears that I refused to let fall, even though they burned at the back of my throat. I wasn't sure what I was feeling anymore—betrayal, anger, or a hollow, aching sadness that made my chest feel tight. Everything was too much. Too much to understand. Too much to carry on my own.

I opened my eyes, staring at the bare walls of the apartment. The emptiness of the place mirrored how I felt inside—empty, lost, like something was missing, but I didn't know what.

Dad's words were still echoing in my mind. "I don't know how to fix it." But the truth was, I didn't know either.

I didn't know how to fix this. How to fix us.

And as I sat there, staring into the distance, I realized that maybe this wasn't something that could ever be fixed. Maybe the pieces we once had were too scattered now, too far apart to ever be put back together.

CHAPTER 16: A NEW LEAD

Ryan gently tugged at my arm, coaxing me out of the apartment. It wasn't that I wanted to leave—it was more like I couldn't stay there, in that suffocating space with my father and the wreckage of our family. I followed him without protest, my mind too clouded with confusion and anger to put up much of a fight.

We stepped into the cool evening air, the low hum of traffic in the distance. Ryan led me toward a small park at the end of the block. The benches were empty, save for a couple of elderly women walking slowly, their coats pulled tight against the wind. The evening light was fading, but the sky still held on to a faint blush of orange, like it couldn't quite let go of the day.

"Can we talk?" Ryan asked, his voice soft but insistent.

I crossed my arms, not wanting to look at him. "You're the one who dragged me out here."

He gave me a look, but I could see the concern in his eyes, the way he was trying to gauge me without pushing too hard. I wasn't in the mood for delicate probing, but I didn't pull away. I was too tired for that, too worn out from everything—my dad's confessions, my own anger, the raw edges of a family that had already frayed beyond recognition.

"I know you're angry," Ryan said, leaning against a lamppost, his breath visible in the chill air. "Hell, I'm angry, too. But you can't keep shutting your dad out like this."

I glared at him. "He's the reason everything's falling apart."

"I know that." He nodded, his tone gentle. "But he's also the reason it's still possible to fix things. If we help him... if we help him recover even a little bit of that money... maybe it'll make things a little better."

I shook my head. "You think money's going to make up for all this? All the lies? All the years he wasted?"

Ryan stepped closer, his hands in his pockets. "Maybe not. But it's something, Nat. And if we can get that money back, maybe your dad can use it to do something good. Something that might actually make up for a fraction of the things he's screwed up. He could use it to help you go to college next year. Think about that."

My chest tightened at the mention of college. My future had always felt like something just out of reach—like a promise dangling in front of me that I could never quite grab. But maybe this was a chance to change that, to take something back from the mess my dad had left behind.

"You're serious?" I asked, the bitterness in my voice barely masking the flicker of hope that was starting to light up inside me.

"I am," Ryan said, his voice steady. "I don't think your dad's a lost cause. But we need to do this, Nat. We can help him."

I was still angry, still hurt, but Ryan's words hung in the air, impossible to ignore. Maybe this was the only way forward. Maybe it wasn't about forgiveness just yet. Maybe it was about doing something for me, for us. Something that might help rebuild at least one part of this fractured life.

With a reluctant nod, I finally said, "Fine. Let's do it."

Ryan's face lit up with a brief smile, but his expression quickly sobered as we headed back to the apartment. When we returned, Dad was pacing, his feet shuffling against the thin carpet. He looked up when we walked in, the exhaustion evident in the slump of his shoulders.

"What happened?" he asked, his voice tentative.

"We're going to help you," Ryan said, his voice firm. "But you need to give me everything. All your devices. Your phone, your laptop, whatever you have."

Dad blinked, caught off guard. "What? Why?"

"We need to trace the scam," Ryan explained, his voice patient. "We're going to figure out where this came from, and we're going to find the people behind it. The sooner you give me what I need, the sooner we can start working on it."

For a long moment, Dad just stared at Ryan, then at me. There was a hesitation in his gaze, like he was trying to decide if he could trust this plan, if he could trust us. Finally, with a heavy sigh, he walked over to the small desk, his fingers trembling as he gathered his things. His laptop. His phone. Even a small notebook with scribbled details of the scam. He handed everything over without a word.

Ryan immediately sat down at the desk, his fingers flying across the keyboard, the soft glow of the laptop casting shadows across his face. I perched on the edge of the couch, arms crossed, feeling the weight of the moment settle over me like a heavy blanket.

The silence between us was thick, but not

uncomfortable. I was watching Ryan work, his focus so intense it almost seemed like he was pulling the world apart with just his fingertips. I could see how much he wanted to fix things—how much he believed this was a way out for my dad, for me, for us.

But I couldn't bring myself to look at Dad. Not yet. Not with the images of the last few hours still fresh in my mind—the lies, the anger, the broken trust. I wasn't ready to make him part of this. Not in a way that made him feel like he was still my dad.

"Got it," Ryan said finally, his voice triumphant, and I looked up just in time to see him lean back, his grin wide.

"What do you mean, 'got it'?" I asked, my heart pounding in my chest.

Ryan turned the screen toward me. "I traced the IP address from the messages your dad got. Whoever scammed him is operating out of Marseille. France."

Dad froze, his entire body stiffening. His eyes widened, and for the first time since I'd walked into that apartment, he looked like a man truly terrified. "Marseille?"

Ryan nodded. "If we go there, we can track them down."

My head spun. This was it. This was the lead we

needed. We were one step closer to finding out who had done this to my father, to making sure he could fix what he had broken. But a part of me couldn't shake the feeling that even if we did find the people responsible, there were things that would never be the same again.

"I'm not sure this is a good idea," Dad muttered, rubbing the back of his neck. His voice was low, like he was trying to talk himself out of something. I could tell he wasn't convinced, but neither was I. Not anymore.

I stood up, pushing my chair back with more force than necessary, the scrape of it on the floor harsh against the silence. "You don't get to back out now. Not after everything."

Dad winced, his face tightening. "I'm not backing out," he replied, but the words were strained, like he was trying to convince himself. "I just don't see how confronting them is going to fix anything. They're criminals, Natalie. Dangerous ones."

I crossed my arms, fighting the way my chest tightened. "And you were their victim." My voice cracked on the last word, but I didn't let it stop me. "You can't keep running forever, Dad. You owe it to us—to yourself—to see this through. You made a mess of things, and now we're all tangled in it. But we can fix it. Together."

Ryan stepped in, his voice softer, trying to bridge the gap between us. "She's right. We're not saying you have to do this alone. We're here to help."

I looked at Ryan, his steady gaze reminding me that even when everything else felt like it was collapsing, I had someone who didn't shy away from the hard things. My breath caught in my throat, but I quickly turned my focus back to my dad, hoping to hide the rawness I felt.

For a long moment, Dad didn't say anything. He looked at the floor, his hands clenched, his shoulders hunched like he was carrying a weight too heavy to bear. But finally, after what felt like an eternity, he sighed deeply, his breath heavy. He looked up, meeting my eyes. "Okay. I'll help."

I didn't know if that was relief or resignation on his face, but either way, it was a step forward. A small one, but still a step. And that's all I could ask for right now.

But maybe, just maybe, this was the start of something new. Something that could heal at least part of the mess my father had made.

Ryan, as usual, jumped into action, taking the edge

off the tension with his quiet efficiency. "I'll help you get something going for dinner," he said, pulling open the small cupboard in the kitchen. "It won't be much, but at least it's food."

Dad and I both watched as Ryan went to work. There wasn't much in the cupboard—just canned soup, a few boxes of pasta, and some stale bread. It wasn't the comforting meal I'd imagined for the evening, but it was something. Ryan heated up the soup and set out the bread, making the best of what little was there. As he worked, I could hear the clink of the can opener, the hiss of the microwave, the steady rhythm of him moving through the motions like this was just another normal evening.

I didn't have the energy to help, and I didn't want to. My mind was too heavy with everything—my dad's betrayal, the weight of our broken family, the confusing mess we'd found ourselves in. I couldn't bring myself to join them in the kitchen, so I stayed where I was, on the couch, staring at the cold, dimly lit walls of the apartment.

But then, when I thought they were both too caught up in the task of dinner, I overheard them talking, their voices low and tentative.

"I didn't know how bad it had gotten," I heard

Dad say, his voice thick with exhaustion. "I thought it would stop. I thought if I gave them what they wanted, it would be over."

Ryan's voice was quieter, but I could hear the note of disbelief. "You should've come to us. We could've figured something out."

"I couldn't," Dad muttered. "I thought it was too late. I thought if I told anyone, it would be worse. I didn't want to drag you all into this mess. And... I didn't want to admit how stupid I'd been. It was... easier to just keep pretending everything was fine."

I could feel the anger in my chest, rising like a slow burn. Pretending everything was fine? Was that what he'd been doing all these years? Pretending, while he tore our family apart? While he lied to us? I could barely breathe through the bitterness that tightened around my ribs.

"Yeah," Ryan said, his tone soft but blunt. "It's easier. But you know what, John? Sometimes doing the right thing isn't easy. And sometimes, you've gotta face the mess you made."

I could hear the sharpness in his voice, but there was something else there, too—something like compassion, or maybe pity. He wasn't angry the way I was. He didn't have the weight of a thousand unanswered questions pressing down on him.

I couldn't listen to it anymore. The truth—the painful, ugly truth—was too much for me to bear right now. So, I stood up abruptly, my feet moving before my mind could catch up. I didn't want to hear my dad's excuses. I didn't want to feel sorry for him, or even try to understand why he'd done it.

I grabbed my jacket, my heart pounding in my ears. But as I was about to slip out the door, Ryan's voice stopped me.

"Hey, Nat, hold on."

I turned to see him standing in the doorway of the kitchen, his eyes softer than they had been a moment ago. "You okay?"

I just nodded, my throat tight, my eyes burning with a mixture of anger and sadness. But I couldn't explain. Not now. Not when everything felt like it was about to crack wide open.

Ryan stepped closer, his hand brushing against mine for just a second before he pulled back. "You don't have to talk about it if you don't want to," he said, his voice gentle. "But just know you're not alone in this. We'll figure it out. All of it."

I didn't know how, but I felt the truth of his words settle inside me, like a pebble sinking into the depths of a pond. Maybe I didn't have all the answers. Maybe things were still broken beyond repair. But I wasn't alone.

I turned back toward the door, taking a deep breath. "Thanks," I whispered, even though I wasn't sure what I was thanking him for.

Then I walked out, into the night, the cold air biting at my skin as if it could freeze all the hurt inside me. But it couldn't. It was still there, simmering just below the surface.

I needed space.

I needed to clear my head, to let the weight of everything we'd just discussed—everything I was still trying to process—settle a little.

The streets of the neighborhood were quiet, save for the occasional car rumbling past, its headlights cutting through the night. I walked, my footsteps echoing in the empty space around me, and tried to not think about the fact that I was angry with my father, disappointed beyond words, but still… a part of me wanted him to be something he wasn't. Something better. The man I'd once believed in.

But that man was gone. He wasn't just a victim of a scam anymore. He was a man who had abandoned us in every sense of the word, running away when things got tough, thinking he could outrun the consequences of his actions.

I turned a corner and walked aimlessly, trying to outrun my thoughts, even as they kept chasing me. There was something about the night that felt colder now, emptier. I kept walking, not sure where I was going or what I was looking for. Maybe I just needed to feel the rhythm of my own body moving, to drown out the noise in my head. The echoes of Ryan's words, Dad's apologies, my own anger. The guilt. It was all too much.

After a while, I slowed down, realizing how far I'd walked. The streetlights flickered on as I glanced up and noticed how quiet it had become. Everything seemed to pause for a second, and I let myself be still, letting the cool air fill my lungs and clear the fog in my brain. I stood there for a few more minutes, letting the silence settle around me, and then turned back toward Dad's apartment.

When I walked back in, the warmth of the tiny space felt almost oppressive after the sharpness of the night. The smell of the canned soup still lingered in the air, and I could hear the faint clink of spoons as Ryan and Dad were still sitting at the table.

I didn't want to go back to the conversation. But

I knew I had to. I had to face the mess. I had to face him.

The moment I stepped inside, Dad looked up from his bowl, his tired eyes lighting up just slightly. Maybe he thought I'd disappeared for good, or maybe he was just relieved to see me walk back in.

"You okay?" he asked quietly, and I saw the flicker of uncertainty in his gaze. He didn't know what to expect from me anymore, and I didn't blame him. I didn't know what to expect either.

"Yeah," I said, my voice quieter than I intended. "Just needed a minute."

Ryan glanced up, his eyes soft with understanding. He didn't say anything, just gave me a small nod, like he knew I needed the time to cool off. I appreciated that, more than I could put into words.

"It's not much," Dad said as he handed me a chipped bowl of soup, the tomato broth steaming slightly in the dim light. "But it's better than nothing."

I looked down at the bowl, my throat tight again. The irony of it wasn't lost on me. The man who used to make gourmet pancakes on Sunday mornings, who would whip up omelets with fresh herbs and toast slathered in homemade jam, was now living off food that barely qualified as a meal. It hit me in a way I wasn't ready for, like the sharp pang of a wound that hadn't fully healed.

"You don't have to live like this," I said softly, before I could stop myself. The words felt heavy as soon as they left my mouth. I wasn't just talking about the soup, I realized. I was talking about his whole life—his choices, the mess he'd made, the things he hadn't fixed.

Dad didn't answer right away. Instead, he just looked at me, his eyes tired, his face worn like the weight of his own guilt was enough to collapse him in on himself. "It's what I deserve," he murmured, his voice distant, like he had already accepted his fate.

"No, it's not," Ryan said firmly, his voice cutting through the quiet like a knife. He looked at Dad with an intensity that matched his words. "You screwed up, yeah. But you don't fix that by hiding in some run-down apartment."

I glanced around the room as he spoke, taking in the cracked walls, the creaky bed shoved into the corner, the mismatched furniture, and the single photograph of me and Trevor taped to the fridge. For the first time, I really saw it—the absence of warmth, the hollow feeling in every corner of this place. It was a reflection of everything that had gone wrong.

And for the first time, I saw just how much my dad had lost—not just his money, but his sense of self. The man I had looked up to, the one who used to stand tall and proud, had shrunk. He was nothing like the father I had once known.

I felt a rush of sadness mixed with frustration, a tight knot forming in my chest as I pushed back from the table. I couldn't look at him anymore. I couldn't look at the man who had let us down in every possible way and then expected us to understand.

But Ryan, somehow, was still holding it all together. I could see it in the way he looked at Dad— his gaze was steady, unwavering. He didn't see a failure. He saw someone who had made a mistake and was trying to get back on track.

I envied that, honestly. The ability to see the potential for redemption, even when everything seemed lost.

I took a deep breath, trying to steady my thoughts. I didn't have the answers, but I had to believe that we could still fix things. Even if it seemed impossible.

But for now, I had to live with the truth that things were broken. And it was up to us to decide how—if— things could ever be repaired.

Later that night, after the soup was eaten and the

last crumbs of stale bread had been swept off the table, I found myself staring at him. My father. The man I used to see as invincible, a rock who could weather any storm. The one who had always held me up when I was small and afraid, who'd fixed things with a smile and a joke, or at least pretended that everything would be okay.

But that man was gone. In his place sat a stranger, or maybe just a version of him I wasn't ready to face. He wasn't the man I'd built up in my head anymore. He was flawed, broken, and trying—so painfully trying—in his own messy, half-hearted way, to make things right. The whole night had been a mess of apologies, half-truths, and the heavy weight of everything unsaid.

As I rinsed the soup bowls and stacked them on the drying rack, I could hear him in the next room, shuffling around, his footsteps echoing in the silence between us. My heart clenched. I wanted to stay angry. To stay mad at him for abandoning us, for running away instead of dealing with the mess he'd created. But as I looked at the man who used to be so full of life, who used to be my hero, something else twisted inside me—something softer, gentler. Something like pity.

It didn't erase what he'd done. The financial ruin.

The lies. The missed years. The destruction of our family. But maybe, just maybe, it was a start. Maybe he was trying to put the pieces back together, even if he didn't know how.

I dried my hands on a dishtowel, the fabric rough against my fingers. The apartment was quiet now. Too quiet. It felt like we were all holding our breath, waiting for something to happen. But what? The clock ticked loudly in the background, and I could hear the low hum of the refrigerator, the only sound in the otherwise still room.

I glanced at Dad again. He was standing by the window now, staring out into the dark street, the dim glow of the city lights casting shadows on his face. He looked smaller somehow. Defeated. The weight of his own mistakes pressing down on him.

"You don't have to stay here, you know," I said, my voice quieter than I meant it to be. "There's more. You don't have to hide."

He didn't answer right away, and I almost regretted saying it. It felt like opening a door that was better left shut. He'd made his choice to be here, in this sad little apartment, with his ruined life and his empty promises.

"I can't go back," he finally muttered, his voice

heavy with something like regret. "Not yet. Not until I fix this."

The words stung, not because they weren't true, but because they were. He had to fix this. And we were all caught in the mess he'd made. My stomach twisted again, the ache settling deeper inside me. But as I watched him—this broken man who used to be so full of confidence and hope—I realized something. I wasn't going to fix this for him. He had to do it himself. But that didn't mean I had to abandon him completely.

I wanted to hate him. To walk out and never come back. To leave him to stew in the consequences of his own actions. But somehow, in the quiet moments between us, I understood that hating him wouldn't fix anything either. It wouldn't make the hurt go away.

Ryan had been right. My dad needed help. And maybe, just maybe, that's what I was here for now. To help him take the first step, even if it felt like we were walking in circles. Maybe it wasn't forgiveness I was after. Not yet. Maybe I just needed to let him try.

I wiped down the counter, trying to ignore the ache in my chest, trying to block out the soft whispers in my head telling me that I could never go back to the way things were. I wanted to scream. To let the frustration out in some tangible way. But I stayed quiet.

I was so tired of fighting.

Dad turned to face me, his eyes meeting mine. For a split second, I thought I saw something flicker in them—something like hope. But maybe that was just me projecting.

"We'll figure this out," he said, his voice thick with emotion. "I'll make it right. I promise."

I nodded, even though I wasn't sure what "making it right" would look like. But I had to believe him. I had to believe that somewhere beneath the mistakes and the lies, there was still the man I used to love. I wanted to believe that there was still something left worth saving.

I didn't know if that was enough, but I was trying to believe it.

❖

CHAPTER 17: BONDING ON THE ROAD

The road stretched before us, winding through rolling hills dotted with olive trees and quaint stone houses. I could see the morning sun casting golden rays over the land, painting the hills in shades of soft green and amber. We had just passed through Florence, on our way to Marseille, but the journey felt longer than the actual distance. Maybe it was the silence between us, or the weight of everything left unsaid. Whatever it was, it made the hours feel heavier, like we were all carrying something we couldn't quite name.

The train car hummed gently, the soft sway of the tracks rocking most of the passengers to sleep. The rhythmic motion was calming for everyone else, but not me. I couldn't seem to relax. My mind wouldn't shut off. It was too loud inside my head, too full of questions I didn't know how to ask. I kept glancing at my dad, watching his fingers curl around the lukewarm cup of coffee, the faint tremble betraying the tension in his body. His eyes flickered to the window, but they weren't really looking at anything. It was like he was somewhere else, somewhere far away.

The silence between us had shifted since that first night—less sharp, less raw—but still there. It wasn't comfortable, not by a long shot. But it wasn't as unbearable as it had been in the days before. Maybe that was a step in the right direction. But what did it mean? What was enough? How many small steps would it take before we could be… whole again? I didn't know. I just knew that right now, sitting across from him in this crowded train car, it felt like we were both floating in a sea of almosts. Almost okay. Almost back to normal. But not quite.

The quiet was broken when Ryan, who had been lounging across the aisle, stretched his legs out and leaned forward. "You guys, I need a distraction," he said, his voice louder than necessary, but the way he said it, with that goofy smile, made me smile despite myself.

"What now?" I asked, raising an eyebrow.

"I'm bored," Ryan said with exaggerated drama. "Like, it's not enough that we're crossing borders and continents. I need some action."

I rolled my eyes, but it was hard not to laugh. "What kind of action are you hoping for? An international spy mission?"

"You never know," he said, eyes twinkling. "There could be secret agents hiding in this train. Or worse, undercover croissants."

I couldn't help the laugh that escaped me at that. "Undercover croissants? What does that even mean?"

"It means," he said, gesturing vaguely with his hands, "they look like pastries, but inside, they're carrying top-secret info. Or, I don't know, they're tracking our every move. All I'm saying is that no one's ever seen a croissant too suspicious to be a spy."

I laughed harder, shaking my head. "Well, if that's what's on your mind, I'm pretty sure we're all safe. The croissants look pretty harmless to me."

Dad, who had been quiet until now, chuckled softly, shaking his head. "He's got a point, though. Nothing is ever quite as it seems."

For a second, I felt the old familiar weight of that statement—the kind of weight that had been part of my life for so long, the kind of weight that made everything feel like it was always just on the edge of something bigger, more dangerous. But Ryan's joke, and the easy way Dad had joined in, somehow lightened it. I wasn't sure if it was just the timing, or the fact that Dad hadn't shut down the moment the way he used to, but it felt like a tiny crack in the wall that had been keeping us apart.

"Do you remember the camping trip to Yosemite?" Dad asked, breaking the stillness in a way that surprised me.

I blinked, caught off guard. "The one where Trevor got poison ivy?"

Dad laughed quietly, a sound that seemed unfamiliar and yet, strangely comforting. "Yeah. He was scratching for days, and your mom nearly lost her mind over it."

I smiled, despite myself. "I thought she was going to have a meltdown. It was like the poison ivy had a vendetta against him."

"And you were convinced we could hike Half Dome without a map," he added, a glint of amusement in his eyes. "I'll never forget how sure you were, like we were some kind of wilderness experts."

I laughed, shaking my head at the absurdity of it. "That was a terrible idea. Especially when we got caught in that thunderstorm."

Dad grinned, like the memory had brought something lighter back into his chest. "We almost made it. If it hadn't been for that storm…"

"That soaked all our gear and turned our tent into a soggy mess," I finished for him, the image clear in my mind. "I thought Mom was going to kill you that day."

We both laughed then, the sound rich with the comfort of a shared past. It was a small, simple moment, but it was the kind of moment that made the heavy silence feel like something we could survive. The tension between us eased, slowly, like the rain finally letting up. There was something about laughter that had the power to heal, or at least to soften things enough to make them bearable. I hadn't expected this—this return to something close to normal. Not after everything that had happened. But here we were, laughing over something so small, so mundane, and it almost felt like old times.

The train passed through the hills, the landscape outside shifting with the changing light. I could feel the rhythm of the tracks beneath us, steady and sure, and for the first time in a while, I allowed myself to breathe a little deeper. Maybe we weren't as lost as I'd thought. Maybe we weren't as far gone as I feared.

I glanced over at Dad. He was staring out the window again, but his shoulders were a little less tense now, and his face wasn't as closed off. The silence was still there, but it felt more like something we could live with. It didn't have to be the end of everything. Maybe it was just the beginning of figuring things out.

Ryan, his eyes sparkling with a new idea, leaned forward again. "So, what's next, huh? We can't let our croissant spy mission go unresolved."

I laughed again, feeling lighter. "Next stop, Marseille. You can start your investigation there."

Ryan winked, clearly pleased with himself. "Well, I've got my passport, my secret agent gear, and my map… kind of."

I looked at him, shaking my head but smiling, and for a moment, everything felt just a little bit more like it could be okay.

But the moment passed quickly, like a gust of wind, leaving only the steady rhythm of the train as its echo.

Dad's expression grew serious, his voice quieter now. "I didn't mean to mess everything up, Natalie."

I glanced up, my heart tightening at the rawness in his words. The pain that lingered in his eyes was something I couldn't look away from.

"You didn't just mess things up, Dad," I said, the words coming out sharper than I intended. I swallowed, trying to keep my voice steady. "You left."

There it was, the truth between us. The thing I'd been holding inside for years, ever since the day he walked out. The bitterness was still there, but I couldn't ignore the way his eyes softened, like the weight of the years hadn't made him forget everything he'd left behind.

His voice cracked when he spoke again. "I thought it was the only way to protect you and Trevor. But I see now that I was wrong." His words were heavy, almost like he was carrying a weight too big for him to bear.

I stared out the window, the scenery blurring by in soft streaks. My throat tightened. I couldn't turn my eyes away from the landscape, even though I knew what I wanted to say. The years of abandonment, the lies, the broken promises—all of it swirled inside me. I couldn't just erase that. But I could feel a shift in the air, something that whispered of understanding. Of something fragile, but there.

"We needed you, Dad. We still do."

His gaze softened, and for the first time in years, I saw him as someone human—not the distant figure I had built up in my mind, but the man who had once been a part of our family. The weight of his regret settled between us like a heavy fog.

He nodded slowly, his voice quieter this time. "I'm here now. For whatever that's worth."

I didn't know what to say. There was so much I wanted to say, but the words got stuck somewhere deep inside me. Could I forgive him? Not yet. I wasn't sure I could ever forgive him fully. But the walls I had built between us, the ones I'd spent so long fortifying, seemed just a little less solid now.

I didn't know what the future held. I didn't know what came next. But for the first time in a long while, I felt a flicker of something that didn't feel like anger. Maybe it was hope. Or maybe just the possibility that we could start to find our way back to each other.

I couldn't be sure. But at least, for now, I wasn't alone on this road.

Ryan sat beside me, his head tilted back against the seat, eyes half-closed, pretending to nap. But I knew him too well. His lips twitched with amusement, and I could practically hear the thoughts behind that impish grin he was doing his best to hide.

I couldn't help it. I nudged him with my elbow. "What?"

He opened one eye just enough to peek at me, his gaze playful. "Nothing. It's just... it's nice, seeing you two like this."

"Like what?"

"Like people who don't hate each other," he said with a teasing smirk.

I rolled my eyes, but deep down, I knew he was right. Dad and I weren't fixed, not by a long shot. But the walls between us, the distance that had felt so insurmountable for so long, were starting to crack. We were trying. That had to count for something, right?

"Well, don't get too excited. I'm not going to start knitting him a sweater anytime soon," I said, trying to make light of it, but there was a warmth in my chest, unexpected but undeniable.

Ryan chuckled softly. "Yeah, I'm sure he wouldn't know what to do with it anyway. But seriously, it's good to see you giving him a chance. Not everyone would."

His voice dropped a little, a rare seriousness slipping into his words. The sincerity in his tone caught me off guard, and I felt a warmth spread through me that had nothing to do with the sun streaming through the train window.

"Why?" I asked, eyebrows furrowed in genuine confusion.

"For giving him a chance," he repeated simply. "Not everyone would."

I opened my mouth to protest, to tell him that it wasn't as simple as he was making it out to be, but the words got stuck in my throat. Because, in some ways, it was that simple. I wasn't ready to forgive everything, but maybe, just maybe, I could let him try. And maybe that counted for something.

"You're pretty amazing, you know that?" Ryan added, the humor gone from his voice now, replaced by something quieter, more thoughtful.

I met his eyes for a moment, the earnestness in his expression making something flutter uncomfortably in my stomach. He was so easy to talk to—sometimes, too easy.

I couldn't help the smile that tugged at the corner of my lips. "Why?"

He shrugged, his easy smile returning. "Just… you are. I think people don't give you enough credit for the way you deal with things. You've been carrying a lot for a long time, and you still keep going."

I wasn't sure how to respond to that. It wasn't the first time Ryan had said something like that, but hearing it now, in the middle of this strange trip, made it feel like the world was shifting beneath me. It was strange to hear him speak with such depth, when all I'd ever known was his lighthearted banter and sarcastic comebacks.

Before I could find my words, he added, "Anyway, I'm just glad to be here with you, helping you get through this."

I smiled, a little crookedly, and shook my head. "You sure you're not just here for the ride to France? I'm pretty sure this train's more of a vacation for you."

Ryan laughed, raising his hands in mock surrender. "I'd be lying if I said I didn't enjoy the view. But yeah, I'm here for you. No getting out of it."

I couldn't help but laugh, the tension in my shoulders easing just a little. "You're impossible, you know that?"

"I'm also incredibly charming," he said with an exaggerated wink. "Don't forget it."

As the train carried us closer to Marseille, the world outside blurring into a wash of soft green hills and endless fields, I felt the weight of the moment pressing in around me. This trip wasn't just about finding answers anymore. It wasn't just about catching some faceless criminal who'd torn our lives apart. It was about rebuilding—rebuilding my dad, rebuilding our fractured family, and maybe—just maybe—rebuilding myself.

I hadn't realized how much I'd needed this trip

until now. I'd been so focused on the past, on all the things that had gone wrong, that I hadn't really thought about what came after. What if I didn't have to fix everything? What if, in the process of trying to find my dad's lost money, I found something else instead? Something bigger. Something I'd forgotten even mattered.

Maybe there was still hope for the pieces of my life that felt too shattered to fix.

And maybe, just maybe, there was room for forgiveness, even if I wasn't quite sure what it looked like yet.

I turned my head to look out the window again, feeling the rhythm of the train beneath me, the motion of the world outside matching the quiet, steady thrum of my own thoughts. For the first time in a long while, the storm inside me felt still. The road ahead, both literal and metaphorical, was long. But maybe, just maybe, we were on the right path.

And maybe that would be enough.

The train ride stretched endlessly, the rhythmic clatter of the wheels beneath us the only constant. The motion rocked me, a comforting lull, but the silence in the air felt heavier with each passing mile. Outside the window, the countryside unfolded in soft, rolling waves—hills that gave way to flat plains dotted with yellow sunflowers, their heads turning toward the fading light. It was beautiful in a quiet, lonely sort of way. A far cry from the chaos swirling inside my mind.

Ryan sat beside me, his head resting back against the seat, his eyes closed as though pretending to nap. His occasional sighs gave him away, though. He wasn't really sleeping. He was just biding time. I could practically feel the impatience radiating off him.

"Are we there yet?" Ryan asked, the words coming out with mock petulance, his voice thick with exaggerated annoyance.

I smirked, not bothering to look up from the battered book I'd been pretending to read. "We still have three hours. Want me to draw you a map of the route again?"

He groaned, slumping dramatically in his seat. "You're enjoying this, aren't you?"

"A little," I admitted, my lips curling up slightly at the corners. He always knew how to lighten the mood, even when I wasn't sure how to crack the tension myself.

Across from us, Dad sat quietly, his face expressionless as he stared out the window, his eyes fixed somewhere in the distance. He hadn't said much since we left Florence, and I couldn't shake the feeling that the silence between us was only getting heavier, more loaded. His profile was drawn tight, etched with something I couldn't quite place—dread, maybe, or resignation.

"You okay?" I asked softly, unable to stand the quiet anymore.

Dad didn't immediately respond. When he did, his voice was distant, like he was talking from somewhere far away. "I'm fine."

I frowned, not convinced. Ryan leaned in closer, his voice dropping low so Dad wouldn't overhear. "He's not fine."

"I know," I whispered back, my stomach twisting at the thought. I hated seeing him like this, but at the same time, part of me couldn't bring myself to care. Not yet. Not after everything.

The hours dragged on, a blur of endless fields and restless anticipation. Despite the scenic views outside, I felt like I was suffocating in the tension that clung to the air between us. I wanted to believe that this trip would change things, that it would somehow fix everything that had gone wrong, but part of me knew better. The mystery of what had happened to Dad's money still loomed over us, and I couldn't shake the fear that it wasn't just about the money anymore. It was about all the things that had been left unsaid for too long.

Ryan broke the silence with a sudden grin. "Alright, who wants food? I'm starving."

I glanced up from my book, a bit surprised at the sudden change in mood. "What are you, a vending machine now?"

"Pretty much," Ryan said, already unzipping his bag. "I'm going to go see what they have. We've got nothing but a couple of stale crackers and your endless optimism."

I rolled my eyes but let him go. After a few minutes, he returned with a tray of food that smelled like it had been reheated a dozen times. The sight of the meager offering made me laugh despite myself. He handed over a sad-looking sandwich and a plastic cup of pasta, its sauce glistening with too much oil.

"I didn't even get to have pasta in Italy," Ryan muttered with a wistful sigh, poking at the spaghetti like it had personally offended him. "This is the worst."

I snorted. "You realize we're on a train from Florence to Marseille, not on a luxury cruise, right?"

"I know, but still," he said, looking mournful. "I was expecting better than this." He waved the sandwich around for emphasis. "I mean, who even puts mayo on a sandwich with ham? What is this?"

I couldn't help but laugh again, the sound bright and genuine despite everything. It felt good to share a moment of lightness in the middle of all the uncertainty.

As Ryan dug in with exaggerated enthusiasm, Dad finally spoke, his voice quiet and hesitant, as though testing the waters. "What about... about Marianne? And Trevor?"

I froze, the words hanging in the air like a sudden gust of wind. The mention of Mom and Trevor felt like a punch to the gut. I hadn't expected him to bring them up, not now, not like this.

Ryan looked between the two of us, sensing the shift in the atmosphere. "It's been a long time, hasn't it?" he said, his voice soft, almost apologetic.

Dad nodded, his fingers tapping nervously against the edge of his cup. "I... I don't know how to fix it, Natalie. I don't know how to make it right."

I couldn't look at him. Not yet. I wasn't ready for the rawness in his voice, the vulnerability that spilled out in the silence between us. Part of me resented it. Part of me wanted to tell him that it didn't matter, that nothing would ever fix the years of mistakes he had made. But another part of me... a quieter, more honest part... wanted to reach out. Wanted to say that maybe it wasn't about fixing things. Maybe it was just about trying.

For a moment, I couldn't speak. The words caught in my throat, and I felt the weight of everything—the past, the pain, the unspoken regrets—settling over us all.

Ryan, ever the diplomat, changed the subject, his voice light and casual as he dug into his meal. "Anyway, if you're not going to eat that sandwich, I'll take it. It's not gourmet, but it's food, right?"

I managed a weak smile, grateful for the distraction. As Ryan chattered away, I glanced at Dad, his eyes distant, his thoughts clearly elsewhere. I didn't know how we were supposed to move forward. But maybe—just maybe—this trip wasn't about having all the answers. Maybe it was about finding the pieces that still mattered, the ones I hadn't realized were still there.

I could feel the weight of it in my chest, a mixture of hope and uncertainty. I didn't know what was going to happen next. But for the first time in a long time, I was willing to find out.

CHAPTER 18: TRACKING THE SCAMMER

As the train made its way toward Marseille, the landscape started to change. The golden hills, so comforting in their rural simplicity, slowly gave way to the sprawling urban expanse of the city. The sky above us was a painter's canvas, with pinks and oranges swirling together, the sun sinking lower with every passing minute. The closer we got, the more the city felt alive—like the beating heart of France itself.

The urban sprawl was like nothing I'd seen before. Ancient stone buildings stood shoulder to shoulder with sleek glass high-rises, their modern surfaces reflecting the last rays of daylight. I felt like I was crossing through centuries, stepping into a place where history and progress collided in the most unexpected ways.

Ryan nudged my arm, his voice full of excitement. "We're almost there."

I turned to look at him, seeing the thrill in his eyes.

Even he, who normally couldn't sit still for more than ten minutes, seemed at ease, almost eager. The weight of what we were doing—the mystery we were trying to unravel—was settling over me in heavier doses the closer we got.

I glanced over at Dad. He was sitting straighter in his seat, his hands gripping the armrests, as if he was trying to ground himself. I watched him for a moment, trying to read his expression. There was tension in his posture, but it was more than just nerves. It was a quiet anticipation—something deeper that I couldn't quite place.

"You sure you want to do this?" I asked softly, the question hanging between us like a delicate thread.

Dad didn't respond at first, his eyes fixed out the window. His silence spoke volumes, the weight of everything unspoken pressing down on him, and on me. After a few seconds, he gave a brief nod, but his hands tightened their grip on the armrests. His silence felt more telling than words could ever be. It wasn't the reassurance I had hoped for, but it was all he was willing to give.

I exhaled slowly, trying to calm the storm of emotions swirling inside me. I knew why we were here—why Dad felt like he had to come. The man who had swindled him out of everything, who had left him broken and desperate, was somewhere in this city. Somewhere in this tangled mess of old streets and new buildings, the answers we needed were waiting. I couldn't let myself think too much about it, couldn't let myself feel the pressure of everything we had at stake.

But as we neared the city, it became harder to ignore the unease growing inside me.

Ryan, noticing my quiet, nudged me again. "Come on, don't go all serious on me now. This isn't the 'end of the world' situation you're making it out to be."

I shot him a look, but he was grinning, and I couldn't help but laugh. Ryan had this way of lightening the mood when things felt like they were about to break wide open.

"Right, because nothing screams 'good idea' like chasing down a scammer who ruined my dad's life in a foreign city," I said, raising an eyebrow.

He smirked. "You know, this isn't the first time we've been here. Remember that whole 'farewell forever' moment we had a few weeks ago? Yeah. We're back. Plot twist." He rolled his eyes dramatically, making me snort.

"You're unbelievable," I said, laughing, but the

sound felt forced, even to me.

"It's what I do best." He grinned, and for a moment, it felt like things were normal again. Like we were just two people on a trip, not tangled in the mess of betrayal and broken promises.

But as the train began to slow, and Marseille came into full view, that normalcy slipped away, replaced with something far heavier.

The closer we got to the station, the more I could feel my heart pounding in my chest. I wasn't ready for what we were about to face. The city looked beautiful, the streets alive with movement, but it felt distant to me now. Too far away from the small town I'd come from, too far from the life I knew before everything had fallen apart.

Dad cleared his throat and stood up, shifting uncomfortably. The tension in his body was obvious now. He looked back at me, his eyes meeting mine briefly, then flicking away. He wasn't saying anything, but I could tell—he was scared. Not just for what we were about to do, but for what it would mean once we found this guy. I don't think he was ready to face the truth. But then again, I wasn't sure I was either.

The train screeched to a halt, and I felt my stomach lurch as I stood up with Ryan. We stepped off the platform together, but as I glanced back at Dad, I felt that familiar pang of doubt and fear. It was like we were walking into a storm, and I didn't know if I could hold on long enough to weather it.

Ryan, sensing my shift in mood, bumped my shoulder with his. "You're gonna be fine," he said, his tone more serious now.

I nodded, even though I wasn't sure I believed it. As we made our way toward the exit of the station, the city of Marseille buzzing around us, I couldn't help but feel the weight of everything—of the lies, the mysteries, the uncertainty—bearing down on me.

I wasn't ready for the answers I might find here. But I had no choice but to keep moving forward.

The air in Marseille was damp, clinging to my skin and filling my lungs with the briny tang of the nearby sea. The streets were a maze of cobblestones and narrow alleyways, the kind that twisted on themselves until you weren't sure if you'd walked this way before or if every corner just looked the same.

Ryan walked ahead, his phone clutched in one hand as he muttered to himself, his brow furrowed. "This doesn't make sense. The signal should've bounced again by now."

"What doesn't make sense?" I asked, trying to

keep up. My boots scuffed against the uneven stones, the sound echoing faintly in the alley.

"Whoever this scammer is, they're either a genius or an idiot," Ryan said. "The IP trace keeps looping back to a fixed location. It's too obvious, almost like they want to be found."

"Or they think no one would be crazy enough to actually follow through," I muttered.

Ahead of us, Dad stopped suddenly, squinting at a street sign written in looping French script. He frowned, then turned to Ryan. "Rue de la Charité," he said, his accent flawless. "You're looking for a building just past the bakery on the right."

Ryan and I froze.

"Wait, what?" I asked, staring at him.

"I said—"

"No, no," I interrupted, pointing at him. "Since when do you speak French? Like… fluently?"

He hesitated, then shrugged, as if it were no big deal. "Highschool French. It comes back."

My mind spun as I tried to reconcile this version of my dad—the man who once claimed ordering pizza in another language was the height of sophistication— with the one standing in front of me now.

"What else don't I know about you?" I asked, my

voice quieter.

He didn't answer, just turned back to the street. "We're close."

The building wasn't much to look at—three stories of cracked plaster and windows streaked with grime. A rusty balcony jutted out above the entrance, its railing sagging under the weight of tangled vines.

"Cozy," Ryan muttered, glancing up at it.

The faint smell of mildew grew stronger as we stepped inside, the narrow staircase creaking under our weight. My heart thudded in my chest, every step amplifying the growing knot in my stomach.

I kept glancing at Dad, trying to read his expression, but his face was a mask—calm, focused, unreadable. I hated that I couldn't tell what he was thinking, couldn't connect this version of him to the one who used to tuck me in with corny bedtime stories.

"Are we sure about this?" Ryan whispered when we reached the third floor, his voice low.

"No," I admitted, wiping my palms against my jeans.

Dad stepped forward, his jaw set. He raised his hand and knocked firmly on the door.

The sound echoed down the empty hallway, and I held my breath, my pulse quickening. Every worst-case scenario I'd ever imagined raced through my mind—a gang of scammers, a trap, or worse, finding nothing at all.

The door opened a crack, and the figure on the other side wasn't at all what we expected.

"You've got to be kidding me," Ryan exclaimed.

I wasn't ready at all for the face that appeared—young, barely older than Trevor, with scruffy hair and a defensive scowl that made him look like a feral cat cornered in an alley.

"What do you want?" he asked, his voice rough but thin, like he was still growing into it.

Dad spoke, his voice low and tense. "I think you know."

My mind blanked. I glanced at Ryan, who was already taking a step forward. "We want to talk. That's all," he said, his tone calm and measured.

"I don't talk to strangers," the boy snapped, trying to push the door closed.

Dad caught it with his hand, his voice cutting through the tension like a blade. "Écoute-moi," he said, his French sharp and commanding. "We're not here to hurt you. But we will get what we came for."

The boy froze, his eyes narrowing as he studied Dad. His eyes flickered with recognition before he quickly tried to close the door. Ryan was faster, sticking his foot in the gap.

"Hey!" the boy protested.

"We're not here to hurt you," I said quickly, my heart racing. "We just want answers."

After a moment, he sighed and stepped back, opening the door just enough to let us in.

The flat was as run-down as the building's exterior had suggested. The faint smell of old cigarettes lingered in the air, and mismatched furniture was shoved against the walls, creating a cluttered but oddly efficient workspace.

"You're the scammer?" Dad asked, his voice incredulous.

The boy folded his arms defensively. "What do you expect? Some big, scary criminal mastermind? I'm just making a living."

"A living?" Dad's voice rose. "You ruined mine!"

The boy rolled his eyes. "Don't be so dramatic. You're not the first guy to fall for it, and you won't be the last."

Dad staggered back slightly, his face pale. "How... how did I not see it?"

The boy shrugged, smirking. "People believe what they want to believe. You wanted to feel important, like someone cared about you. I just gave you what you wanted."

The words landed like a punch, and I saw Dad flinch. His face crumpled, the weight of his shame and regret etched in every line.

Ryan stepped between them, his tone sharp. "You're a kid. You don't get to ruin lives and call it 'making a living.'"

The boy glared at him but didn't respond.

A laptop sat open on a battered desk, the screen glowing with an email inbox that I didn't have to read to know was full of lies. Stacks of prepaid phones and SIM cards littered the surface, along with half a sandwich and a crumpled can of soda.

Ryan walked over, his eyes scanning the setup with a mixture of awe and disgust. "This is it. This is your whole operation?"

The boy bristled, crossing his arms. "It works, doesn't it?"

I stepped forward, my voice shaking. "Do you even care about the people you hurt? About what you've done to my family?"

His scowl deepened, but there was a flicker of guilt in his eyes. "It's not personal. It's just… business."

"Business?" Dad's voice was quiet, but it cut

through the room like ice. "You call stealing everything from people business?"

The boy looked away, his posture defensive. "I don't have a choice. You think I like doing this? It's this or nothing."

"Then maybe try nothing," Ryan snapped, slamming a hand down on the desk.

The boy jumped, his eyes darting to Ryan's laptop. "What are you doing?"

"Tracing," Ryan said, his voice clipped. "And locking you out of all of this while I'm at it."

"Wait—what?" the boy stammered, rushing toward him. "You can't—"

"Sit down," Dad said, his voice sharp.

The boy hesitated, then sank into a chair, his face pale. For the first time, he looked less like a scammer and more like a scared kid.

"Are you okay?" I asked Dad, hesitant.

He shook his head, his voice barely above a whisper. "I don't think I'll ever be okay again."

I didn't have the words to comfort him. I wasn't sure they even existed.

As I stood there, watching Ryan work and Dad hover like a storm ready to break, I felt a strange mix of emotions—anger, pity, confusion. This boy had turned our lives upside down, and yet he didn't seem like the villain I'd built up in my mind.

I didn't know if that made things better or worse.

CHAPTER 19: CONFLICTING MINDS

The flat was as cold and unwelcoming as the man sitting in front of us. It smelled faintly of stale coffee and cheap cologne, the dim lighting casting long shadows that seemed to stretch into the corners of the room like secrets waiting to be uncovered. The walls were bare, save for a few posters of clubs and events that felt too loud for the quiet tension in the air. It was as if everything about this place was a façade—hiding something, masking the real truth.

Dante, the scammer we'd come to confront, leaned casually against a chair. His arms were crossed, his stance trying too hard to scream nonchalance. But I wasn't fooled. There was something about the way his eyes darted to the door every few seconds, the slight twitch of his hand that betrayed his unease. He wasn't as calm as he was pretending to be.

"You're wasting your time," he repeated, his voice smooth but too practiced, like a rehearsed lie. "The money's gone."

I stepped forward, my heart pounding in my chest, though I wasn't sure if it was from fear or anger. It felt like both, mixed together in a cauldron, ready to spill over. The feeling was one and the same right now—sharp, raw, and unforgiving.

"Gone?" I repeated, my voice steady despite the fury twisting inside me. "How does money just disappear, Dante?"

He shrugged, that lazy, smug smile curling at the corners of his lips. "Ask your dad. I'm just the middleman."

I felt my breath catch. My eyes shot to Dad, who was standing off to the side, arms folded tight across his chest, his face tight with controlled emotion. His usually stern features were pinched now, the lines of worry deeper than I'd ever seen them. He looked like a man grappling with the ghost of who he used to be—the version of himself that he thought could trust people, could make things right. But now? Now he was facing the wreckage of all those choices. He was a stranger to me in this moment, and that feeling hit harder than I wanted to admit.

I turned back to Dante, my hands clenching at my sides. "You know who my dad is, don't you?" My voice dropped, becoming colder, like a blade scraping the skin. "You know what he lost. So don't stand there and pretend like you have any excuse for what you did. People like you always have excuses."

Dante met my eyes, but there was a flicker of something in them that I almost didn't catch—a crack in the otherwise smooth, practiced exterior. For a split second, there was uncertainty, a hesitation that betrayed his calm façade.

"Listen, kid. You've got your info all wrong. I'm just doing what I have to do," he said, his voice carrying a hint of defensiveness.

I stepped closer, my breath coming faster now. "And that's your justification for scamming people? Destroying lives?"

Dante sighed, an exaggerated motion, as if the conversation bored him. "People make choices," he said flatly, his eyes hardening again. "That's life."

I saw it then—the tension in his jaw, the slight flex of his hands at his sides, as if he was waiting for something. Or someone.

Suddenly, there was a low growl behind me. I turned just in time to see Dad's face turn crimson with fury. His fists clenched at his sides, his posture rigid, as if every ounce of control was being tested in that moment. Without warning, he lunged forward, grabbing Dante by the collar with a ferocity I hadn't seen in years.

"You think you can just ruin lives?" Dad's voice was a low, guttural growl. "You think you can walk away from this without consequences?"

I froze for a moment, the sight of Dad losing control sending a shockwave through me. It was like a dam breaking—years of anger, frustration, and confusion flooding to the surface. But I knew if I didn't act, things would spiral out of control fast.

"Dad, stop!" I shouted, my voice sharp with panic.

I reached out, grabbing his arm, trying to pull him back, but he was stronger than I realized. "He doesn't deserve it!" I added, my voice strained as I struggled to get him to release Dante. "He's not worth it!"

Dante, wide-eyed, was practically choking now, his hand clawing at Dad's fingers as if he didn't know how to handle the intensity of the moment. I felt a twinge of guilt for him, but it didn't matter. He had chosen this path. He had chosen to hurt people.

Dad's eyes flickered to me, something darker in them—something like regret, or maybe realization. It only lasted for a second, but in that moment, I saw the man I used to know, the man who could be kind and protective and strong. And then, just as quickly, it was gone.

I pulled harder on Dad's arm, not willing to watch him destroy what little was left of his dignity. "Please," I whispered, my voice trembling. "Don't."

For a long, heavy moment, neither of us spoke. The air was thick with the sound of Dante's labored breathing, the weight of everything we were carrying. Finally, Dad let go, pushing Dante back into the chair with a sharp shove. His breath was ragged, his fists still clenched. But he didn't say anything more. Didn't need to. Dante had gotten the message.

I stood there for a moment, catching my breath. My heart was still racing in my chest, the adrenaline pumping in my veins like a drug. But underneath it, there was a cold, sinking feeling. The anger still simmered inside me, but it wasn't just for Dante anymore. It was for everything—everything I had lost, everything that had been taken from us.

Dante sat back in his chair, wiping his mouth, his eyes darting between me and Dad. "You'll never get that money back. It's gone. And your father's mistakes—well, they're his to live with, not yours."

I wanted to lash out, wanted to scream at him, but something in me held back. Part of me had known it wouldn't be easy to fix what had been broken, that the answers we were looking for wouldn't come clean and simple. But hearing it from him—it hurt. It hurt more than I expected.

Dad didn't speak. He stood there, arms folded, looking at the ground as though he was weighing something heavy, trying to decide what to say. But the truth was, there was nothing left to say. Nothing that could make it right.

I looked at Dante, my eyes narrowing. "You're wrong. This isn't over."

He smirked, but it was a hollow thing. "We'll see about that, kid."

And as the tension in the room continued to linger like smoke in the air, I knew we hadn't come close to finishing this fight.

But I wasn't going to let it go. Not yet. Not until I got the answers I needed.

I glanced at Dad, unsure of what to say, but his face was unreadable. That was the worst part. I didn't know who he was anymore.

And I wasn't sure I knew who I was either.

Ryan was at the table, his laptop open in front of him, his eyes scanning the screen with sharp focus. His fingers moved across the keys, almost too quickly, as if the information was already burned into his memory. I had seen him in action before—he was good at this, but this time was different. His lips pressed together as he navigated through screens, clicking, typing, his face drawn tight in concentration.

"Give me a second," Ryan said, not looking up from the screen. "This guy's got a setup here that's more complex than we thought."

I glanced at Dad, who was clearly trying to hold it together but was failing. His eyes flickered nervously between Dante and Ryan, his hands running through his hair, but he didn't speak. His silence felt like a weight pressing down on me.

Dante shifted in his seat, clearing his throat. "Don't listen to him. I've told you, it's all gone. No one's going to get anything back."

But Ryan didn't flinch. He kept typing, pulling up information at a speed that made my head spin. "Yeah, well," Ryan said, leaning forward to adjust something on his screen, "I'd say otherwise."

I couldn't see the details from where I was standing, but Ryan's face was tight with focus, his brows furrowed as the screens shifted. "This guy's been scamming multiple people at once. Thousands of dollars at a time. And it's all connected—well, not all of it, but enough to make things interesting."

"What do you mean?" I asked, my throat dry, my heart picking up speed again.

Ryan clicked a few more times, then sat back in his chair, looking up at Dante. "What I mean is, you're not just some random scammer. You've been running this for a while, haven't you? Thousands of people, all getting conned at the same time. There are multiple networks, different names, different faces. You've been playing the game from all sides. But you're slipping now. You think we didn't notice the overlap?"

Dante's face paled slightly. He glanced toward the door again, like he was considering an escape route. His bravado wasn't fooling anyone anymore. The truth was catching up with him.

I looked back at Dad, who still hadn't said a word, and I felt something shift between us. This was the man who'd once been so sure of himself, so full of ideas and plans and hope for a future. Now, all he had was the ruins of a life he'd never imagined losing. I wanted to reach out to him, to give him something— some reassurance, some way to ease the burden of his regret. But all I could offer him right now was this— catching the person who had done this to him.

"You think you're untouchable, don't you?" I said,

my voice low, my anger simmering beneath the surface. "You think no one's ever going to come for you. Well, guess what? You're wrong."

Dante smirked again, but it was weak now. "So, what's your big plan? Report me to the cops? Like that's going to do anything."

Ryan's eyes flicked to mine, a look of grim determination there. He closed the laptop with a decisive snap, the weight of the moment pressing down on all of us. "We don't need the cops," he said softly, but there was a finality in his tone.

The room was silent for a moment, except for the distant sound of traffic outside, the low hum of the city that felt so far removed from everything that was happening here.

Dante's bravado was all but gone now. "What do you want from me?" he asked, his voice suddenly smaller, defeated.

Dad took a deep breath, his eyes still fixed on Dante. "The money you took from me," he said, his voice cracking slightly but steady enough. "I want it back. And I'm not leaving here until I get it."

I felt a shift within me, a weight lifting slightly. This wasn't just about catching the bad guy—it was about something else, something deeper. It was about justice, about taking back what had been stolen. It was about giving my dad, and myself, a sense of closure.

But as I stared at Dante, waiting for his next move, I couldn't shake the feeling that this wasn't the end of the story. It was just another chapter.

The room felt too small, too stifling, like it was holding its breath. The low hum of the city outside seemed distant, muffled by the weight of the tension that hung in the air. Dante, the scammer who had twisted my family's life into a knot, stood in front of us, trying to maintain some semblance of control. But it was all unraveling, and I could feel the weight of it pressing on my chest.

"It's gone," Dante repeated, his voice cracking slightly, though he tried to keep his tone flat. "All of it. You can't get it back."

I clenched my fists at my sides, my nails digging into my palms. Gone. That was the word that had haunted my every thought for the past few days—the thing I kept hearing over and over again, even as we traveled halfway across Europe chasing shadows. And now, it was the word I couldn't escape.

Ryan, standing next to me, was already ahead of me, his mind working faster than mine. He had always been the sharp one. The steady one. He was already moving, his fingers tapping over the laptop's keys with an easy precision that made everything feel colder, sharper.

"No, see, that's where you're wrong," Ryan said, his voice cool but firm. "Because I'm not here to ask nicely."

Dante's brow furrowed, and I saw that familiar flicker of uncertainty cross his face. He was starting to realize he wasn't in control anymore.

Ryan set the laptop down on the cluttered desk in front of him, his eyes scanning the screen as his fingers flew over the keys. "You've been sloppy," he continued, almost too casually. "You didn't even try to mask your IP on some of these accounts. Rookie move."

The smirk that had been plastered on Dante's face faltered for a split second. For the first time, he wasn't the one pulling the strings.

Ryan leaned closer, his voice lowering, still casual. "And these burner phones? Useless if someone knows how to backtrace your transactions." He turned the screen toward Dante, and for a moment, I thought I saw a flash of panic in the scammer's eyes.

"W-what is that?" Dante stammered, taking an instinctive step back, his bravado slipping further with each word that left Ryan's mouth.

Ryan's lips barely twitched into a smile. "Everything I need to blow up your entire operation," he said, as if it were nothing. "I can send this to the local police. Or Interpol. Your pick."

Dante's confidence faltered completely now. He pushed off the wall, standing straighter, but it wasn't the same. The cocky, untouchable act was gone. "You wouldn't," he said, his voice desperate, but still trying to hold on to some semblance of defiance.

Ryan didn't budge. His eyes were locked on Dante's, unflinching. "Try me," he said, his tone calm, but with an underlying steel I hadn't heard before. "You've scammed a lot of people, haven't you? How many of them do you think will want payback when they find out where you live?"

I could feel the air in the room growing thick. The room itself seemed to shrink, the walls closing in on us. Dante's face paled, and I saw a faint tremor in his hand as he slowly reached for the edge of the desk. He wasn't the predator anymore. He was the prey, and the realization that there was nowhere left for him to run was sinking in.

"Fine!" he snapped, throwing his hands up in defeat. His voice cracked, and he looked over at Ryan like he was begging. "I'll give the money back. Just… don't do anything crazy."

Ryan's expression didn't change, his eyes cold and calculating. "All of it. Now."

Dante hesitated, his gaze flicking nervously to the door, then to the open window, and finally, his eyes landed on Ryan. For the first time, he looked small—cornered, like a caged animal who had nowhere to go.

With a defeated sigh, he muttered something under his breath and moved to a drawer in the desk. He pulled it open, and the sound of the drawer scraping against the wood felt too loud in the quiet of the room. He reached inside, pulling out a stack of cash, and my heart pounded harder in my chest.

"It's not all here," he admitted, his voice barely a whisper. "Some of it's digital."

Ryan didn't even blink. "Then transfer it," he said, his voice flat, like this was just another business transaction to him, nothing more than a necessary step.

I couldn't breathe for a moment, the weight of the moment pressing down on me. This wasn't just about the money. It was about what had been taken from us—the trust, the security, the belief that things could go back to normal. It was about reclaiming something that had been stolen, piece by piece.

Dante slowly lowered the stack of cash back into the drawer, and then hesitated again. The air in the room seemed to thicken, my chest tightening as the silence stretched between us. I could hear the faint buzz of the city outside, the distant hum of life continuing as if nothing had changed. But everything had changed.

Ryan's voice broke through the silence again. "Transfer it," he repeated, his tone growing sharper.

Dante's face twisted with frustration and fear, but he didn't protest again. With shaking hands, he pulled out his phone, his fingers moving quickly as he accessed an account I couldn't see. I could feel my heart beating faster, the minutes stretching out like hours as he made the transfer. I watched him closely, every motion of his hands making my skin crawl. How many other lives had he ruined? How many people had been as desperate as we had been, searching for something they'd lost, only to be led down this twisted path by him?

I couldn't help but watch, a little stunned, as Dante's fingers hovered over the screen of his phone. The once confident, smug expression that had been plastered on his face was now gone, replaced by something far less certain. He was scrambling, his eyes darting from the phone to Ryan and back, like a cornered animal trying to figure out its next move.

I felt the weight of the moment pressing down on me, the kind of weight that made everything else in the room fade into the background. The low hum of the city outside, the stale smell of the flat, the flickering light from the overhead bulb—all of it became distant, insignificant. All I could see was Dante, breaking before us, and Ryan, steady as always, unmoving and relentless.

Ryan wasn't just resourceful; he was fearless. He'd been calm from the start, methodical, like he had nothing to lose. The way he'd so effortlessly dismantled Dante's defenses made something in me tighten. Ryan had a way of taking control, of finding cracks in walls no one else noticed. But this—this was different. This wasn't just about the scam. It was about everything that had happened to us. The lies. The betrayal. The feeling of helplessness. And Ryan, he was the one who was fixing it. No hesitation. No second thoughts. Just action.

I glanced at him, my heart doing something strange in my chest. He wasn't doing this for us—at least, not just for us. He was doing it because he couldn't stand to see anyone take advantage of people, take what wasn't theirs, and leave them broken in their wake. His expression was focused, but there was something else there, too—a kind of quiet righteousness, like he was giving Dante a chance to make things right, but only because he knew it wouldn't be the last one.

Finally, he handed the phone over to Ryan, who quickly scanned the screen and nodded. The transaction was done. The silence that filled the room afterward felt almost too loud. Dante was small now, no longer the predator, but the prey.

Ryan didn't flinch. His eyes remained locked on Dante's, his posture unwavering. He was the one in charge here. "If I find out you're still running this scam, I'll make sure you regret it," he said, his voice quiet but cutting through the air like a knife.

Dante nodded quickly, his face pale, his eyes avoiding Ryan's gaze. It was clear he just wanted to vanish, to escape the crushing weight of everything that had gone wrong.

For a moment, I didn't know what to do with myself. The anger that had burned through me for days felt like it had been replaced with a kind of numbness. I stood there, frozen, watching as Dante shuffled back to the corner of the room, away from us, retreating into his own misery.

Ryan glanced at me, his expression unreadable, and I felt an inexplicable mix of relief and unease wash over me. The money was back, sure. But it didn't feel like the resolution I'd hoped for. There was no closure, no neat ending. Nothing would ever go back to the way it was before.

And yet, there was something about this moment—about the way Ryan had handled it—that made me feel a little less lost. A little less broken. I wasn't sure if it was his quiet confidence or the fact that he'd stepped up when I didn't know how to—but I was grateful, even if I couldn't fully understand it.

I looked away, my gaze falling to the floor as my mind scrambled to make sense of everything. The tension in my chest hadn't loosened. In fact, it only seemed to grow tighter, like a knot that had been pulled too many times.

I could hear Ryan's steady breath, feel his presence at my side, grounding me, even if I didn't know what to say or how to process what had just happened.

Finally, I turned to him, my voice barely a whisper. "Do you think... we're done here?"

Ryan didn't answer immediately. He glanced back at Dante, his face impassive. Then, slowly, he shook his head. "No. Not yet."

His words hung in the air between us like a warning.

And I knew, even without asking, that this wasn't over. Not by a long shot.

CHAPTER 20: SMALL STEPS

The train rumbled beneath me, a low, steady hum that seemed to reverberate deep into my bones. Outside the window, Marseille's lively streets faded away, replaced by soft fields of lavender stretching out under the late afternoon sun. The city's chaos, its noise, its people, slowly blurred into a tranquil patchwork of purple and gold, like the world was holding its breath for a moment of peace. The landscape, so calm and picturesque, felt like a lie. Everything outside the window seemed effortless, perfect, while inside, I was drowning in a storm of questions, of fear, of what-ifs.

Dad sat across from me, his posture stiff, his hands clasped tightly in his lap like he was trying to keep them from shaking. His eyes were fixed somewhere beyond me, distant, as if the world outside was easier to look at than the one in front of him. Ryan was a few rows away, giving us space. I couldn't tell if I appreciated the distance or resented it. Alone with Dad, with the weight of everything unsaid between us,

I felt like I was holding my breath, waiting for the moment when the words would finally break free— when I'd finally say what I'd been carrying for years.

Ryan was a few rows away, his presence like a quiet wall between us. He gave us space, but that distance only made everything feel more raw. I couldn't tell if I appreciated the space or resented it. On one hand, it was easier not to have someone looking over my shoulder, waiting for me to say the things I had been too scared to say for so long. On the other hand, it felt like another way of pretending everything was fine, like there was no weight of history between me and my father.

I shifted in my seat, the worn fabric of my jeans rubbing against the upholstery. I could feel my pulse in my throat, that familiar, tight knot of anxiety creeping in. The words were still there, just beneath the surface, but they felt like a wound that hadn't healed, and no matter how much I pressed, I couldn't make them bleed. I felt like I was suffocating in the silence, in the things we hadn't said, in the way we used to be able to talk without thinking and now couldn't even find the right words to begin.

"I don't know," I finally muttered, my voice quieter than I meant it to be, slipping out between clenched teeth. The words tasted bitter, like they'd been stuck in my throat for too long. "How do we just… start again? After everything?"

Dad's head shifted slightly, and I thought, for a moment, he hadn't heard me. But then his voice came, low and hesitant, like it had been locked away for years, too.

"I wish I had an answer for you," he said, the words slow, careful.

I looked at him, waiting for more, but he didn't elaborate. It was like he was afraid to say too much, afraid to break whatever fragile thread was holding us together. I wasn't sure how I felt about that—whether I was relieved or disappointed. In some ways, I just wanted him to take the words out of my mouth, to say everything that I couldn't. But that wasn't how it worked, not anymore.

The silence stretched out, thick and heavy, pressing down on me until I could barely breathe. But Dad finally spoke again, his voice so quiet it barely rose above the hum of the train.

"I don't even know where to start," he said, his voice rough, like it had been shredded by too many years of keeping things inside. "Everything I say feels… inadequate."

I turned my gaze to the window, not trusting myself to say anything in response. The clouds were gathering on the horizon, and I couldn't tell if they were a sign of an impending storm or just the dying light of a day that had been too long.

"I've been trying to figure out how I let it all get so bad," Dad continued, his voice tight, like every word was a struggle. "How I could convince myself that running away was the answer." He exhaled shakily, the sound like air being forced through a cracked pipe. "I never wanted to hurt you, Nat. Or Trevor. Or your mom. I thought… I thought I was protecting you. But I see now that I was just running from the mess I made."

His words hung in the air between us, raw and unpolished. I could feel them like a weight on my chest, each sentence sinking deeper into the quiet that had surrounded us for so long. His apology wasn't clean, wasn't tidy, but it was there. And that was enough. Or it should've been.

But it wasn't.

I couldn't bring myself to respond right away. The wound was still too fresh, and I wasn't sure I even had the strength to unpack everything he had just laid out.

"Do you have any idea what it was like for us?" I

asked, my voice trembling before I could stop it. I hated how fragile it sounded, how broken I felt. "Not knowing where you were, if you were even alive? Watching Mom fall apart? Trevor—he's still not okay, Dad." My throat constricted, and I turned my face toward the window again, desperate to hide the way my eyes burned.

Dad's shoulders slumped under the weight of my words. I could see him wince, could feel the remorse radiating off him, even without looking at him. "I know," he whispered, his voice raw, too soft. "And I'm so, so sorry for what I put you through."

I turned toward him then, my heart heavy in my chest. I wanted to say something, but the words wouldn't come. I wanted to scream at him, to tell him everything I had been feeling all these years. But the anger felt small now, swallowed up by the enormity of it all. Instead, I just shook my head, my throat tight with something I couldn't name.

"I don't know if I can forgive you for that," I said, my voice barely above a whisper. The words tasted like acid in my mouth, but they were true. And it felt important to say them, even if they were impossible to take back.

Dad's face fell. I could see the shame in his eyes,

and it hurt in a way that made my chest ache. But he nodded, like he expected nothing less. "I understand. But I want to try to fix things. If you'll let me."

There it was. His offer. His fragile hope. And I wasn't sure what to do with it. I wasn't sure what to do with him.

The train swayed, the rhythm of the tracks beneath us lulling me into a trance-like state. I didn't know what came next. Maybe I didn't even want to know. But something in me softened. I couldn't turn my back on him—not completely. Not yet.

"I don't know if I'm ready for that," I whispered, the truth of it hitting me as soon as the words left my lips. "But maybe… maybe…"

Dad nodded, a quiet relief washing over his face. It wasn't much, not yet, but it was a start. A small step toward something I wasn't sure I was ready for. But maybe it didn't matter. Maybe that was the point. There was no magic fix, no perfect resolution. But I was willing to try.

The train swayed gently as it rounded another bend, and I could see the Mediterranean in the distance, its surface sparkling like a thousand diamonds under the fading sun. For a moment, I forgot everything—forgot the weight of my dad's apology, the churning thoughts that had kept me up for days, the mess of emotions I didn't know how to navigate. The world outside felt so much simpler. So vast, so quiet, so unbothered.

I let the silence settle between us, the rhythm of the wheels beneath the train lulling me into a rare, almost meditative state. I wasn't sure if I wanted to speak or if I wanted to stay in this suspended moment forever, where nothing was expected of me, where everything could just exist as it was.

But when my dad shifted in his seat, exhaling a long breath that seemed to come from the very bottom of his chest, I knew it was time to say something.

"I don't know how we fix this," I said finally, my voice quieter than I meant it to be. I wasn't sure I even had the answer.

Ryan, who had been quiet up until then, leaning against the window a few rows away, turned toward me. He was studying me with that look I couldn't quite decipher, as if trying to gauge how deep the cracks went.

"We start small," he said, his voice steady. "One day at a time. I'm not expecting everything to go back to normal. I just… I want to be better. For you. For all of us."

His words hung in the air, and I felt something in me tighten, a flicker of hope mixed with disbelief. His voice cracked a little on the last word, a vulnerability that felt almost out of place on someone so often so composed. I didn't know how to respond. Maybe I didn't have to. Maybe I just needed to let him say it.

I turned back to my dad, and something in me softened, but not completely. I didn't let him finish. I didn't want him to keep apologizing, not now, not like that. I didn't know how to let him off the hook, how to make him understand that it wasn't about fixing the past, about erasing everything that had happened. What I needed—what I wanted—was for him to see me, to really see me for the person I was now, not the one he wished I still was.

"You broke us, Dad," I said softly, the words slipping out without me fully realizing it. I wasn't sure if I was talking to him or to myself. "And we're not going to be the same. But..." I hesitated, fighting the lump in my throat. "Maybe we don't have to be."

I wasn't ready to forgive him, not fully. But maybe I didn't need to, not right now. Not in this moment.

When I looked at my dad, his face was crumpled, the years of guilt and regret finally catching up with him. His eyes were shiny, wet with the unshed tears that seemed to have been waiting for the right moment. I wasn't sure if he was crying because of the weight of everything he'd done or because of what I'd said—or maybe it was both.

"Thank you," he whispered, his voice breaking.

I nodded, feeling the smallest shift between us—not a repair, not yet, but the faintest crack in the wall I'd built. A crack I didn't know if I was ready to widen, but one that didn't feel so terrifying anymore.

Just then, my dad stood up from his seat and stretched, his back stiff from the long hours spent on the train. "I'm going to take a walk," he said, his voice low, like he didn't want to disturb the fragile moment we were sharing. He glanced at me quickly, a little hesitant, but then his eyes dropped, like he was already retreating into himself again. There was a tension in the air, the kind that happens when too much has been left unsaid, and it made the space between us feel miles wide.

I watched him move toward the door, his figure retreating down the narrow aisle of the train car, until he was out of sight. The moment he disappeared, I let out a breath I hadn't realized I was holding. My chest felt tight with all the things I hadn't said, the questions I didn't know how to ask, the things I was too afraid to know. And yet, I knew I was waiting for something. For him to come back and say the thing that would make it better. But I wasn't sure what that thing was anymore.

The silence that followed felt heavy, like it was pushing in on me from all sides. I turned to Ryan, who was sitting across the aisle, his eyes distant, but not cold. He looked like he was giving me space to breathe, like he understood that I needed it, even if I hadn't asked for it.

"Thanks," I whispered, my voice barely above a murmur. "For… being here. For not letting me shut everything down."

Ryan glanced over at me, and for the briefest moment, I saw something in his eyes. A flicker of understanding, maybe. Or maybe just the recognition that we were both standing on the edge of something that could either break us or help us rebuild. He gave a small shake of his head, as though he could hear the doubt in my voice and wanted to stop it before it turned into something bigger.

"Don't be so hard on him," he said, his tone gentle, but firm. "It's not easy for anyone. And… you don't have to fix everything in one go. It's okay to take it slow."

I wanted to argue. I wanted to tell him that it wasn't about making excuses for my dad. That it wasn't about going slow—it was about the fact that we'd never even gotten a chance to try. I could feel the tension building inside me, the urge to say something sharp, something that would break the silence and shatter the fragile thing that was growing between us. But when I opened my mouth, the words didn't come. Not the way I expected.

Instead, I found myself just sitting there, taking in Ryan's quiet, almost patient gaze. Maybe he was right. Maybe I was expecting too much. Maybe, after everything that had happened, I couldn't expect my dad to suddenly fix it all in one go. The idea of forgiving him, of letting go of the anger I'd held onto for so long, felt impossible, but something about the way Ryan said it made me want to try. Slowly.

Before I could say anything else, the sound of footsteps approached, soft but unmistakable. When I looked up, I saw my dad returning, slipping back into his seat without a word. He sighed as he settled in, his shoulders a little less tense than before, like the walk had helped in some small way. But we didn't talk. Not yet.

The train was still moving, its wheels clicking

steadily on the tracks. Outside the window, the lavender fields and olive trees stretched out in quiet rows beneath the sinking sun, casting long, slanted shadows that seemed to stretch with the same tiredness that I felt inside. The world was changing, but it wasn't changing fast enough for me. The long silence that followed felt like it was pulling us back into something unresolved, but I was too tired to fill it with words. There was something about the stillness that felt safer than saying too much.

I leaned back in my seat, the worn leather creaking under my weight. The sun's glow seeped through the windows, painting everything in a hazy, golden light, but the warmth did little to ease the knot in my stomach. The future loomed ahead, uncertain and jagged, like the landscape outside—beautiful, but difficult to traverse.

My heart still ached for the father I thought I knew, the man who had been a stranger for so long, and yet, sitting here next to him, I wasn't sure who I was anymore. Was I the daughter still waiting for an apology that might never come? Or was I the one who had to let go, to move forward even if it meant leaving behind the version of him I'd wanted to believe in?

I looked over at him, his face lined with fatigue,

his eyes tired but not entirely closed off. He wasn't the same man he'd been before, and maybe I wasn't the same girl who had left home months ago. But I didn't know how to reconcile those versions of us with who we were right now.

I didn't know how long it would take to piece everything back together. I didn't know if I even wanted to. Part of me still clung to the hope that things could be fixed, that we could somehow get back to the way we were before, when things had felt simpler. But another part of me wondered if we were both too broken for that now.

As the train rolled toward the next chapter of our journey, I let myself drift into the rhythm of its movement, the gentle rocking that felt like a lullaby for all the questions I didn't know how to ask.

I didn't know what the future held. I didn't know what would happen when we finally got to the end of this road.

But for the first time, I didn't feel like I had to have all the answers.

Maybe, for once, I could just take things step by step.

CHAPTER 21: A FATHER'S GIFT

The train station was a blur of movement—bags being dragged across the stone floors, the low hum of announcements echoing through the air, and the distant whistle of a train pulling away. But amidst the chaos, everything between Dad and me felt oddly still, as if the world had kept going, but we were suspended in this tiny moment together. His presence was there, steady, but still fragile. The weight of everything unspoken hovered in the air like a thick fog, thick enough that I almost felt like I couldn't breathe.

We stood on the platform, not close enough to touch, but not far apart either. His hands were shoved into the pockets of his jacket, his eyes darting between the tracks and the bustling crowd. Ryan had disappeared to grab a coffee, leaving Dad and me alone for the first time in days. I wasn't sure how I felt about the solitude. Some part of me wanted to fill the silence, to make it less uncomfortable, but another part of me didn't want to rush this—didn't want to rush the slow, tentative steps we were taking toward something that felt almost like healing.

Dad shifted slightly, clearing his throat. His voice, when it came, was low and hesitant. "I need to give you something."

I turned to face him fully, startled by the sudden seriousness in his tone. "What is it?" I asked, trying to keep the suspicion from creeping into my voice.

He pulled an envelope from his jacket pocket and held it out to me. It was thick, the edges worn from the handling, sealed with a careful fold, like he'd put a lot of thought into the presentation. For a moment, I just stared at it, unsure of what to say. The last time I'd received something from him like this, it had been a birthday card I found months after the fact, shoved under a stack of bills.

"What is this?" I asked again, my brow furrowing. The envelope felt heavier than it should have, like it carried the weight of more than just paper.

"Everything Ryan helped recover," Dad said, his voice thick with an emotion I couldn't quite place. "The money. It's not all of it, but it's enough to help with whatever you need—college, traveling, whatever you decide." His eyes locked onto mine, and for the first time in a long while, I saw something in them that wasn't regret or guilt. It was sincerity, a hope I hadn't realized I'd been missing.

I stared at the envelope, the weight of it making my fingers tremble slightly. It felt like an offering, but not one I was sure I could accept. "Dad, I can't—" My voice trailed off, and I realized I didn't know how to explain why this felt so wrong, why I couldn't just take the money and move on.

"You can," he interrupted gently but firmly, stepping closer. His gaze softened, but his words didn't falter. "And you will. I don't deserve to decide how to fix things, but this... this is one thing I can try to make right."

His words caught in my throat, a lump forming that had nothing to do with the envelope, but with the hollow space that had once been filled by him. I swallowed hard, feeling something inside me break open. "Thank you," I whispered, my voice so quiet that it felt like it would be lost in the sounds of the station.

Dad gave a tight nod, his hands still shoved into his pockets. There was nothing else to say—no grand apology or explanation that would make everything okay. But somehow, in that moment, the small act of him handing me that envelope felt like the first step toward something—something I couldn't define yet, but something that wasn't entirely hopeless.

I stared at the envelope for a long time, the weight of it heavy in my hands. I wasn't sure what to do with it, or what to do with all the things it represented—regret, responsibility, and the thin thread of trust that was slowly beginning to weave itself back between us. I wasn't sure if I could forgive him for all of it. But for the first time, I felt like he was trying. And that was more than I'd had from him in a long time.

As I slipped the envelope into my bag, I felt a strange, almost ridiculous impulse. I pulled something from my jacket pocket and turned to face him again.

"Here," I said, holding out a small, wrapped bundle.

Dad blinked, confused. "What's this?"

I smiled, though the smile was small and tight, as I unwrapped the cloth to reveal a tiny fish-shaped piece of wood, painted in soft shades of rainbow. "It's a lucky fish bait," I said, trying to make my voice sound casual. "You know, the one you always talk about. Your lucky charm for when you fish."

Dad's eyes softened, and his lips twitched as if he were holding back a laugh. It was an old inside joke, one that had faded a little over the years but never really disappeared. The fishing trips he used to take me on, where he'd pull out that ridiculous bait, convinced it would bring him the biggest catch of the day.

"Don't drown again, okay?" I said, the words escaping before I could stop them.

He chuckled softly, the sound of it breaking the tension that had wrapped itself so tightly around us. "I'll try not to," he said, his voice lighter now, a genuine smile on his face. It was the first time in so long I'd seen him smile without that hard edge of guilt behind it.

And for a brief moment, I felt like maybe, just maybe, he wasn't the man who had walked away from us. Maybe he was the dad who had stood by me, laughing over something silly. Maybe there was still a chance to find that version of him again.

I swallowed the lump in my throat, trying to hold onto the moment before it slipped away. "Promise?"

He reached out, taking the tiny wooden fish from my hand and tucking it into his jacket pocket, as if it were something sacred. "Promise."

The train station buzzed with movement—luggage wheels scraping against tile, muffled announcements echoing overhead, and the soft hum of conversations blending into white noise. But in that moment, the world around us faded. It was just me,

Dad, and a small envelope he held out, his hand trembling like it weighed more than it should.

I stared at it, the corners slightly bent and the faint scent of his cologne clinging to the paper. My chest tightened. "You could give it to her yourself," I said, my voice sharper than I intended.

He shook his head, his eyes dropping to the ground. The fluorescent lights cast harsh shadows across his face, emphasizing the lines I hadn't noticed before. "I can't. I've done enough damage, Nat. Coming back would just make things worse."

"That's not true," I said quickly, the words tumbling out before I could think. But even as I said them, they felt hollow.

He looked up, his gaze meeting mine, and in that moment, I saw it. Regret. Guilt. Something deeper, something raw and unfixable. "It is. You're all better off without me there," he said, his voice quiet but steady. "I need to figure out who I am, Natalie. And I can't do that by going back."

A lump formed in my throat, and I clenched my fists around the envelope. "So that's it? You're just... leaving again?"

His face softened, and he reached out, resting a tentative hand on my shoulder. "I'm not disappearing," he said softly. "Not this time. You know where I am. But I can't come home. Not yet."

The words hung in the air, filling the space between us like a fog I couldn't see through.

"You think this fixes anything?" I asked, my voice cracking as I held up the envelope. "A letter? Some money? You think that erases everything?"

"No," he admitted, his hand dropping to his side. "I know it doesn't. But it's a start. It's all I can give right now."

I wanted to scream at him, to tell him that it wasn't enough. That it would never be enough. But the anger felt heavy, like carrying it any longer would break me.

"Do you know what it was like?" I asked instead, my voice shaking. "Do you have any idea what it felt like for us? For me? Thinking you were dead, gone, and then finding out you left because you couldn't face us?"

He flinched, his shoulders sagging. "I think about it every day. About what I did to you, to your mom, to Trevor." His voice cracked, and he looked away, his jaw tightening. "I can't take it back, Nat. I can't undo it."

"But you can try," I said, my tone softer now, almost pleading. "You can come back and try."

He smiled faintly, but it didn't reach his eyes. "I

don't deserve that chance. Not yet."

I didn't know how to feel. Part of me wanted to hate him, to shove the envelope back into his hands and walk away. But another part—the part that still remembered the dad who made pancakes on Saturday mornings and taught me to ride a bike—wanted to hold onto him, to force him to stay.

"I don't know if I can forgive you," I whispered, the words barely audible.

He nodded, his expression unreadable. "I don't expect you to. But maybe someday, you'll understand why I have to do this."

I wasn't sure I ever would.

The train announcement crackled overhead, garbled but clear enough to signal it was almost time. My train. My departure. My escape.

Dad glanced at the oversized clock hanging above the platform, the heavy kind you only see in old train stations. His shoulders sagged slightly, the weight of everything unsaid pulling him down.

"I'm sorry," he said again, his voice barely above a whisper. "For everything."

The words hung in the air between us, fragile and uncertain. For a moment, I wondered if I'd imagined them.

I wanted to be angry. To tell him it wasn't enough. That 'sorry' didn't even begin to cover what he'd done—what he'd broken in me, in Mom, in Trevor. I wanted to yell, to lash out, to demand he fix it somehow.

But the words wouldn't come.

Instead, something else happened. My feet moved before my brain caught up, and suddenly, I was stepping forward, wrapping my arms around him.

It surprised us both.

He froze for a moment, like he didn't know what to do, and then his arms came around me hesitantly, almost like he was afraid he'd shatter me if he held on too tightly.

But then something shifted. His grip tightened, and it felt like he was holding on for dear life, like he was trying to memorize the moment—every detail, every feeling—because he knew it was slipping away.

I pressed my cheek against his shoulder, and for a second, I could almost trick myself into believing he was still the dad I used to know. The one who sang off-key in the car, who taught me to skip rocks, who made pancakes shaped like stars.

But when I pulled away and met his eyes, the illusion shattered.

There was nothing left of that man. What stared back at me was hollow, fragile, a shell of someone who had once been whole. I searched his face for something to hold onto—some piece of him I could still love. But it wasn't there.

I swallowed hard, the lump in my throat threatening to choke me.

The train whistle blew, sharp and insistent, pulling me back to the present. Ryan appeared at my side, his footsteps quiet but grounding. He handed me a coffee, its warmth seeping into my hands as I clung to it like a lifeline.

He gave Dad a small nod, the kind you give to someone you don't quite trust but can't bring yourself to hate. Dad nodded back, his hands shoved deep into his coat pockets.

"You ready?" Ryan asked softly, his voice steady in a way I desperately needed.

I nodded, though I wasn't sure I believed it.

As I stepped onto the train, I turned back one last time. Dad stood alone on the platform, his figure dwarfed by the vastness of the station. His coat hung loose on him, and his hands stayed buried in his pockets like he didn't know what to do without them.

He looked smaller somehow, like he was already

fading into the background. A shadow of the man I thought I'd known.

The train doors slid shut with a soft hiss, and I sank into my seat by the window. Outside, the platform blurred into motion, a swirl of colors and movement as the train began to pull away. I turned my head, watching him—Dad—standing there, his figure growing smaller and smaller until he was swallowed entirely by the city's chaos.

He didn't move, didn't wave. He just stood there, his hands shoved deep into his coat pockets, his shoulders hunched like he was already bracing for the cold absence of us.

As the train gained speed, the French countryside opened up, fields of green and gold stretching endlessly under a pale blue sky. It was beautiful in a way that felt distant, like the world was mocking the storm inside me with its calm.

I pressed my forehead to the window, letting the cool glass ground me. The rumble of the wheels beneath my feet filled the silence, steady and unrelenting. Across the aisle, Ryan scrolled through his phone, but even he seemed quieter than usual, as if he could sense the weight of the moment and knew better than to fill it with words.

The envelope sat in my lap, its corners creased from where I'd held it too tightly. My name wasn't on it—Marianne was written in Dad's familiar handwriting—but somehow, it felt like it belonged to me too. Like it carried pieces of answers I didn't know I needed.

I hesitated, my fingers brushing against the seal. Part of me didn't want to know what was inside. Another part—the one that couldn't stop digging, couldn't stop chasing—knew I had to.

With a deep breath, I slipped my finger under the flap and tore it open.

The paper inside was worn, the ink smudged in places, as if he'd rewritten it over and over until the words felt right. I unfolded it slowly, my hands trembling as my eyes scanned the lines.

Dear Marianne,

I don't know if you'll ever forgive me. If I were you, I'm not sure I could.

When I left, I told myself I was protecting you and the kids. But the truth is, I was running. Running from my mistakes, my shame, and the man I'd become. I was a coward, and in doing what I thought was right, I broke the people I loved the most.

You were always the strong one, Marianne. You held us together even when I was falling apart. I should have leaned on you, trusted you, but instead, I left you to clean up my mess. For that, I'll never forgive myself.

I don't expect you to take me back or even understand. But I want you to know that I see what I've done, and I will spend the rest of my life trying to be better. For you, for Natalie, for Trevor.

Thank you for everything—for the life we built, for the family we shared. I'll always love you for that, even if I don't deserve to say it.

John

The tears came before I could stop them, hot and silent as they rolled down my cheeks. I folded the letter carefully, my hands shaking as I tucked it back into the envelope, as if sealing it again might contain the flood of emotions threatening to overwhelm me.

"Hey," Ryan said softly, leaning forward, his voice cutting through the haze. "You okay?"

I nodded quickly, but the lump in my throat made it impossible to speak. I could feel his eyes on me, steady and patient, but I didn't look up. I couldn't.

Instead, I stared at the envelope, the weight of Dad's words pressing against my chest. They were heavy, not because of what they said, but because of what they meant—that he understood, in his own fractured way, the pain he'd caused.

The weight of everything hit me all at once. My hands gripped the letter so tightly I thought it might tear.

I didn't know how to feel. There was anger, yes, a simmering resentment that he could leave, shatter us, and still think an apology might fix it. But there was something else too—something quieter. Sadness, maybe. Or pity.

He wasn't the man I'd idolized. He wasn't the father who'd read me bedtime stories or built me forts out of couch cushions. He wasn't even the man I'd gone to Europe searching for.

He was human. Broken. Flawed in ways I wasn't sure he'd ever be able to repair. And yet, despite everything, I couldn't bring myself to hate him completely.

The train rocked gently as it sped into the horizon, the fields outside shifting into a blur of green and gold. I stared out at the passing scenery, my reflection faint in the glass. He was gone now, but in some ways, he'd been gone for a long time.

I took a deep breath, letting the warmth of the coffee Ryan had handed me seep into my hands. It grounded me, kept me from spiraling too far into the ache of it all.

"Hey," Ryan said again, his voice softer this time. "You okay?"

I turned to him, his expression open and steady, and I nodded slowly. "Yeah," I said, surprising myself with the truth in the word.

Because for the first time in a long time, I wasn't sure where I was going.

But maybe, just maybe, that was okay.

CHAPTER 22: HOMECOMING

By the time we reached the airport, the weight of everything that had happened still clung to me. The envelope was tucked securely in my bag, buried beneath the layers of clothes and junk. It felt like a stone, pressing against the side of my hip, never letting me forget it was there. Every time I shifted my bag, every time I moved just a little, I could feel it, heavy and constant, reminding me that I hadn't made up my mind yet—not fully. It was a decision that lingered, hanging in the air like a fog I couldn't clear, and it gnawed at me with every step I took.

Ryan stood beside me in line for our tickets, his eyes more on me than the counter in front of us. The line stretched long in front of us, filled with chattering people pulling their luggage along, their voices blending together in an almost harmonious buzz. But for some reason, the noise only seemed to amplify the pressure, making the air feel thicker, heavier.

"Are you going to give it to her?" Ryan asked

quietly, his voice cutting through the noise like a thread pulling at the fabric of my thoughts. I hadn't even realized I'd been staring off into the distance, lost in the swirl of my own mind.

I shook my head, unable to form the words I needed. I wasn't sure I even knew what to say. My gaze dropped to my shoes, shifting uncomfortably, trying to ignore the knot of anxiety forming in my stomach. "I don't know," I murmured.

Ryan frowned, his brow creasing in that way that always made him look like he was trying to solve a puzzle that just wouldn't fit together. "Why not? Don't you think she deserves to read it?"

The question hung in the air, and I could feel it all over again—the memory of my mom after Dad had left. I could still picture her face, her eyes red from crying, the exhaustion in every line of her face. She had been so strong, pretending to be okay when I knew she was breaking inside. There were nights I'd find her sitting at the kitchen table, the bills spread out before her, her hand rubbing at her temple like she could will away the exhaustion. She had done it all for us—worked tirelessly to keep Trevor and me afloat while her own heart was shattered.

"She deserves to heal," I said softly, almost to

myself. The words felt like an anchor in my chest. I wasn't sure if I was trying to convince myself or Ryan. "And this…" I glanced down at the envelope in my hand, the weight of it making my fingers tighten around the edges. "This would just rip the wound open again."

Ryan didn't argue, though I could see the conflict in his eyes. His gaze softened, but he didn't push, which was more than I expected from him. He simply nodded, his hand brushing against mine briefly before pulling away. The touch was gentle, soft, warm—like a reminder that maybe I wasn't as alone as I thought. For a fleeting moment, everything felt a little easier, like the distance between us wasn't quite so wide.

We stood in silence for a few moments, the noise of the airport continuing around us, but the weight of everything pressing down on me. I wanted so badly to know the right thing to do, but the truth was, I wasn't even sure if I could ever know. How do you choose between healing and truth? Between protecting the people you love and facing the things that scare you the most?

Eventually, we made our way onto the plane, the hum of the jet engines filling the cabin as we settled into our seats. But my thoughts didn't quiet. I slipped the envelope back into my bag, making a silent promise to myself that I'd decide what to do with it later. But deep down, I knew. It wasn't for Mom. It was for me. I wasn't sure if I was ready to face it, but maybe that was the hardest part of growing up—facing things even when you're not sure you're ready.

The plane lifted off, the earth below us shrinking into a distant patchwork of fields and streets, the sky stretching endlessly above us. The sense of disconnect grew as we soared into the air, the distance between where I was and where I'd come from widening like an endless chasm. The view outside the window was beautiful, clouds and blue skies in all directions, but the storm inside me was far from over. No matter how far we flew, I could still feel the weight of everything—of the past, of the truth, of the choices I'd made. It felt like everything had changed, but at the same time, nothing had.

Ryan shifted beside me, his voice breaking into my thoughts. "So, uh…" he said, a grin tugging at his lips. "You wanna hear something absurd?"

I looked over at him, half-expecting another one of his sarcastic remarks, but he was actually serious, if not a little sheepish. "Sure," I said, trying to shake off the tension, even if it was just for a moment.

Ryan's face scrunched up as he rummaged through his bag, pulling out a croissant he'd bought at the airport before we boarded. He winced the second he saw it. "I swear, I've never seen a croissant look more disappointed in itself. It's like it's giving up on life."

I couldn't help it. I laughed—genuinely laughed. It was such a small, silly thing, but it was like a breath of fresh air. The sound of Ryan's lightheartedness, his ability to find humor even in the most ridiculous of things, felt like a momentary escape from all the heaviness that had been weighing me down. I was grateful for it, even if just for a second.

As we settled into the flight, the conversation drifted into the kind of meaningless banter that you have with someone you trust—talking about the movie on the screen, making fun of the airline food, pretending that the weight of the world wasn't pressing down on us. Ryan was good at that—making it seem like everything would be okay, even when it felt like it might not be.

After what felt like hours, the plane began its descent, and soon enough, the familiar outline of our small town emerged in the distance—just barely visible through the window. A patchwork of rooftops and streets, stretching out like a puzzle I used to put together as a kid. I stared at it, trying to reconcile the sight with everything I had been through. How was it possible that everything looked the same when I felt like I had changed in ways I couldn't even begin to understand?

The streets, the houses, the shops—I could practically picture it all in my mind, the memories of my childhood still etched into every corner. But somehow, it didn't feel like home anymore. Not the way it used to, at least. The houses were the same, the streets the same, but there was something about it that felt foreign. Like I had been away for a lifetime, and now, nothing could ever be the same. Maybe it was the fact that I wasn't the same. Not anymore.

As the plane touched down and we taxied toward the terminal, I felt a strange mix of relief and dread. Relief because it was over—because we had come back. But dread because it meant facing everything I had left behind. And I wasn't sure if I was ready for that.

I wasn't sure if I ever would be.

Ryan walked beside me as we exited the terminal, his bag slung over his shoulder. He gave me a small, reassuring smile, his eyes soft but steady. "You ready for this?" he asked, his voice steady, though I knew he was probably just as unsure as I was.

"Not even a little," I admitted, gripping the strap of my bag tighter than necessary.

I felt a rush of nerves and uncertainty, like everything I had known was slipping away from me, and I had no idea where it would land. The weight of what had happened still hung around me, pressing at my chest like a storm cloud. The thought of seeing Mom again, the town that I had once known so well—nothing seemed familiar in the way it should have.

My heart beat a little faster as we approached the exit, the cool air of our hometown greeting us, sharp and familiar. I took in a shaky breath, as if I was about to step into a world I wasn't sure I belonged in anymore.

Ryan looked at me, his expression open, waiting for me to lead the way. His presence was the only anchor in a world that suddenly felt unsteady, as if nothing was ever going to be the same again.

"I don't know how to do this," I said, the words coming out before I could stop them. I felt a kind of vulnerability I hadn't known I was carrying, as if just being back here exposed all the parts of me I hadn't yet figured out.

Ryan didn't say anything for a moment, just walked beside me, his footsteps in sync with mine. "You don't have to know," he said, his voice low, but full of conviction. "Just take it one step at a time. You'll figure it out."

Mom was waiting at the curb when we finally made our way out of the airport. She was leaning against the car, her arms crossed over her chest, the familiar sight of her soft blue cardigan instantly making me feel a little more grounded. It was one of her favorites—the one she always wore when she wanted to feel put together, even if the rest of the world wasn't cooperating. She looked exactly like herself, yet somehow... different.

When she saw me, her face lit up, and before I could even say a word, she dropped her arms and rushed toward me, pulling me into one of those tight, engulfing hugs that felt like home.

"Natalie!" she exclaimed, her voice full of relief and warmth, and I had to swallow the lump in my throat to respond.

"Hi, Mom," I said, my voice muffled against her shoulder, her scent—sweet lavender and faint traces of her perfume—filling my senses in a way I hadn't realized I missed.

She pulled back slightly, holding me at arm's length. Her eyes scanned me, concern flickering across her face. "Look at you," she said softly. "You've lost weight. Are you eating enough? You look… tired."

Ryan, who had been hovering just behind me, cleared his throat awkwardly, obviously trying to give us a moment. "I'll leave you two to it," he said, his voice deliberately loud.

"Oh!" Mom said, her eyes immediately brightening. "Ryan! Thank you for bringing her back in one piece." She reached out to him, squeezing his shoulder. "Honestly, you're a lifesaver."

"Anytime," Ryan grinned, a touch of his usual mischief returning. "Although, I can't promise she didn't drag me into more trouble than I signed up for."

Mom's laughter rang out, light and genuine, and I couldn't help but feel a little lighter myself. The sound was like a balm, a reminder of who she used to be before everything had turned upside down. I hadn't realized how much I'd missed her laugh until now.

As we climbed into the car, I noticed the small, almost imperceptible changes. Her posture was steadier, and though there was a weariness in her eyes, it was tempered with a new sense of calm. Even the small decorations on the dashboard had shifted. There was a new air freshener in the shape of a sunflower, and a framed picture of the three of us from a vacation we'd taken years ago—something I didn't remember her ever keeping on display before. It was as though she had found her footing again, like the house had been rearranged and now it was more in tune with who she was becoming.

"Mom…" I began, but before I could finish, Ryan jumped in from the back seat.

"Speaking of trouble," he said, a mischievous gleam in his eye. "My parents weren't exactly thrilled about me going on this trip, so they made me wear a tracker." He pulled out a small device from his jacket pocket, its sleek, black surface glinting in the sunlight.

I couldn't help but laugh, the image of Ryan, of all people, wearing a tracker, amusing me more than it probably should have.

"You're like a dog with a collar," Mom said, her voice deadpan but her eyes twinkling. "Next thing I know, you'll have a leash, too."

Ryan raised an eyebrow. "Hey, I'd prefer the collar over the leash."

"Well," Mom said with a grin, "I'm just glad you're safe. Honestly, I don't know what I would've done without you keeping an eye on her." She looked at me, her smile softening just slightly. "Thank you, Ryan, for looking out for my girl."

Ryan gave a small nod, looking uncharacteristically serious for a moment. "No problem," he said, voice low, but sincere. "That's what friends are for."

The car settled into a quiet hum as we drove away from the airport, the familiar streets of our small town gradually coming into view. I felt a strange sense of detachment as we passed houses I recognized, the trees that lined the roads, the same old storefronts. It all seemed so... unchanged, like it had stood still while my life had spun out of control.

Ryan's voice broke through my thoughts. "You okay?" he asked, his gaze flicking between me and Mom in the front seat.

I nodded, though I didn't quite believe myself. "Yeah. Just... taking it all in."

Mom turned to me, her expression softening, her hand reaching out to brush a strand of hair behind my ear. "You look so grown up, Nat. I know it's been a rough road, but you've come so far."

I smiled faintly, but it felt more like a reflex than anything real. "I'm still trying to figure out who I am, Mom."

She gave me a knowing look, her gaze soft. "You don't have to have it all figured out. You never have to have it all figured out. You're allowed to be lost sometimes."

I swallowed hard, my chest tightening. "I don't know if I want to be found."

Mom's hand tightened on the steering wheel, her fingers curling around it like she was holding on for both of us. "Maybe that's okay, too. For now."

The house felt different, but not in the way I'd imagined. It wasn't just the new throw pillows on the couch or the fresh coat of paint in the hallway, though both of those things were new. It wasn't even the small adjustments that had been made in my absence, like the way the kitchen had been reorganized or the new picture frames scattered across the mantel. No, it was the energy. It was lighter. Less stifling. There was a calm that I didn't remember being there before. A kind of breath that filled the space, as though the house itself had finally exhaled after years of holding everything in.

Mom made tea while I sat at the table, fiddling with the edge of my mug, not quite sure where to start. It felt strange, talking to her like this—like we had never been so far apart, and yet, here we were.

"So, how's everything?" I asked, trying to sound casual. My eyes flicked to the small pot of honey she'd set out. The golden syrup glinted in the light from the window.

"It's been nice," she said, setting a steaming mug in front of me. She sat down across from me, wrapping her hands around her own cup. "Keeping busy. Meeting new people. I didn't realize how much I needed it."

I nodded, watching her closely. There was something about her, something different that I couldn't quite place. It was as though the years of struggle had been sculpting her into someone new. Stronger, more at ease with herself. Not the woman who'd been treading water for so long, but someone who had learned how to swim.

"You seem… good," I said hesitantly. It felt like a strange thing to say, like I was commenting on someone else's life, not my mom's.

She smiled, the kind of smile that reached her eyes—soft, but full of an unspoken understanding. "I think I am. It hasn't been easy, but I've learned that I can stand on my own. And that's something."

I swallowed hard, not sure if I should say anything more. It was good to hear her speak like that, but it also made something inside me twist. Standing on her own? I hadn't really imagined that she would have to. Growing up, she had always seemed like the rock. The one who held everything together. But now, I was seeing her in this light that I didn't quite know how to navigate.

"I'm proud of you, Mom," I said quietly. The words sounded a little hollow in my ears, but I meant them, more than I could explain.

She reached across the table, her hand warm as she placed it over mine. "Thank you, Nat."

I wasn't sure how to follow that up, so instead, I took a sip of the tea she had made for me. It was warm and soothing, though my stomach felt a little tight. It had been a long time since I'd felt like this—so distant, yet so close. It was a new kind of intimacy, and I wasn't sure how to manage it.

After a moment, Mom broke the silence. "How's Ryan?" she asked, her voice light, but with an undercurrent of something deeper—something I hadn't expected.

"He's… good," I replied, my mind flashing to the way his smile had looked when we'd left the airport. The way his hand had brushed mine in the terminal, a silent reassurance that everything was okay between us.

"I think he's going to be okay."

"Good," she said, nodding like she was weighing something in her mind. "It's good to have people like that in your life."

I blinked, feeling her words settle around me. The way she said it wasn't just about Ryan. It was about everyone who had been there, who had carried the weight with me while I was away. People like that. The thought of it made me want to say more, but the words didn't come.

Instead, I excused myself, needing a break from the heavy silence that seemed to be creeping in.

I found Trevor in his room, the door cracked open just enough for me to hear the rapid-fire of mouse clicks and loud explosions, the sounds of a game I couldn't quite place. His curtains were drawn, the only light coming from the cold glow of his computer screen. The dimness of the room felt almost suffocating, like it was holding everything inside, wrapping itself around Trevor in a way that kept the outside world from touching him.

It was familiar. Too familiar. The way he disappeared into his world, the way he shut everyone else out like a wall between him and the mess we had all found ourselves in. A mess that I had walked away from, and now it felt like I was being pulled right back into it—whether I wanted to be or not.

I knocked lightly on the doorframe, my knuckles barely making a sound, but it felt too loud in the quiet of the room. "Hey," I said, my voice softer than I meant. The words felt too heavy, like I was carrying a weight I couldn't get rid of.

Trevor didn't look up. "What do you want?" His tone was flat, disinterested, like I was interrupting something that mattered more than anything I could say.

I shrugged, stepping inside and letting the door close behind me. "Just saying hi." I could almost hear the lie in my own voice.

"Hi," he muttered, not bothering to shift his attention. His fingers moved furiously over the keyboard, his expression locked in concentration, his eyes glued to the screen like the rest of the world didn't exist.

I walked over to the bed and sat on the edge, watching him for a moment. The rhythm of his game was fast and relentless, a series of clicks and sudden bursts of noise. It felt like a world I didn't belong in anymore. I didn't know when it had changed—when everything between us had gotten so... distant.

"I missed you, you know," I said quietly, trying to fill the silence that seemed to stretch between us.

"Yeah, well, you missed a lot," he muttered, his voice carrying a sharp edge that made me flinch. Still, his eyes stayed focused on the screen, his fingers moving with precision, like he was chasing something down that I couldn't see. His words were like a slap, though. A reminder of the time I'd been gone, the time I'd spent away, while everything around me kept changing.

"Trevor, I know you're angry—" I began, but he spun around in his chair so quickly that it made my heart skip a beat. His eyes flashed with frustration, his jaw tight, like I had just pushed the wrong button.

"Angry?" he snapped, his voice bitter, sharp. "I'm not angry, Nat. I'm done. With him. With everything."

The words hit me harder than I expected. I knew something had shifted. I knew that he'd been struggling, that everything about Dad's disappearance had taken a toll on him. But hearing him say it, hearing him call it like it was—done—felt like I was standing on the edge of a cliff, waiting to fall.

I blinked, unsure what to say. His face, that face I used to know so well, was unreadable now. It was like the person I'd left behind in the house was gone, replaced by someone I didn't understand.

"Trevor—" I started again, but he shook his head sharply, cutting me off.

"No," he snapped, his voice harsh. "You don't get it. He left. He doesn't care about us, so why should I care about him?"

I felt my throat tighten, a lump forming there that I couldn't swallow. It wasn't like I hadn't expected this—hadn't seen the anger building in him like a storm. But hearing the words out loud, seeing the way his anger had crystallized into something hard and permanent, made my chest ache. He was right, in a way. Dad had walked away from us. He had chosen to leave, and there was nothing any of us could do to change it. But this—this version of Trevor—felt like something I couldn't fix.

I wanted to say something—anything—that would make it better. Something that could put the pieces of him back together. But nothing came. There were no words that felt like they would make a difference.

Trevor turned back to his computer without another word, clicking his mouse so violently that it almost felt like he was trying to destroy whatever was on the screen. The conversation was over. He'd closed the door on it, and on me.

I sat there for a few minutes, the silence pressing in on me, making the room feel smaller and smaller. The weight of his words crushed the air around me. Somehow, he'd turned bitter while I was away, and I hadn't even seen it happening. It was like he had built this wall brick by brick, and now I was standing on the outside, looking in, unable to get through.

The room felt suffocating, and I stood up without another word. As I walked down the hall, I could still feel the weight of the conversation clinging to me, pressing on my shoulders. It felt like the distance between us had grown too wide, too deep to ever cross again. The thought of it—of Trevor pulling further away from me, of us becoming strangers—felt like a punch to the gut.

I didn't know how to fix any of this. I didn't know how to fix him.

I walked into my own room, the familiar sight of my bed and books and half-empty suitcases only making things worse. My hands were shaking, the kind of tremble that comes when you're caught between wanting to move forward and being terrified of what lies ahead.

I sat on the edge of my bed, looking at my hands,

trying to make sense of the knot in my stomach. It had been easier when we were all pretending, when everything was normal and the cracks were just small enough to ignore.

But now, the cracks were wide open, and nothing could be the same.

I missed my brother. The way he used to be—before everything fell apart. But that version of Trevor felt like a ghost now. And I couldn't figure out how to bring him back.

CHAPTER 23: A CHRISTMAS MIRACLE

Mom was moving forward, piece by piece. Slowly, but surely, she was stitching herself back together. It wasn't as dramatic as some days when you could see the world shifting in an instant, but there was something beautiful in the way she was learning to find her footing again. I didn't realize how much we needed it until I saw her humming along to the Christmas carols while decorating, the soft melody weaving through the house like a thread tying everything together. Her hands were steady as she worked, gently hanging the ornaments on the tree, adjusting the lights until they flickered in perfect, quiet harmony.

It felt almost magical, the way she could turn a space that had been so cold, so quiet, into something warm, inviting, almost alive again. The wreaths and garlands had a softness to them that matched the way she was beginning to move through her days. More than anything, there was a steadiness about her, a quiet strength that hadn't been there before.

I could still see the traces of what she'd been through, though. The pain was never far, lurking just beneath the surface like a shadow that refused to fade away. But for the first time in a long while, she seemed to be finding her way back, inch by inch, one moment at a time. It wasn't perfect, but it was real. And somehow, in the midst of everything else, I realized that was all any of us could ask for.

I stood in the living room, my gaze fixed on the soft glow of the tree. The lights were dim, casting gentle pools of warmth across the room, and I could hear the distant sound of Mom's humming, her voice barely audible beneath the layers of memory. It should have been peaceful, should have felt like something close to home. But there was a strange, unsettled feeling in my chest that I couldn't shake.

Trevor.

He was still stuck.

While Mom was rebuilding, Trevor had become this version of himself I couldn't reach. The anger that radiated off him felt like a thick, impenetrable wall, one that kept him separated from all of us, like he was caught in a place he didn't know how to leave. It was a rage that I couldn't begin to understand, and I felt helpless in the face of it, unsure of how to break through.

I hadn't seen him laugh in weeks. No real smiles. Just the same cold expression, the same rigid posture. The game controller in his hands was like a lifeline he couldn't bear to put down. The few times we spoke were brief, clipped, like he was guarding his emotions with everything he had left, hiding behind his anger, because maybe that was easier than facing the truth of everything that had happened.

But sometimes, there were small glimpses of him. Moments when the mask would slip, just for a second, and I'd catch a flash of my brother—the one I used to know. It was like seeing a flicker of light in the distance, fading before I could touch it. But it was enough to keep me hanging on, to keep me trying. I just wasn't sure if I'd ever find the way to him again.

The truth was, I wasn't sure if I could fix anything. Maybe no one could. But the way Mom was rebuilding herself—slowly, carefully, one step at a time—gave me a strange kind of hope. Maybe there was a way forward for all of us, even if it didn't feel like it right now.

I wandered into the kitchen, the smell of cinnamon and sugar filling the air, and I found Mom at the counter, carefully frosting sugar cookies. The soft red apron she wore—something she'd bought after Dad left, a small act of rebellion against the dark cloud hanging over our house—was a small sign of how much she'd changed. It wasn't much, but it was something. I didn't say anything at first, just leaned against the doorframe, watching her move.

She glanced up and smiled, that small, peaceful smile she wore these days. It was the kind of smile that didn't promise everything was perfect, but it promised that we were okay for now. And that was enough.

"Want one?" she asked, her voice gentle.

I nodded, crossing the room to grab a warm cookie from the tray she had just pulled out of the oven. I bit into it, savoring the sweetness, and for a moment, I could almost pretend things were normal. That this—this holiday, this house, this family—was what it had always been.

But the ache in my chest, the gnawing doubt, reminded me that it wasn't that simple.

"Where's Trevor?" Mom asked, her tone light but tinged with a quiet worry.

I swallowed, the cookie suddenly feeling dry in my throat. "I don't know," I said softly. "Probably in his room."

"Is he... is he okay?" Her eyes held something I

couldn't name—concern, maybe, or a kind of helplessness she wasn't used to feeling.

I hesitated. I wasn't sure what "okay" even looked like anymore. "He's just… not talking much," I said finally. "He's really shut off."

Mom's shoulders slumped slightly, a subtle shift, but I saw it. The weight of everything she'd carried for so long was still there, in the way her movements slowed when the conversation turned to Trevor. I could see the same longing in her eyes—the same desperate desire to make things better. But we both knew it wasn't that simple.

"I don't know how to fix him, Mom," I said, my voice barely above a whisper. "I don't even know if he wants to be fixed."

Mom set down the frosting knife, her hands still and steady, and met my eyes. "We just have to be here for him," she said quietly, her words soft but firm. "Sometimes, that's all we can do. He'll come around when he's ready."

I nodded, even though I wasn't sure I believed her. Sometimes, it felt like we were all waiting for something—waiting for Trevor to forgive Dad, waiting for me to find my way back to who I used to be, waiting for something to change. But the waiting didn't feel like progress. It felt like time slipping through our fingers, taking pieces of us with it.

I grabbed another cookie, biting into it with a little more force this time. Mom was right about one thing. We could only take things one day at a time. And today, I was trying my best to believe that, even if the ache in my chest made it hard to breathe.

Ryan had left for college right on the nick of time. I could tell he was excited—more than excited, even—but there was something else, too, something unspoken. A quiet sadness, like a piece of him didn't quite want to go, even though he was running full speed toward everything he'd dreamed of. The reality of it, though, was harder to face. Ryan, my constant, my best friend, was walking away. And it felt like an end I wasn't ready for.

The airport was overwhelming, the noise reverberating through the cavernous terminal. People bustled past, their faces a blur, too wrapped up in their own goodbyes and reunions to notice the weight of my own. The coldness of the metal floors seemed to echo in my chest, and the distant hum of the announcements felt like a backdrop to the growing emptiness inside me.

I stood there, frozen for a moment, watching

Ryan adjust the strap of his backpack as he paced in front of the security checkpoint. He looked different— older, somehow—but I couldn't quite put my finger on it. Maybe it was the way he moved, more purposeful now, or maybe it was just the way his eyes lingered a little longer on things he used to glance at without thinking. I could tell that when he boarded that plane, everything would change. We wouldn't be the same. The air would feel different without him in it.

"Are you sure you packed everything?" I asked, trying to sound casual.

Ryan smirked. "Yes, Mom. I've got everything. Toothbrush included."

I rolled my eyes, but it didn't stop the lump from forming in my throat. "It's going to be weird without you here," I admitted, almost in a whisper. The words tasted foreign on my tongue, like they didn't quite fit. How could I even explain it? How could I make him understand that in a world where nothing felt stable anymore, where everything was shifting and breaking, his absence felt like the final straw?

"You'll survive," he said, but his teasing tone softened. "You always do."

We'd always been close, even when things were at their worst. He had been the steady anchor during all the chaos, the one I could always count on. Before he left, he told me something I hadn't expected, something that surprised me in the way only Ryan could.

"I've been working with the French police," he said, his tone casual, like it wasn't a big deal. "After our run-in with Dante, they asked for my help. I've been in contact with them about some other cases."

I stared at him, blinking. "Wait, what? You're working with the French police?"

He grinned, that mischievous glint in his eyes that always made me second-guess everything. "Yep. Always one step ahead, right?"

I laughed, shaking my head in disbelief. "You really can't sit still, can you?"

Ryan shrugged, the grin never leaving his face. "Guess not. Just wanted to make sure you're okay. But hey, if you need anything, you know how to reach me."

The announcement for his flight crackled overhead, and he glanced at the gate. "Guess that's me."

"Guess it is."

He stepped closer, pulling me into a tight hug. For a moment, neither of us said anything, the noise of the airport fading into the background.

"I'll call you," he said finally, his voice quiet against my hair. "Every day, if you want."

I smiled against his shoulder. "Don't make promises you can't keep."

He pulled back, his hands lingering on my arms. "You're going to be okay, Nat. I mean it."

I nodded, but the lump in my throat only grew. I wanted to say something, anything that would hold this moment in place. That would make him stay. But I couldn't. There was nothing to say.

Instead, I reached out, giving him a quick hug, a tight squeeze that I wasn't sure how to let go of. When we pulled apart, I could see the words that had been hovering between us, just below the surface, wanting to break free. The words that felt like too much to say.

"I'll miss you," I said, finally. It felt too small, like it couldn't possibly contain everything that was tumbling through my heart.

He smiled, but it was the kind of smile that didn't quite reach his eyes, the kind of smile that said he was trying to make it easier on both of us. "I'll miss you too, Nat."

And then he was gone, stepping through the security gate, walking away into the new chapter of his life. I watched him go, the finality of it pressing against me, until he disappeared into the crowd, until the whole world went back to its noise and chaos. But I stayed there, standing alone in the middle of it all, feeling a little bit more empty than before.

I hadn't realized just how much I relied on Ryan, on his constant presence in my life. His jokes, his sarcastic remarks, the way he could make me laugh even on my worst days—those things were anchors, tiny pieces of stability in a world that was anything but. And now, he was gone. And it felt like I was drifting.

I tried to push the feeling away, but it lingered, an unwelcome guest in my chest. The world had a way of shifting beneath your feet when you weren't looking, and for the first time in a long time, I felt like I was losing my balance. Everything had changed. The pieces of my life were still scattered, still out of reach, and I wasn't sure how to put them back together.

I missed him more than I cared to admit, even if our texts were fewer than I wanted. He was living his life, and I was happy for him. But I couldn't help but feel a little left behind.

As for me, I was somewhere in between. Caught in the messy, complicated space of healing and remembering. It was like trying to walk through a fog, not sure which direction to take. But for the first time in a long time, it didn't feel so impossible. The weight wasn't as heavy, and the path forward, while still unclear, felt like something I could face.

I spent my days helping out Grandpa at his store. The quiet, slow rhythm of his shop was a kind of therapy. The smell of old wood, the soft murmur of customers chatting, the feeling of my hands wrapped around a broom or a rag—it was grounding, like I could breathe again. The routine was simple, and for a little while, it was exactly what I needed.

The house smelled like pine and cinnamon, the scent of Christmas filling every room. The low hum of Christmas music from the old radio Mom insisted on using this time of year made everything feel like it was wrapped in a soft, nostalgic blanket. It wasn't a perfect Christmas, but it was close enough. The tree stood in the corner of the living room, its lights casting soft shadows across the walls. Trevor and I had argued over ornaments, as usual, but somehow, despite the bickering, it ended up looking perfect.

The laughter, the small scuffles over which ornaments went where, the quiet moments of reflection—there was something about this Christmas that made it feel real. Mom moved through the house like she was trying to soak it all in, her eyes scanning every corner, every decoration, every little detail. She hummed along to Silent Night as she rearranged the stockings on the mantle, her steps lighter than they'd been in years.

Christmas gave Trevor something to focus on, something to be part of. He wasn't completely open, still holding a lot inside, but the distance between us seemed to shrink just a little, and for that, I was grateful.

It felt like a Christmas miracle—small, quiet, but undeniable. A miracle that wasn't about big gestures or grand changes, but about the slow, steady work of healing. About learning how to live with the hurt, without letting it define us.

And maybe that's all we could really ask for. A little peace. A little room to breathe.

As I sat on the couch, watching the light from the tree twinkle in the window, I felt it—what had been missing for so long. I felt like maybe, just maybe, everything wasn't lost. Not yet.

The living room felt warmer than it had in years. The Christmas tree stood in the corner, its lights casting a soft, golden glow over the worn furniture and neatly wrapped gifts. The faint scent of pine mingled with the aroma of Mom's tea—peppermint, her favorite during the holidays.

Trevor was sprawled on the couch, one foot propped on the armrest, his game controller clicking rhythmically. Mom sat in her favorite chair by the window, cradling her tea with both hands, her gaze distant but peaceful.

I perched on the edge of the coffee table, turning the idea over and over in my mind. The words were on the tip of my tongue, but I wasn't sure how to say them. How to make them real.

Finally, I spoke. "I think we need to stop talking about him."

Trevor's controller stilled mid-click. He frowned, glancing at me. "What?"

"Dad," I clarified, my voice steadier than I felt. "I think... I think it's time we let him go."

Mom's cup paused halfway to her lips. She set it down carefully, her lips pressing into a thin line. "You mean pretend he doesn't exist?"

"No," I said quickly, shaking my head. "Not that. Just... stop letting him take up so much space. In our lives, in our heads. We can't keep waiting for something to change. He's not coming back."

Trevor stared at me for a long moment, his expression unreadable. Then, with a sigh, he dropped the controller onto his lap. "Fine by me. I'm sick of hearing about him anyway."

His tone was sharp, but there was an undercurrent of hurt there, too, one I didn't think he'd ever admit.

Mom didn't respond right away. Her gaze shifted to the twinkling lights on the tree, her fingers tracing the edge of her cup. I could see the conflict in her eyes—the tug of old memories, the weight of years spent holding us together without him.

Finally, she nodded. "You're right," she said softly. "It's time. We've spent too long trying to figure out the 'what ifs.' We have to focus on what we have, not what we've lost."

Her words hung in the air, and I felt something shift. It was subtle, but it was there—a loosening of the knot I hadn't realized I'd been carrying for so long.

Later that night, Mom called up the stairs, her voice light but a bit frantic. "Natalie! Trevor! I need your help getting the box from the attic!"

"I'm busy!" Trevor's voice floated through the thin walls of his room, a few gunshots and rapid clicks from his video game seeping through the door.

"I'll do it," I said, already moving before I'd even finished the sentence.

The attic was one of those places that felt both

familiar and forgotten. The air was thick with dust, the wooden beams sagging slightly under the weight of memories. The only light was from a single bare bulb that flickered as I reached up and pulled the ladder down. The scent of old wood and forgotten things hit me immediately—a musty mixture of cardboard, fabric, and time itself.

I climbed up the rickety stairs, my hand brushing against old toys, forgotten furniture, and shelves stacked with things we hadn't touched in years. The box Mom always asked for, the one labeled Christmas Memories, sat where it always did, tucked into the corner. I pulled it down and felt the weight of nostalgia hit me, but as I lifted it, another box shifted slightly underneath it.

"What's this?" I murmured to myself, reaching for the smaller box wedged in the shadows.

I didn't remember it being there. There were no labels, just a plain cardboard box, sealed with old, crinkled tape. Curiosity got the better of me. I tugged it free from its hiding place and carried it downstairs, the silence in the house thick around me.

"Mom, what's this?" I asked, entering the living room with the box in hand. She was at the sink, drying off a dish, the scent of cinnamon from the candles still in the air.

She glanced up, brow furrowing slightly as she wiped her hands on a dish towel. "I have no idea. What does it say?"

I shook my head and gently placed the box on the table. "Nothing. Just a plain box."

Her eyes flicked to it, then back to me, and I could see the hesitation in her movements as she wiped her hands again, her focus on the strange box now. "Well… let's see, then."

She carefully pried open the box with a kind of reverence, like it might contain something too delicate, too precious to rush. Inside was an envelope, crinkled with age, and when she pulled it out, I saw what was inside. Bundles of cash, tied neatly together with rubber bands.

"Mom…" I said, the words hanging in the air as she stared down at the money.

Her fingers trembled slightly as she touched the cash, flipping through the bills, her face slowly draining of color. "What on earth…" she whispered, her voice faltering.

I stepped closer, unsure of what to say, unsure of what was happening.

She opened the envelope slowly, and the look on

her face shifted from confusion to something softer, something I couldn't quite place. Her breath caught in her throat, and she brought her hand to her mouth. Tears welled in her eyes, and she whispered again, "How was this here? How..."

I stood frozen in place, feeling the weight of the moment. I'd kept the secret from her—the money wasn't from John. It wasn't from some mysterious benefactor. It was from me. A part of what we'd recovered from the scammer, money I'd hidden for her, knowing she needed something tangible, something real to hold onto. Something to give her hope when she didn't know where to find it.

"Mom, I..." My voice faltered, but she held up a hand, cutting me off, her face a mixture of awe and something deeper.

"This is a sign," she said, her voice stronger now, her grip on the money tight. She looked up at me, her eyes filled with something like relief, like she had finally exhaled after holding her breath for far too long. "This is a sign that we can move forward. Really move forward."

Her words hung in the air, heavy with meaning. For a second, I almost didn't want to tell her the truth. I didn't need to. I could see it in her face—this was her peace, her moment of closure. Her hand gently clutched the cash to her chest as if it were a promise, a new beginning.

I watched her, my heart twisting in my chest. There was something in her face, a softening I hadn't seen in a long time, something that made me feel like maybe, just maybe, everything was going to be okay.

And for the first time, I didn't feel the need to explain. I didn't need to tell her that I was the one who'd given her the money. The truth, in this moment, didn't matter. It was her belief in something bigger, her ability to see hope in the smallest of things, that made all the difference. The world could be falling apart, but if she could believe, if she could move forward, then maybe I could, too.

"Thank you," she said softly, her voice thick with emotion. "Thank you for this, for believing we could."

I swallowed the lump in my throat, nodding. "I'm just glad you're okay."

She smiled, and I saw that it was genuine—like she had finally found a way to heal, even if it was just a little bit. For the first time in what felt like forever, I wasn't sure if it was my actions that had fixed things, or hers. Maybe we both had a role in this.

And in that moment, the weight of everything—

the anger, the confusion, the hurt—seemed just a little bit lighter.

Maybe, just maybe, we were already moving forward.

That night, the house was quiet. Trevor had gone to bed early, and Mom was in her room, humming a tune as she wrapped the last of the presents.

I slipped outside, the cold biting at my cheeks as I settled near the fire pit. The sky was clear, stars scattered like tiny diamonds against the inky blackness.

In my hands was the envelope I'd carried all the way from France, the letter Dad had written to Mom still tucked neatly inside.

The paper felt heavy, its edges softened from where I'd unfolded and refolded it countless times. It wasn't just a letter—it was a reminder of everything we'd lost, everything we'd tried to hold onto.

I stared at the flames, their warmth licking at the chilled air, and took a deep breath.

For so long, I'd clung to the idea of my father as someone perfect. Someone who could do no wrong. But the man I'd found in Europe wasn't perfect. He was flawed, broken in ways I might never fully understand.

And that was okay.

He wasn't the father I thought he was, but he wasn't a villain either. Just human.

Slowly, I held the letter over the fire. The edges curled and blackened, the paper folding in on itself as the flames consumed it. Ash rose into the night sky, disappearing into the darkness.

I let go of a breath I didn't realize I'd been holding.

Letting go didn't mean forgetting. It meant moving forward, carrying the memories without letting them weigh me down.

It meant choosing to remember the good, without being haunted by the bad.

As the last of the letter disappeared into the flames, I felt something inside me settle. It wasn't a perfect peace—there was still hurt, still questions—but it was enough.

I looked up at the stars, the cold air biting but invigorating. For the first time in a long time, I felt like I could breathe.

CHAPTER 24: A NEW YEAR

The snow had started falling a few days after Christmas, blanketing the yard in a soft white glow. It was the kind of snowfall that made everything feel quieter, softer, as if the world had decided to hush itself just for a moment. I sat on the porch swing, wrapped in a thick sweater, watching the flakes drift lazily under the streetlamp. The world felt peaceful, the kind of quiet that makes you feel like you're the only person awake, the only one who can still hear the muffled rhythm of your heartbeat, your breath in the cold night air.

It had been a quiet Christmas. The house was fuller than it had been in months, but something about it felt incomplete without Ryan, without his jokes and his laugh, the way he always knew how to break the tension when it crept into the room. I missed him more than I thought I would. But then, just a few days after Christmas, he made it home—arriving in time to ring in the New Year with me. That felt like a Christmas miracle of its own.

Ryan appeared in the doorway a moment later, two steaming mugs in his hands. "Hot chocolate," he announced, his voice light but warm in the cold night. "Extra marshmallows, because I know you're a purist."

I couldn't help but smile. "Thanks."

He handed me one of the mugs, and I wrapped my fingers around it, feeling the warmth seep into my hands. The night air was biting, but with the mug in my hands, everything felt a little more bearable. He sat beside me, the swing creaking slightly under his weight. For a while, we just sat there in silence, watching the snow pile up on the railing, the world outside quiet except for the occasional sound of a car crunching over the snow-covered road.

"Feels weird, doesn't it?" Ryan finally said, his voice low but steady.

"What does?"

"Being back. After everything." He paused, glancing over at me, his expression a little uncertain, but also understanding. "I don't know. It's like we're here, but not all the way here. Like we left a piece of ourselves somewhere along the way."

I nodded, taking a sip from my mug. "Yeah. Exactly. It's like I'm here, but I'm not. Like I left some part of me behind."

Ryan's gaze softened, and he shifted next to me. "That's not a bad thing, Nat. It means you grew. You're not the same person you were when we left. None of us are."

I glanced down at my mug, swirling the marshmallows around with the tip of my finger. "I don't know what happens next, Ryan. Everything feels... unsettled. Like nothing is really certain."

He leaned back against the swing's frame, his shoulders relaxed. "That's the best part, isn't it? Not knowing." He shot me a grin. "Makes life more interesting, don't you think?"

I rolled my eyes, but a small laugh escaped me. "You and your endless optimism."

"Hey, it got us through Europe, didn't it?" he said with a wink.

I chuckled, the sound lighter than I'd expected. "I guess it did."

The night stretched out around us, the snow falling gently, the only sounds the occasional scrape of boots against snow and the faint music from inside the house. There was a peacefulness between us now, something comfortable and real. We didn't need words to fill the space; just the steady swing of the porch, the crackling warmth from our mugs, and the shared understanding that, despite everything, we were here together.

Ryan shifted again, leaning slightly toward me. "You know, you were amazing through all of this. You never gave up, even when everything felt impossible."

I felt the heat rise in my cheeks, embarrassed by the unexpected compliment. "Ryan…" I started, but he held up a hand, stopping me.

"Let me finish," he said, his tone quieter now, more serious. "You're stronger than you think, Nat. And yeah, maybe you leaned on me a little. But you don't realize how much I leaned on you, too. You kept me going, even when I thought I couldn't keep going."

His words made my chest tighten, and for a second, the warmth from the hot chocolate didn't feel like it was enough to explain the heat rushing to my face. I didn't know how to respond, not without feeling exposed.

"You're not too bad yourself," I managed, my voice barely above a whisper.

He smiled then, the kind of smile that made his dimples appear, the one that always made my heart skip a beat. And before I could overthink it, before I could second-guess myself, I leaned in and kissed him.

It wasn't perfect. The swing wobbled beneath us, and I nearly spilled my mug in the process, but it was real. It felt like the final piece of something I hadn't even known was missing. Like something I had been waiting for without even realizing it.

When we pulled apart, Ryan's grin widened, the playful edge returning to his voice. "Took you long enough."

I laughed, the sound bubbling up without restraint, and I nudged his shoulder, feeling lighter than I had in a long time. "Shut up."

We fell into a comfortable silence again, but this time it felt different. It felt like the beginning of something new. The snow continued to fall around us, soft and silent, as if the world was giving us the space to breathe, to settle into this moment.

The morning kitchen smelled like coffee and fresh-baked banana bread, a cozy, comforting warmth that filled the room with a sense of peace I hadn't felt in months. For a moment, it felt like everything could be okay, at least for a little while. The world outside, with all its complications and unanswered questions, seemed far away. Here, in this moment, it was just me and my mom—silent, but together.

Mom sat across from me at the table, her fingers

wrapped around her mug. I watched as she traced the rim absently, the faint lipstick stain a small sign of a life lived beyond the kitchen. Her eyes were distant, focused somewhere just past the window, as if she was gathering her thoughts—or maybe preparing herself for something. I didn't push her. I knew better by now. When she was ready to speak, she'd speak.

Finally, she looked up, her gaze steady but soft. "You know, I've been thinking a lot about your dad," she said, the words falling between us like a confession.

Here it was. The conversation I'd been avoiding but knew was coming, the one I'd been bracing myself for without even realizing it.

"Yeah?" I said, trying to keep my tone even, to sound like it was just another ordinary conversation.

She nodded, her fingers tightening slightly around the mug as she took a slow sip of coffee. She set it down gently on the table, but I could see the weight of what she was about to say, the quiet hesitation in her eyes.

"I think I've spent so much time being angry at him that I never really thought about us," she said softly. "About what we were before all this."

I couldn't breathe for a moment, the air suddenly thick with her words. "What do you mean?"

She glanced out the window, her eyes flicking to the backyard, where the sunlight made the snow glitter like tiny stars. "Your dad and I… we were never in love the way you'd hope. Not in the storybook sense, anyway. We got together because it made sense. We were young, we cared about each other, and then life just… happened."

I leaned forward, surprised by the sudden vulnerability in her voice. "You're saying you never loved him?"

She shook her head, and a small, rueful smile touched her lips. "It's not that simple. I did love him, in my way. But it wasn't the kind of love that makes you want to run away to Paris together. It was the kind that gets up early to make school lunches and fixes leaky faucets. Practical love."

The honesty of her words hit me harder than I'd expected. For so long, I'd clung to this image of my parents as perfect partners, as the unshakable foundation of our family, and here she was, dismantling that picture piece by piece. The idea that love could be something less than this grand, sweeping gesture felt like an entire worldview shifting beneath me.

"Then why stay?" I asked softly, the question

slipping out before I could stop it. "If it wasn't like that, why stay?"

"Because it was the right thing to do," she said simply, her voice steady, as if she had said this a thousand times before. "For you, for Trevor, for the life we built. Responsibility, Natalie. It's not as romantic as love, but sometimes it's what keeps things together."

Her words hung in the air, a quiet truth that filled the space between us with a heaviness I hadn't expected. I had always believed that love was the thing that made everything worth it. But this… this was something different. Something far more complicated.

She reached across the table, her hand warm as it covered mine. The touch was small, but it felt like the bridge between everything we had been and everything we might become. "But that doesn't mean that has to be your story," she said, her voice low but firm.

I stared at her, confused. "What do you mean?"

"I mean, don't do what I did," she said, her voice stronger now. "Don't settle for what feels safe. Don't let responsibility keep you from going after what you really want. Love, adventure, freedom—whatever it is, go after it unapologetically."

I sat there, staring at her, the weight of her words

sinking in. The idea that I had permission to live differently, to choose something bigger than the life I had known, felt like a permission slip to the life I had never dared to imagine. Could I really do that? Could I go after what I wanted, even if it meant breaking the rules, defying expectations?

"You really think I can do that?" I asked quietly, not entirely sure if I was asking her or myself.

"I know you can," she said, squeezing my hand. "You've already proven it. Look at what you've done this summer, Natalie. You faced the hardest truths head-on, even when they scared you. If anyone can live freely, it's you."

Her words washed over me, a wave of understanding that felt like the first time someone had ever seen me for who I truly was—who I could become. For the first time, I saw her not just as my mom, the woman who took care of everything, who kept the house running and the family together, but as a woman who had made choices, sacrifices, dreams deferred. She had carried burdens I might never fully understand, and now, she was asking me to take a different path. A path where I could choose for myself, without fear of what came next.

"I'll try," I said finally, my voice quieter but full of

the kind of determination I hadn't known I had until that moment.

She smiled, her eyes glistening. "That's all I ask."

I sat there, my mind racing, the weight of her words settling into my chest like a seed, ready to grow. And in that moment, I knew—this wasn't just a conversation about my future. It was about my mother, too. About the things she had sacrificed, the dreams she had let go of for the sake of our family. And now, she was passing that chance on to me.

The question was, would I take it?

The New Year's eve air was crisp and biting as Ryan and I trudged through the snow-covered field, our breath visible in the cold night. My hands were stuffed deep into the pockets of my coat, but even that wasn't enough to keep them warm.

"You know," I said, my teeth chattering, "when you said 'romantic New Year's surprise,' I didn't think it would involve frostbite."

Ryan turned to me, his nose red from the cold, and flashed that crooked grin of his. "Trust me, it'll be worth it. Just a little further."

"A little further?" I muttered, glancing down at my boots, which were now dusted with snow. "This better include hot chocolate or I'm never forgiving you."

He laughed, the sound warm and familiar, cutting through the icy stillness of the night.

We finally reached the spot—a small clearing just outside of town, surrounded by tall, frost-covered trees. Ryan had laid out a blanket, complete with fairy lights and a thermos sitting in the middle.

"Ta-da," he said, spreading his arms as if unveiling a masterpiece.

I stared at him, then at the setup. "You do realize it's, like, twenty degrees out here, right?"

He rubbed the back of his neck, sheepish. "It seemed more romantic in my head."

"Romantic hypothermia," I teased, dropping down onto the blanket anyway.

He joined me, opening the thermos and pouring steaming hot cider into two mismatched mugs. "Okay, so maybe it's not perfect. But at least we've got this."

I took the mug, cradling it in my hands for warmth. The cider smelled of cinnamon and apples, and I couldn't help but smile. "You're lucky this is good cider."

"Lucky, huh?" He bumped his shoulder against mine, his grin softening.

The stars above us were bright, scattered across the sky like someone had spilled glitter on a black canvas. For a moment, the cold didn't matter.

Then a sudden gust of wind cut through the clearing, making us both shiver.

"Okay, plan B," Ryan announced, grabbing the blanket and thermos.

"What's plan B?" I asked, following him as he headed toward the car.

He held up the keys, jingling them like they were the answer to everything. "A front-row seat to the countdown… with heated seats."

Minutes later, we were huddled in his car, the engine running and the heater blasting. The blanket was draped across our laps, and the thermos sat between us in the cup holder.

"This," I said, holding up my mug, "is way better."

"Noted for next year," he replied, his voice warm with amusement.

The radio played quietly in the background, a countdown ticking closer to midnight. Outside, the world was still, the snow glowing softly under the moonlight.

"Thanks for trying, though," I added after a moment. "The effort was… sweet."

His expression softened. "You know I'd do anything to make you happy, right?"

I looked at him, the words catching me off guard. They weren't grand or flashy, but they felt real. Honest.

And that's when it hit me—clear and undeniable.

I didn't just like Ryan. I loved him.

The countdown on the radio reached its final moments, the announcer's voice rising with excitement.

"Ten… nine…"

Ryan turned to me, his eyes catching mine.

"Eight… seven…"

I swallowed, my heart pounding.

"Six… five…"

"Nat," he said quietly, his voice cutting through the noise.

"Four… three…"

"Yeah?" I whispered, my breath catching.

"Two…"

Instead of answering, he leaned in and kissed me, his lips warm and soft, chasing away the cold.

The announcer's voice shouted, "One! Happy New Year!"

But I barely heard it.

When we finally pulled back, I couldn't help but laugh, my cheeks burning despite the cold. "Happy New Year," I murmured.

"Happy New Year," he replied, his grin as bright as the stars outside.

In that moment, I knew for certain. Ryan wasn't just my best friend. He wasn't just the boy who'd been there for me when I felt lost and broken. He was more.

And for the first time in a long time, I felt like I knew exactly where I was supposed to be.

CHAPTER 25: THE LAST SUMMER I REMEMBER

The winter had faded into spring, and now summer was slowly giving way to autumn. The world felt like it was exhaling, the frost melting into tiny streams that trickled along the edges of the sidewalk. The trees were shedding their summer coats, turning golden and auburn, the leaves swirling around in a slow dance before settling on the ground. It was the kind of day that felt both peaceful and melancholic, like the universe was sighing with relief, as though it too had been holding its breath for far too long.

I sat on the porch swing, wrapped in an old woolen blanket my mom had knitted years ago. The swing creaked slightly as the breeze moved through the trees, but the rhythm was calming, like a quiet heartbeat. My mind, however, wasn't still. It never was. Even after everything, I hadn't learned to quiet the noise that lived inside me. But today, it was different. The ache was there, tucked somewhere in the back of my chest, but it no longer screamed. It had settled, become a part of me, a constant hum I carried with me instead of a roar that threatened to overwhelm.

Grandpa sat beside me, his eyes on the horizon where the last light of the day was casting long shadows over the yard. He wasn't saying much, but I could feel him there—steady, a presence that somehow made everything feel more manageable. Like he was still holding on to the thread that kept everything from unraveling.

"How are you holding up, kiddo?" he asked, his voice as gruff as ever, but there was a softness in it now, like the years had worn away the sharp edges.

I shrugged, pulling the blanket tighter around me. "It's… a lot. Still processing, I guess. But I'm okay. I think I'm okay."

He didn't respond right away, his gaze still focused on the fading light. "I always thought you were tougher than you let on," he said quietly. "You've got more strength in you than most people realize."

I chuckled softly, the sound almost surprised. "I think I've learned that the hard way."

Grandpa looked over at me then, his expression soft but knowing. "Sometimes the hardest lessons are the ones that stick. And you've been through your fair share of them."

I nodded, feeling the weight of his words settle over me like the blanket I was wrapped in. It hadn't been an easy road, and it wasn't over. I'd lost pieces of myself along the way, pieces I wasn't sure I'd ever get back. The mystery of my dad had unraveled in ways I hadn't expected, and while the truth had come to light, it hadn't been the neat, satisfying conclusion I'd imagined. Instead, it had left a trail of confusion and questions, things I didn't know how to fit together. But the urgency had faded. The need to have all the answers had slipped into something quieter—an understanding that some things weren't meant to be fully understood.

I thought about Ryan, how the connection between us had deepened over the months, how we had grown together, learning how to trust each other with pieces of ourselves we hadn't shown anyone else. Our love wasn't perfect, but it was real, and it was enough. Sometimes that was all I could ask for.

"I miss Grandma," I said suddenly, my voice softer than I expected. It had been a while since I'd said her name out loud.

Grandpa gave me a small, sad smile, but there was no bitterness in it. Just the quiet understanding that comes with years of remembering. "I miss her too, Nat. She was one of a kind."

I smiled faintly, the weight of my own grief suddenly feeling like a gentle tug on my chest. It wasn't the sharp pain it used to be. It had dulled over time, like a wound that had started to heal, but still left a scar. "Do you ever wish you could just… talk to her again? Like you used to?"

He paused, his gaze drifting to the trees lining the yard. The sun was setting now, casting a golden glow over everything. "Every day," he said quietly. "But she's still with us, in the ways she taught us to love, the ways she showed us how to keep going. You carry that with you."

I looked at him, studying the lines in his face, the way time had etched its mark on him. He had always been a man of few words, but there was something in his eyes now that I couldn't quite place. Vulnerability, maybe. Or perhaps just the knowledge that life was slipping away, bit by bit, and we couldn't hold on to everything.

"I wish I could tell her about everything that's happened," I said, my voice barely above a whisper. "About everything I've learned."

Grandpa nodded slowly. "She already knows,

sweetheart. Somewhere out there, she knows."

A quiet silence settled between us, the kind that felt like it could stretch on forever, but didn't need to be filled with words. I was learning how to sit in moments like this—how to feel the weight of everything that had come before without letting it define me. I didn't have all the answers. I didn't have a perfect plan for what came next. But I was starting to realize that maybe that was okay. Maybe the point wasn't to have everything figured out, but to just keep moving forward, one step at a time.

The world around us was shifting again, the seasons changing, the air growing cooler. And as I sat there with my grandpa, wrapped in the blanket, I felt like I was finally starting to understand what it meant to let go of the past while still carrying the pieces of it that mattered.

It had taken many months of silence from the police before I got the call.

"Miss Donovan?" The officer's voice was clipped, professional, but not unkind. "I wanted to let you know we're officially closing your father's case. It'll remain listed as inactive, but there's no further investigation planned at this time."

I felt the words drop into the pit of my stomach,

heavy and unyielding. Part of me wanted to argue, to demand that they keep looking—keep searching, keep asking questions that would lead to answers. Anything, just to keep the possibility alive. But I knew, deep down, that no amount of arguing would change the fact that we were out of answers. That the man I had spent so long trying to understand was now just a ghost, and no amount of police reports or unanswered questions could bring him back.

"Thank you for letting me know," I said finally, my voice thick with a bitterness I couldn't swallow down fast enough.

The officer paused, the hum of the phone line filling the silence. "There's one more thing," he said, his tone shifting slightly. "Your dad's Jeep... it's been released from impound. You can pick it up anytime."

The Jeep. It hadn't crossed my mind in months, but the mention of it hit me like a freight train. I remembered the endless drives we used to take, the wind rushing through the windows, music cranked up so loud it drowned out the rest of the world. It felt like a different lifetime, back when Dad had been alive, and everything had felt... possible. It was a piece of him, still waiting, collecting dust in a forgotten lot, just like me.

"Okay," I whispered, barely able to choke out the word.

That was how it began—the Jeep wasn't just a reminder of the life we'd lost. It was a piece of him that I couldn't let go of, a chance to reclaim something that felt like it was mine again. So, the next weekend, I picked it up from the impound lot. It was dusty, its once bright red paint dulled by time and neglect, but underneath, it was still solid, still standing.

"I think we can fix you up," I whispered to it, running my hand along the hood. The Jeep, like me, had seen better days. But unlike me, it could be repaired.

The house was quiet when I brought it home, Mom sitting at the kitchen table with her hands wrapped around a mug of tea, her eyes tired and distant. "It's yours if you want it," she said quietly, almost as if she didn't want to disturb the silence that had become our new normal. "But if it's too much, we can sell it."

Trevor didn't even look up from his phone. "I don't care what you do with it," he muttered.

I didn't say anything right away. I just stood there, staring at the Jeep in the driveway, at the way the fading light made the dust on it look like a thin veil over the memories we used to make inside it. It was more than just a vehicle. It was the last connection to a life I had wanted to preserve, and I wasn't ready to let it go.

That weekend, I spent hours in the garage, going over every inch of it, tracing the lines of the body with my fingers, pulling off the parts that were worn and rusted. There was something therapeutic about it, about getting my hands dirty, about the process of turning something broken into something that could still work.

I was halfway through trying to replace the spark plugs when Jamie Garner showed up.

"Your hands are covered in grease," he said, his voice flat, but the concern underneath was unmistakable. His eyes were focused on the engine in front of me, a subtle tension in his jaw.

"I noticed," I replied, wiping my hands on an old rag. "You want to help?"

Jamie, who had always been the quiet genius, leaned in, his fingers moving with precision as he started pointing out things I'd missed, offering advice like he could see every part of the car's inner workings in his head before even touching them. His mind worked in a way mine didn't—logical, precise, always five steps ahead. But this wasn't just about fixing the

Jeep. It was about him, in his own way, offering me something I didn't even know I needed: understanding.

"That's not how you align the carburetor," he muttered under his breath, adjusting the tool in my hand with a precision that made my head spin. "The angle's off. It'll never run right."

I blinked, trying to absorb what he was saying. "How do you know all of this?" I asked, half-laughing.

Jamie shrugged, his eyes focused entirely on the task at hand. "I read the manual. A few hundred times. Plus, I've watched YouTube videos. They're not as good as real experience, but they're close."

I couldn't help but smile at him, feeling an unexpected burst of gratitude. "You're a freak, you know that?"

He glanced up at me, his lips twitching with the ghost of a smile. "You've said that before."

The hours passed with Jamie guiding me through the mechanical maze, each step more frustrating but also more rewarding. It wasn't about the Jeep anymore—it was about what I was learning along the way. About letting go of what was broken and creating something new. About fixing the parts of me that had felt damaged beyond repair.

By the time the sun had set, the garage smelled like

oil, metal, and the faint scent of the first rain of the season. It wasn't perfect—there were still things to fix, little adjustments to be made—but it was mine now. And in that moment, that was enough.

"You're getting better at this," Jamie said, his voice a little less flat than before.

I wiped my hands on my jeans, a laugh bubbling up from my chest. "Yeah, well, I've had a good teacher."

"You still have a long way to go," Jamie added, turning back to the engine. "But you'll get there."

I nodded, watching him work with a focus that I could never quite match. Maybe that was the one thing I would never have, and maybe that was okay. Because what I had was my own journey. My own way of fixing things, of moving forward.

It wasn't just about fixing the Jeep. It was about what came next.

I spent hours in the garage, hands coated in grease, trying to breathe life back into the machine that had once been a symbol of my dad's presence. But there was more to it than that. The Jeep had become something else over time—a lesson in patience, a symbol of reclaiming control when everything else in my life had felt out of my hands. I practiced in empty parking lots, late at night when the world around me was still, as quiet as my thoughts. There were moments when I stalled out, the engine sputtering, as if the Jeep itself was tired of waiting. My heart would race with frustration, my hands tight on the wheel, but then there were those glorious moments when everything clicked, when I shifted gears smoothly, feeling the hum of the engine beneath me, like a pulse. The first time it happened, I laughed out loud, startled by the sound of my own joy. The crows in the trees above took flight in protest, but I didn't care.

The freedom of it—the control—was everything I hadn't known I'd been searching for. I felt as if I was finally taking hold of my own story, driving it in the direction I wanted to go, instead of letting the past dictate where I ended up.

By spring, I felt ready.

Ready to stop living in the shadow of what was lost, and to start living in the light of what could be. Ready to drive forward, not just in the Jeep, but in my own life. The decision hadn't been sudden, but it felt like a slow unraveling, the way an old knot loosens after you've tugged at it for long enough. There had been grief, yes, but also something more—a growing sense of acceptance. I could never change the past. I could never bring my dad back. But I could choose to move forward, not in spite of the loss, but because of it.

There was a weight to this moment, an unspoken recognition that I was on the cusp of something—maybe something bigger than just a ride in an old Jeep. I wasn't sure where it would take me, but for the first time in a long time, I was okay with that. I wasn't planning to drive the Jeep just to prove I could fix it; I was driving it because I needed to.

On a clear morning, when the air was crisp with the promise of the changing seasons, I packed a bag and climbed into the driver's seat, my fingers brushing the steering wheel with an odd tenderness. The engine rumbled to life beneath me like a pulse, steady and sure. The road to Grey Lake stretched out before me, familiar in its winding curves, the trees along the sides starting to show the first hesitant green, as if the world itself were stretching after a long, cold winter.

When I arrived, the lake was still and quiet, its surface reflecting the pale blue sky like a giant mirror. The world seemed to be holding its breath, and I wasn't sure if it was because of me or because it just always felt this way here. This was where it had all started. The panic, the uncertainty, the questions that swirled around like the fog that sometimes rolled in over the water.

I parked the Jeep under the shade of an old oak tree, the sound of the engine sputtering to silence as I turned the key. I stepped out and let the breeze wash over me. The air smelled fresh—like new beginnings, like growth. It was the kind of morning that made you feel like you could do anything.

I got out of my Jeep, my boots crunching on the gravel as I approached the water's edge. The lake was as still as ever, its surface reflecting the blue sky above like a mirror. I walked to the water's edge, the familiar crunch of gravel under my boots grounding me in the present. There had been so much uncertainty before. The search for my dad, the endless questions about who he had been, who I was, and how all of that fit together. But now, standing there, I wasn't looking for answers anymore.

Dad had always loved this lake, and I suppose, in a way, I always had too. It wasn't because of its beauty—though it was beautiful, in its quiet way. It was because this lake had held pieces of my life that I needed to release, pieces I didn't even know how to let go of until now.

I pulled the Paris snow globe from my bag and stared at it for a moment. The Eiffel Tower inside it sparkled, a tiny glimmer of something beautiful, something I could never quite touch.

I knelt by the edge of the water, the gentle ripples sending small waves across the surface, and stared at the snow globe in my hand. It felt heavier than it ever had, filled with memories I wasn't sure I was ready to release. But it wasn't about keeping it anymore. It was about accepting that the past couldn't define me anymore.

"I think I understand why you liked Paris," I said softly, the words carried away by the breeze before they could go anywhere else. It was more than just a passing thought—it was a quiet admission to myself. I understood why Dad had chased those dreams, why he'd wanted to believe in something far away, something beautiful.

I raised my arm and tossed the snow globe into the water. It hit the surface with a soft splash, and then, like everything else, it disappeared. Gone. Just like that.

The ripples spread, delicate and slow, until they faded into nothing, just like the memories that had weighed on me.

I stood there, watching the spot where it sank, and felt something shift inside me. It wasn't sudden, dramatic. There were no bright lights or fireworks. It was a quiet moment, like the moment after a storm when the sky begins to clear. The tension, the questions, the guilt—it didn't disappear completely, but it began to unravel, thread by thread, leaving me with only the space to breathe, to be.

The girl who had left for Europe, searching for answers about her dad, was still there, still me. But she wasn't the same anymore. She had learned to let go. Not of the love, not of the memories, but of the idea that I could control them. That I could somehow fix everything. I could carry the weight of the past, but it didn't have to crush me.

I climbed back into the Jeep, the familiar smell of leather and old fabric surrounding me as I turned the key. The engine hummed beneath me, steady and strong, like an old friend. As I pulled away from the lake, the sun breaking through the trees around me, I felt something I hadn't felt in a long time: peace. Quiet, fragile peace. Not because everything was figured out or tied up in a neat little bow. But because I had found a way to move forward.

That summer had felt endless while I was living it. Every moment stretched tight with uncertainty, grief, anger, and hope, each day a battle between the old version of myself and the new one that was trying to emerge. But looking back, it was clear: it had been a bridge. A single, transformative season that carried me from one version of myself to another.

It wasn't just the summer I found my dad, or the summer I chased answers across Europe. It was the summer I learned what it meant to let go. To move forward, even when I didn't have all the answers.

It was an end.

It was a beginning.

And that was the best part.

THE END

ABOUT THE AUTHOR

Kathy Winslower is a gifted storyteller with a passion for weaving tales of love, resilience, and triumph. With her captivating narratives and richly drawn characters, she takes readers on unforgettable journeys that explore the depths of human emotions and the power of love to transform lives.

Born with an insatiable curiosity and a love for words, Kathy began her writing journey at a young age, filling countless notebooks with her imaginative stories. As she grew older, her passion for storytelling only deepened, leading her to pursue a career as a novelist.

Drawing inspiration from her own experiences and the world around her, Kathy's writing is characterized by its heartfelt authenticity and emotional depth. She skillfully delves into the complexities of relationships, capturing the raw and tender moments that shape her characters' lives.

When she's not immersed in her writing, Kathy can be found exploring nature, seeking inspiration from the beauty of the world around her. She believes that every moment holds the potential for a story, and it is her mission to capture those moments and share